# Praise for *Planetside*

"A tough, authentic-feeling story that starts out fast and accelerates from there."
—Jack Campbell, author of *Ascendant*

"Not just for military SF fans—although military SF fans will love it—*Planetside* is an amazing debut novel, and I'm looking forward to what Mammay writes next."
—Tanya Huff, author of the Confederation and Peacekeeper series

"*Planetside* is a smart and fast-paced blend of mystery and boots-in-the-dirt military SF that reads like a high-speed collision between *Courage Under Fire* and *Heart of Darkness*."
—Marko Kloos, bestselling author of the Frontline series

"This was a brisk, entertaining novel. [ . . . ] I was reminded a bit of some of John Scalzi's Old Man's War novels." —SFFWorld

"Mammay capably writes Butler's gritty, old-school soldier's voice, and the story delivers enough intrigue and action for fans of military SF."  —*Publishers Weekly*

"The book was an enjoyable read and would likely sit well with any fan of military SF looking for an action-thriller to browse while lying in the sun at the beach."
—Chris Kluwe for *Lightspeed Magazine*

"In *Planetside* Mammay mixes a brevity of prose with feeling of authenticity that would be remarkable in many experienced authors, let alone in a debut novel. Definitely the best military sci-fi debut I've come across in a while."
—Gavin Smith, author of
*Bastard Legion* and *Age of Scorpio*

"A fast-paced tale of military investigation that reads like a blend of Jerry Pournelle and *NCIS*. Michael Mammay brings an exciting and authentic voice of experience to military science fiction."

—Peter McLean, author of
*Priest of Bones*

"*Planetside*, the debut novel by Michael Mammay, is an easy book to love. [ . . . ] a page-turner and an extremely satisfying read."
—*Washington Independent Review of Books*

"If you like military SF you'll love this, or if you like SF mysteries or probably just SF in general. It's a highly impressive first novel that left a real impact."

—SFCrowsnest

# By Michael Mammay

SPACESIDE
PLANETSIDE

# SPACESIDE

## MICHAEL MAMMAY

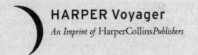

HARPER Voyager
An Imprint of HarperCollins Publishers

SPACESIDE. Copyright © 2019 by Michael Mammay. All rights reserved. Printed in the United States of America. No part of this book may be used or reproduced in any manner whatsoever without written permission except in the case of brief quotations embodied in critical articles and reviews. For information, address Harper-Collins Publishers, 195 Broadway, New York, NY 10007.

First Harper Voyager mass market printing: September 2019

Print Edition ISBN: 978-0-06-269468-3
Digital Edition ISBN: 978-0-06-269469-0

Cover design by Guido Caroti
Cover illustrations by Sebastien Hue

Harper Voyager and the Harper Voyager logo are trademarks of HarperCollins Publishers in the United States of America and other countries.
HarperCollins is a registered trademark of HarperCollins Publishers in the United States of America and other countries.

FIRST EDITION

19 20 21 22 23   QGM   10 9 8 7 6 5 4 3 2 1

*For my wife, for more reasons than I can count.*

# CHAPTER ONE

DESPITE WHAT I did, I never spent a day in prison. That's pretty fucked up.

I spent maybe an hour in a holding cell before what passed for my trial, but that proved to be a formality. The powers that be had decided my fate before I ever came out of stasis after the journey back from Cappa. More accurately, they'd decided upon the politically expedient course, and my fate happened to be attached to it.

In technical language it was called "retirement" in lieu of prosecution. The official judgment included a lot of legalese about my thirty-plus years of exemplary service, exigent circumstances, the role of the commander on the ground, and that sort of nonsense. I even got to keep my pension, though most of that goes to Sharon.

That's probably the real punishment. She left me about eighteen months ago, six months after I returned, though some of that time we staged for the optics. She didn't enjoy being married to a pariah—it didn't suit her. I don't blame her. I'd have avoided it too, if I could have. Being recognized on the street, being followed by the press . . . those things got old fast. So we called it quits as amicably as a couple can do that kind of thing. I took the circus with me, and she took half my money—it's how that goes. She could have made it worse, but she didn't. I will always appreciate that. Soon after, the hoopla mostly died down to a point where I could function, so I was suddenly truly alone.

The transition took a while to set in: leaving the military, where my entire life had followed a pretty tight regimen on a day-to-day basis. Suddenly, I had nowhere to be, nothing that had to be done, no emergencies, no enemies. After about ninety days of that, I decided to do something other than sit around in my new apartment and drink all day. That's how I came to be strapped into a high-tech battle-simulation suit with a bunch of other executives, playing the galaxy's most expensive game of laser tag. Admittedly, there were a few other steps along the path to that moment.

Battlesim!™ was a hybrid live-action/virtual-reality (VR) immersive game where teams of up to twenty players worked physically inside of a simulated city to try to outfight the other team and achieve an objective. In our case, we had to capture a building, which in our virtual-reality world looked like a small three-story hotel. We also got bonus points if we eliminated everyone on the other team. I had some skill in that area. The thing that made it challenging was that the other team always shot back, trying to accomplish the same objective. Battlesim!™ started as WarTrainer 14, designed by Varitech Production Company—VPC—as a combat simulator for the military. Unfortunately, the cost upon completion exceeded the government budget and another company got the bid, so VPC did the next best thing.

They turned it into a game for rich people.

I definitely wasn't rich—far from it. That's why I had to find a job, and VPC was as good a job as any. They really liked doing team-building events for their executives, so it was only a matter of time until somebody in the HR department decided it would be good for morale if we all ran around a little bit inside the simulation one afternoon and tried to virtually kill each other. I held an alternate opinion. But since they employed me and didn't make me do any real work other than schmoozing at corporate events, I gave them a pass and played along.

Inside the game, my team had been led by Albert Claxton, the CFO, who had promptly gotten himself and most of the rest of our players killed in an ill-fated frontal assault. That may have been on purpose, though, since the other team's captain was Javier Sanchez, our CEO. Probably not great politics to wipe out the boss.

Not that I was good at politics.

Still, this left us outnumbered fifteen to three, with me and my two remaining teammates hiding in an out-of-the-way building, discussing strategy as the other team combed the grid looking for us. I came into the game planning to make it look good but not really expecting to expend much effort. I had a chance to make that a reality now by dying valiantly in a heroic charge, then joining in the celebration of the boss's win.

Thing is, I'm not wired that way.

I decided to beat the boss, even if it got me fired. And with all of the higher-ups from my team in virtual body bags, the other two members of my team were staring at me through creepy, bug-eyed virtual-reality helmets, looking for guidance. I'd probably get them fired too.

At least I'd have some drinking buddies.

"We can't attack the building. We don't have enough firepower," I said. They both nodded, either out of understanding or mere acquiescence. "So our only option is to try to draw them out, trap them, then eliminate them. Once they're all dead, we can walk in. They probably won't leave anybody defending, because they'll all want to be part of the hunt."

"But there are fifteen of them," said Kaitlyn Woo, vice president of Engineering. She could see the fifteen red symbols in her heads-up display, same as I did.

"Exactly," I said. "So they'll be overconfident, especially after that first little action we did. They're not thinking about this as a battle right now; they're thinking of it as a mop-up operation. A fox hunt."

"Sure, but five-to-one odds are still five to one," said Derek Birchfeld, deputy VP of Logistics. "And we used up a lot of our assets in the main assault. Sometimes overconfidence is just good sense."

I smiled, though they couldn't see it with the helmets. Claxton had brought in an airstrike at the worst possible time, as our aircraft couldn't fire because we'd put ourselves into the kill zone. So we had no support from above. But I'd scrolled through what we had left, and I had a plan. Everyone playing the game was intelligent—leaders in their field—but they'd stepped into my world. They saw individual moves, where I saw combinations. They thought sequentially, while I thought simultaneously. It wasn't their fault. I had a lifetime of practice, and for all the complexity of Battlesim!™, it was still a game, and simple compared to real combat.

And even if I did something stupid, no one would die.

"Kaitlyn, if I wasn't here and you were in charge, what would you do? Be honest."

She thought about it for a few seconds. "I'd expect them to be out looking for us, leaving the building undefended, like you said. So I'd try to get around to this side over here." She pointed to the three-dimensional map my helmet had projected between us. "I'd move fast, and coming from this direction, there's a good chance they wouldn't see us, so maybe we could take them by surprise. We could get into the building, then make a stand there, from a position of strength."

"Exactly. That's the textbook answer, and the only way to win." I could almost feel her smiling at my praise. I wasn't lying. She'd given the answer any competent junior officer would have come up with.

Except, of course, we couldn't do that.

Because in this case, outnumbered five to one, the textbook way to win meant sure defeat. "What do you think the other side is thinking right now? Not their initial thought. Once they sit for a second and plan. What will they expect us to do?"

After a second Woo nodded her head, getting it. There's a reason she's a VP. "They'll expect us to do exactly what I just said we should do."

"Right. And they'll hit us right here." I indicated a spot about halfway to our target building. "They've got good sightlines from the roof of this building over here, and they can put somebody on the ground over here so we can't slide out the back door."

"So we attack them in those spots," said Birchfeld.

"Not exactly," I said. "As soon as we do that, they'll know we're not doing what they thought, and they have enough people left where they'll change up their plan and beat us anyway."

"That makes sense," said Woo. "So what do we do? The process of thinking through this is interesting, but I know you already have the answer. Can you just give it to us?"

I laughed inside my helmet. "Sure. We need to make it look like we're going the way they expect us to. Once they believe it, they're more likely to commit fully to stopping us. Especially if we make it hard for them. But we also attack the positions we think they'll be in. We hit them on the roof, where they don't have any cover, and we hit their blocking position. Hopefully we can thin their numbers a little bit."

"So how do we do that with only three people . . . and without getting caught in the trap?" asked Birchfeld.

"We're going to show them exactly what they expect to see, then we attack from the opposite direction." I traced another path through the map. "I've already started."

"So we're really going to try to take out the boss?" he asked.

I gave an exaggerated shrug that the VR could pick up. "Yep."

"Sounds good," he said. Woo nodded in agreement as well. Their standing went up in my eyes.

The VR helmet ran on similar specs as things I'd seen in the military, so I had no trouble toggling through our resources via eye movement. I brought in a drone and had it drop smoke pellets along the route we would have taken, to make it look like we were coming that way and trying to obscure our movement. Without waiting, I called for artillery strikes: an airburst against the roof and heat-seeking submunitions against the blocking position down at street level. I expected our opponents to think a little bit two-dimensionally and forget about cover from above. I'd know if I guessed right in about thirty seconds. Yet another advantage of a simulation over real life. The simulation had a scoreboard that told us when we "killed" somebody.

"It's about time to move," I said, and the three of us headed toward the door. "Woo, you keep an eye up top, looking for drones. Anything that might spot us. If you see something, report immediately so we can put up countermeasures to confuse it. Birchfeld, you take point. Follow the route I sent to your heads-up and keep to cover as much as possible. The longer it takes them to realize our true position, the better."

As Birchfeld opened the door, I triggered our last drone to make an electronic strike against the enemy's communications. Jamming didn't work very well on professional units because they trained for it. They had plans in place to bypass network failure, so in real combat it only created a few seconds of advantage. With civilians, however, I counted on it giving us quite a bit longer. If we took some of their people out with artillery at the same time their comms went dead, each group of them would have to make their own decisions until they could regroup on a new frequency. In the confusion, some might rush to the place where they thought we were attacking, some might fall back and defend. Anything that split them up helped our cause.

The thud from the artillery as it impacted compressed my chest, the virtual reality so good that I almost panicked for a second. I took a deep breath and reminded myself where I was. Neither of my companions hesitated, probably because they never experienced real artillery. My feet slapping the synthetic floor pounded in my ears as other noise went away, following the explosions. I toggled my display as much as I dared while running. Seven enemy icons went dark. I'd predicted their locations well. Eight enemy left—still close to a three-to-one advantage for the enemy, but much better than before.

We turned the corner and gunfire erupted directly in front of me as Birchfeld opened up on automatic. By the time I got my bearings, three enemy were down, shot in the back as they'd run the opposite direction. Five on three head count now. Even better odds, and very much needed because I'd used up all of our assets in the deception, leaving us only rifles and grenades.

We staggered our run to the objective, darting from one doorway to the next, hugging the sides of buildings as we ran. It didn't hurt to be cautious, though I thought it more likely that they'd fall back and defend now. They'd have seen the losses as well as we did. They'd have their communications back, so they could organize themselves. These were corporate leaders. Someone would take charge.

"As we approach, watch the upper-story windows for snipers," I told my teammates. Personally I'd have chosen to defend from inside the building, keeping my position hidden from attackers. I'd wait for the enemy to enter, and then cut them down. But I didn't expect that from amateurs. They'd want to see us coming. If they used snipers, they would definitely create problems, so it wasn't a bad plan, just a basic one. We could take advantage of it, because we could get to within about fifteen meters of the target building without having to break into the open.

The first bullet slapped into the building a few centimeters away from Birchfeld's head. The fragments burst off the wall with a snap; the report of the rifle came after the bullet struck. Holy shit. I had to give the VR designers credit for reality.

"Sniper," said Birchfeld, with only a slight inflection betraying his adrenaline rush. He'd make a good soldier.

"Did you see which window?"

He poked his head around the corner, then jerked it back before the enemy could get another line on him. "Third story. Second window from the left. I think there might be a second one, too. I thought I saw a flash of light two more windows down."

That made sense. The building had five windows and they'd taken up positions in numbers two and four. Again, basic, but also effective, as it gave them the widest coverage of the street since they didn't know which direction we'd come from. They probably had two on the opposite side of the building as well, leaving their fifth person as a floater. I wondered whether they'd bring everybody to this side now that they knew our location, or if they'd stay put, thinking we might come from multiple directions. Either way, we had to move. They had the numbers, so I'd have to make some assumptions and take some chances. It was VR, not real life, so we might as well take a shot at glory.

"Birchfeld, you stay here and try to keep them occupied. Provide some covering fire. Woo, you're with me. We're going to hit the east entrance then get upstairs as fast as we can and try to take the snipers out from behind."

"Got it," they both responded.

Birchfeld poked his rifle around the corner and began firing. I didn't have time to watch the result. I tossed a smoke grenade into the street to cover our move, then sprinted for the east door, hoping Woo kept up. A few bullets kicked up dust around us, but the smoke and our movement saw us to the cover of the building unharmed. Speed mattered now. I kicked open the door and went in low. It's a good thing I did, as bullets snapped over my head into the door frame, splintering wood. Woo fired from behind me and an enemy dropped twenty meters down the hall.

"I got him!" said Woo.

"Nice shot. The stairs." I didn't wait to see if she followed. I took the stairs two at a time to the third floor. I didn't know how they'd be arrayed, but I'd already decided to fight it based on how I expected them to set up. Risky, for sure, but I had to hit them fast if we had any chance. With real lives on the line I'd have done it different. Shit, in real life, I'd have backed out and tried to escape when we were down three to fifteen. But in VR, with four of them left, it gave me my best chance at a win. Either way, I'd end it in thirty seconds and we could all go drink.

"You take the second door on the left," I told Woo. "I'll get the rest." I pulled a grenade and moved to the second door on the right. I opened it a crack, tossed the grenade in and slammed it shut. I flipped my weapon to automatic as I ran down the hall. I hoped the simulation had enough realism for my next move to work. A wall separated me and where I expected the enemy, and as beginners, they probably thought that walls protected them. What you can't see can't hurt you . . . that kind of thing. I fired a dozen rounds through the wall and door of the fourth room on the left, then turned to deal with the one on the right.

I kicked the door open. The figure—I couldn't tell if it was a man or a woman—was still looking out the window, which meant that Birchfeld was doing a great job keeping them occupied. The soldier turned as I entered, bringing their rifle around, but not fast enough. I already had my aim and at least two seconds' advantage.

I froze.

It wasn't the system or the weapon. It was me. I didn't pull the trigger. A moment later my helmet went dead. A computerized female voice asked me to sit down, and when I did, video started on my heads-up display so I could watch the rest of the battle by toggling through several camera feeds. It didn't take long. Woo lost her fight and went down, and I hadn't hit the woman I'd fired at through the wall. My grenade had worked, but that still left three of them against Birchfeld. He managed to get one before they got him.

**PERHAPS THE BEST** part of the simulation facility was the full-service bar attached to it, complete with comfortable faux-leather stools and fancy high tables. They had a great whiskey selection, too, which I took advantage of because we were on the corporate bill and I planned to take public transportation home anyway. I sipped on my second very expensive Ferra Three single malt.

A table over, Phillip Tannard, an asshole from accounting, held court, reliving the action of the battle loudly, with half a dozen followers gathered around him listening. "It was just me, alone in a room facing down the most infamous soldier in the galaxy. The Scourge of Cappa. He had me dead to rights, but I was faster."

It had been Tannard who shot me when I froze, but I didn't correct his story. His version sounded better than the truth, and everybody liked a good story. I smiled and raised my glass to him, then downed it and signaled for another. This was part of the job. They didn't expect me to do much in the office, but they liked to have the famous guy from the war around. Somehow it made them feel good to be near me.

Sheila Jackson slid onto a stool across from me as the waiter brought my next drink. She'd changed into a sharp-looking gray suit with a knee length skirt, and somehow looked put together despite having come off the same fake battlefield as the rest of us. She was the one person at VPC I considered a real friend, and she was about to lecture me on something. With friends you can tell.

"Are you okay?" she asked. "Don't pay any attention to Tannard. He's an asshole."

"He is. But I'm fine," I said. She stared me down. "What? Really. I'm fine."

"You know we all had video feeds once we got killed, right? We all saw you enter that room." She sipped a glass of red wine.

I sighed and took a drink, savoring the rich flavor of the whiskey. "Right. I forgot about that." Javier Sanchez, the CEO, approached, saving me from further analysis.

"Carl! Good fight out there."

"Thanks," I said. "It's a great simulation. Very realistic."

"I thought we had you dead when it was fifteen to three, but you really showed us. You caught me on the roof with artillery. How come you didn't bring out that strategy earlier?"

"Didn't think of it," I lied. It was easier to let it go, now that the battle had ended and I had a drink in my hand. He signed my check, but I didn't owe him the truth on this one.

He smiled a big CEO smile. I think he sensed my falsehood. "Right. It was definitely good for the team. Thanks."

I fake-smiled back and raised my glass, playing the good employee. "Of course. Anytime."

"You could have gotten out of it," said Sheila, after Javier left us.

I gave her a half smile, real this time. "What would be the point? They pay me well and don't ask much of me. I can do this one thing."

She hesitated. "Sure. I get it. Okay. But take care of yourself, yeah?"

"Of course." I saw where she was going, and I didn't want to take that trip at the moment. Thankfully, the waiter saved me, handing me a new whiskey. I spent several seconds swirling it and watching the ripples of water course through the amber liquor until Sheila got the hint and changed the subject.

# CHAPTER TWO

"SO YOU FROZE? What does that mean?" Dr. Baqri had brought her chair out from behind her desk, close to me. Psychiatry 101. Somehow the desk represented something coming between us, so she took it out of the way.

"You're the doctor. Aren't you supposed to tell me what it means? I locked up. Couldn't pull the trigger. I don't know why."

"What made you think going into a military simulation was a good idea?"

I leaned back in the expensive office chair. It had a mesh back and excellent lumbar support. Nothing but first class. "I don't know. It didn't seem like a big deal, and it's kind of part of the job."

"I think your boss would have understood if you sat out the event," she said.

"I'm sure he would have. But I didn't want to bring it up, you know? People don't like knowing that they're working around crazy people."

She shook her head and annotated something in her notebook. "We've talked about that word."

"Yeah. Sorry," I said.

"Besides, it's not like they don't know what you've been through. It's pretty well documented in the public domain."

I half snorted. "Yeah, I know." We'd been over that before. The inability to get away from the spotlight, people knowing me—or thinking they knew me— everywhere I went.

"Do you want to talk about that? People thinking they know what you've been through?"

"Not really."

She sighed. "Carl, this only works if you're willing to talk."

I tried to force a happy face. "What's there to say that I haven't said? I killed a shitload of people. I have to live with it."

"There are a lot of people who consider you a hero for what you did." She was right. Half the galaxy saw me as some sort of military savior.

"Sure. And a lot of people are assholes," I said. "The other half think I'm a monster."

"And what do you think?"

I hesitated a second, then laughed. "You're so good, Doc. You always bring it back around to me."

She smiled, and it seemed genuine. "Well that's kind of the job, isn't it? But since you don't want to talk about that, let's go in another direction. How are you sleeping?"

"Fine," I said.

She shook her head. "I think you're lying, Carl." Smart lady. I rarely fooled her.

"Okay. It's the same. I don't sleep much, and when I do, I have the dreams."

"Have they gotten any better?" she asked.

"No."

"You know there are medications we could—"

"We've been over this, Doc. No drugs."

"Alcohol is a drug," she said.

"It is. It's one I know, though. I've had a lot of practice. The chemical stuff, I don't want to mess with that. I never quite know how it's going to affect me."

She sighed again. A lot of our sessions ended with her sighing. I didn't do it on purpose. I guess I wasn't ready to get better.


I LEFT MY appointment and headed to my job late, which nobody noticed, or if they did they didn't say anything, which also worked. I got coffee and sat behind my computer terminal pretending to read email. I mostly checked sports news. The information technology folks almost certainly monitored that, but again, nobody ever said anything, so I didn't care.

My office had clear walls, which on a good day gave me a measure of privacy in a mostly open-floor-plan building. On bad days it reminded me of a fishbowl, where people could view the mass murderer behind the glass from a safe distance. The placard on my door said Deputy Vice President, Security. Technically that title came with a set of duties, protecting Varitech Production Company from all the dangers of the corporate battlefield. In practice, I showed up for corporate events like the war game, and I used the few contacts I had left in the military to arrange meetings for sales reps or to push a new project. It paid well and nobody shot at me.

The knock on my door echoed with that funny sound that rapping on fake glass makes. I waved for them to enter without looking up. My friend Sheila wouldn't have knocked, and other than her I didn't care. Someone from my team of fifteen or so underlings probably wanted me to sign something.

"Colonel Butler?"

"Carl," I said. No matter how many times I told people, they insisted on the title. I looked up and made eye contact. I didn't recognize the woman in the door. She wore a corporate uniform—charcoal business suit—and had her auburn hair pulled back in a bun. I was pretty sure she didn't work for me but not confident enough to say so and risk embarrassment.

"Sir, there's been a security breach, and Mr. Sanchez would like to speak to you about it."

"Mr. Sanchez wants to speak to *me* about it? That seems unlikely. Are you sure he didn't want my boss?" Javier Sanchez and I had talked on many occasions, but none of those instances involved my actual job.

"He was quite clear, sir."

"Huh." I stood. "He could have had his secretary send me a meeting notification."

"I did, sir."

I glanced at my monitor. "Oh. Sorry about that."

She gave me a pretend smile that said I should hurry up. I glanced at my shirt and wished for a moment that I'd spent a few more seconds with the iron that morning, and then followed her to the elevator and up to the top floor.

I'd been to the top floor of the VPC building once before, when they hired me, but I'd mostly forgotten it. It had the same open plan as every other floor of the building except for the four corners, which had opaque-walled offices. Efficient workers sat at efficient desks, speaking softly into communicators or tapping through data on screens. The air seemed to muffle the sound. I followed my guide to the largest of the corner offices. She paused at a desk outside it and said something I couldn't hear into a device. A moment later, the office door whooshed open and a very fit-looking Sanchez walked out, smiling. He was close to sixty, so about my age by calendar, but more than a decade older because of all my cryo time. If I was a proud man, it might have hurt my feelings that he could easily pass for ten years younger than me. His jet-black hair didn't show a touch of gray and only the slightest crinkles marred his brown face, right around the eyes. Okay, it hurt my feelings a little.

"Carl. Good to see you." He strode toward me and I met him halfway and shook his hand.

"No problem, Javier. Sorry I'm late." He insisted that I call him by his first name, though he didn't do that with everybody. I think he wanted to give people the impression we were closer than we actually were. But the boss is the boss, and it didn't bother me as long as they kept hitting send on my pay transfers.

He made an exaggerated face of dismissal. "You're not late. Come on in."

His massive office had two glass walls. Unlike mine, they were huge ones that looked out over a wonderful view of East Park and the city. He walked across the expensive blue carpet to an ornately crafted wooden hutch. "Drink?"

I checked my device for the time. Eleven in the morning. "Still part of the duty day."

He waved me off. "You're not in the army anymore, Carl. Besides, I'm the boss and I insist. It's Ferra Three. The twenty year."

I looked at the bottle he held up, which cost about three hundred marks. "Well I can't say no to that."

"Smart man." He poured a generous amount of whiskey into each of two crystal glasses, splashed in a little water and handed me one. I breathed it in, and then took a sip, savoring it. We stood in silence for a few moments. The Ferra Three had waited twenty years, so it demanded a little respect.

"So I'm guessing you didn't call me up here only for the wonderful whiskey," I said.

He smiled. "That obvious?"

I shrugged. "It's not every day that someone opens a bottle of booze that costs more than most people earn in a day."

"Sometimes it's good to enjoy the finer things." He gestured to a large, straight-backed wooden chair and I took a seat. He pulled another one around and set it at an angle to mine, so we were close, but not directly staring at each other. It was "make-your-guest-comfortable" perfection that I'm guessing he read in a book somewhere. "There's a security issue that I want you to look into."

I didn't know what to say, so I didn't speak for what must have been a little too long, because he spoke again. "You are in security, after all."

"I am. And forgive me if nobody told you this . . . I'd have thought they would have. I don't actually do much with security."

His face tightened. "No, I'm aware."

"But you want me on this anyway," I said, so he wouldn't have to. Once you know where the boss is going, it's good to help him get there.

"I think it fits your skill set."

"Does Wong know?" Xi Wong was VP of Security, and my boss.

"He's aware of the issue. Have you heard of Omicron Technology?"

"Sure," I said. "Everyone has. Weapons, military engines, drones, medical . . . all the stuff that pays."

"Five days ago someone breached their network."

"Wow. That's big." I took a sip of my drink. "How deep did they get?"

"All the way."

I whistled. "That's *really* big. But what does that have to do with us?"

Javier took another sip of his whiskey. "On the surface, nothing. I might even be happy for their misfortune, since some of our business interests overlap. But there's more to this. Whoever hit them . . . it was something unexpected. Omicron has the best security money can buy."

"And you're worried it could happen to us."

"Exactly," he said.

"Got it. What did the attack do? What were they after?"

"Omicron isn't exactly opening up about it, for obvious reasons. That's where you come in. Omicron employs a bunch of ex-military folks. Reach out, see what you can learn. And see what we might be able to do to protect ourselves."

I considered it, running over the scenario in my mind. To do it right called for more of an intelligence operative than somebody with my background, and somebody who had some experience with computer networks, but I could probably find a contact. I took another sip of my drink to buy me a second to think. "Who do you have for my team?"

"I want to keep it quiet," he said. "I'll give you somebody from legal to consult, but that's it."

"Legal?"

"It's sensitive, poking around another company," he said. "We don't want to get into trouble."

I kept my face neutral. What he was really saying was that *he* didn't want to get caught. That could be tricky, because anybody I approached who might talk to me would potentially talk *about* me, too. It was his decision, though, and not unreasonable. I'd find a way to make it work. "How much do we know already? What sort of starting point do I have?"

The side of his mouth quirked up slightly. He knew he had me hooked. "What do you need?"

"Anything we know about how the breach happened. Even if we only know who reported it."

"We don't know much. There's been nothing public."

Of course not. I don't know why I bothered asking. "Let's start with an easy one, then. How did *you* learn about it?"

He looked away from me, pretended to examine his liquor, but he was thinking. Something confidential, then. A source above my pay grade.

"I need somewhere to start," I prompted. "At least give me a hint. Your source. Is it military, political, inside of Omicron?"

"Military," he said.

I didn't respond for a few seconds, hoping that the awkward silence would prompt him to say more. A lot of people can't handle silence. Something flipped in Javier. A small something, but significant. His face hardened a tiny bit, and I knew he'd finished speaking on the matter. "I know it's not much. See what you can do," he said.

"Sure." I downed the rest of my drink. I had thin information, but life or death didn't hang in the balance. I'd do what I could with what I had. "Who's my contact at legal?"

"Jacques Dernier will meet you at your office. Make sure you keep him in the loop. We don't want trouble."

I didn't want a lawyer hanging around, but Javier's body language didn't allow for further debate. "Great. I'll make an initial assessment of the situation and report back on what I'll need to do from there. Give me two days."

His face relaxed slightly. "Good. I knew I had the right man."

**AS PROMISED, THE** lawyer waited for me in my office, sitting up straight in the one chair I had for guests. He stood when I arrived, slightly taller than me, younger, with his black hair in a style I referred to as "executive number one." He offered his hand. "Jacques Dernier."

"Carl Butler," I said, returning the handshake.

"I've been detailed to work for you," he said. "I've taken the liberty of creating a joint page where we can share documents and information. It's in your system, and all my contact information is there as well."

"Great." I walked around my desk and sat. Jacques sat as well, and waited for me to speak. I toggled my screen on and saw what he'd set up for us. Efficient.

I decided right then to cut him out of everything.

Javier told me to share with legal, and I'd fake it a little bit so I didn't get in trouble, but I kind of wanted to see what would happen if I didn't. Javier might get pissed, but he wouldn't fire me. Not without a warning. The main thing was that I didn't need a lawyer. I didn't have any plans yet, legal or illegal, and until I did he'd get in the way and ask annoying questions. I ignored

Jacques and started searching the company directory for his name.

"Is there anything you need me to do?" he asked, after several awkward minutes.

"Sure," I said. "I need a list of everybody who works at Omicron. No, not everybody—executive level."

"Okay. I can do that. What are we looking for?"

I found Dernier on the company registry. He'd been working for VPC for around eight years. Promoted once. Nothing out of the norm. "Like I said, a list of names. I'm looking for somebody I know, or barring that, somebody I can reach out to. I have no idea what direction I'm going with this, so I want a bunch of information. Maybe I'll see something and figure it out."

"Anything else?" he asked.

"If you want, start cross-matching names with recent news articles. See if you find anything interesting." I planned to do the same thing myself, but having an extra set of eyes working on it wouldn't hurt, and it wouldn't give away any of my secrets. Not that I had any yet. It might keep Dernier busy enough that he didn't notice me ignoring him. And it might show me if he missed anything, which would help me evaluate him and see what I could trust him with in the future. "Drop whatever you find into that page you made, and I'll do the same."

"Yes, sir," he said.

"Please, call me Carl."

*Please.*

## CHAPTER THREE

**I LEFT MY OFFICE** maybe an hour later and headed home. I needed to get started on Omicron, but I didn't want to do it on company infrastructure. Anything I did on their system would be visible to someone in the company, and Javier said he wanted to keep it quiet. Thanks to Dernier's efficiency, I could pull the list of Omicron names down from my system at home. His work would leave some tracks, for sure, if somebody really wanted to find it, but I figured legal types knew how to protect themselves.

I descended to the marble palace that VPC called a lobby and exited through the ridiculous revolving doors. A chilly blast of wind whipped down the canyon of skyscrapers and made me gasp as I stepped out onto the sidewalk. I regretted leaving my coat in my office. The wind always blew on Talca 4, at least in the parts I'd visited—the one drawback on an otherwise nice planet. Not that I had had a choice in where I lived. All the big military technology companies headquartered on Talca. They needed access to the politicians, and more important, the military bureaucracy.

I walked a hundred meters to the transportation stop and pulled out my device while I waited. I punched up my contacts and spoke a message to Karen Plazz, a reporter I knew from my time on Cappa. "Call me. I've got a story for you."

A few seconds later the bus hovered around the corner and I stepped on, finding a seat easily as normal people still had to work in the early afternoon. I kept my head down, trying to avoid eye contact with the dozen or so other people on board. I made it to my seat about halfway back thinking nobody had spotted me, but when I looked up the man sitting across the aisle was staring at me with a goofy grin.

"I'm sorry to bother you, but I have to say it's an honor to be on the same bus with you, sir. You showed those alien bastards who runs the galaxy." He kept grinning. I gave him a flat smile and nodded in a practiced gesture of acknowledgment that seemed to make people happy. Alerted by the man's words, the woman a couple seats down looked over and then made an exaggerated show of looking away, as if she wanted to make sure I knew of her distaste. I knew. It happened often enough.

I put my face down into my device again and blocked them out, spending the thirteen painful minutes it took to reach my stop scrolling through the news, searching for anything related to Omicron. Nothing jumped out at me. I got off and walked fifty meters to the door of my building. I didn't have the best address, but the easy access to transportation helped make up for it, and I'd lived in worse places. The nondescript apartment building had a fake stone facing that the architect meant to look sophisticated. Instead it looked cheap. I took the lift to the seventh floor and keyed the dual encryption to turn off my alarm. What I saved in rent I spent on security.

As soon as I got through the door of my two-bedroom unit, I called Sheila Jackson, making sure to use her personal device and not anything associated with VPC.

"Hey. Where are you?" she asked.

"I cut out early," I said.

"Must be nice."

"It is," I said. "Hey, what do you know about Jacques Dernier?" Sheila knew everybody. She had one of those minds that remembered faces and names. I couldn't really relate.

"From legal?"

"Yeah."

"Not much," she said. "He's been with the company six or eight years. Joined up right out of law school, I think."

"Who's his patron?" I asked. "Does he have one?"

"He's tight with Abarri. Deputy VP for legal. I don't know how much there is to that, but they're definitely friendly. They eat lunch together, sometimes."

"That could be business," I said.

"Probably is," said Sheila. "But people tend to find other options for lunch if they don't like somebody."

"Right. So who is Abarri hitched to?"

"You mean other than the CEO?"

"That's what I thought," I said. "Abarri is Javier's person in legal?"

"Pretty much, yeah. Javier doesn't really get along with the VP for legal, so he's got Abarri in the number-two seat."

"So if Javier wanted a lower-level lawyer, he'd probably ask Abarri, who would give him Dernier's name."

"Very possible," said Sheila.

"Thanks. You're the best."

"This is true," she said. "You owe me lunch."

"You got it." I hadn't learned much, but I appreciated the background in case something came up later.

My device hummed before I even set it down. "What do you have for me?" Karen Plazz's voice said. She worked the capital beat now, and we kept in touch every month or so. We always said we should talk more often, being on the same planet, but we never did.

"I need a favor," I said.

"That's funny, I could have sworn your message said that you had a story for me. I should have known you'd have questions."

"I'm wounded," I said.

"Stop me when I say something that isn't true. Do you have a story or not?"

"Sure I do. But I don't know what it is yet."

"Gah! You kill me, Butler. You've got to give me more than that. That's how this reporter thing works. You tell me things."

"Remember that time back on Cappa where I didn't tell you anything, but then it was the biggest story of the year and you broke it, then you won that award? The Jacob Prize, I think—"

"Yeah, yeah," she interrupted. "How long are you going to try to live off of that?"

"I don't know, how long are they going to refer to you as a Jacob Prize-winning reporter?"

"So to be clear," she said, "you're saying I owe you."

"I'm saying that maybe I've earned a little bit of trust, and when I say I've got something, I really have it."

"I'd love to do this all day, Carl, but some of us actually have to work."

"Fair enough," I replied. "There was a security breach at Omicron. Nobody is reporting on it. There's your story."

"What kind of security breach?"

"I'm not sure. Something big enough where important people are interested."

"Which important people?" she asked.

"I'm not sure yet."

"Then how do you know?"

"You really do ask a lot of questions," I said.

"That's kind of the job."

"Right. I can't tell you," I said.

She paused a moment, probably taking notes. "This is thin."

"Yes it is. But it's also real."

"Be honest with me, Carl. Why are you giving me this?"

"Old times' sake?"

She laughed. "So then it's not because you want to know more about something and want me to do the work?"

"You know, you're a remarkably good reporter," I said.

"And you're an asshole."

"I really am. But that's not news. I'm telling you, there's something there. You can get on it, or you can read it somewhere else."

She made an exaggerated gasp. "Carl Butler, are you suggesting that you'd cheat on me with another journalist?"

"Don't be ridiculous. You know I hate reporters. But if I know about the breach, then that means other people know about it, too. It's only a matter of time until it gets out."

"Okay," she said. "I'll see what I can dig up."

"Let me know what you find," I said, trying to sound light.

"You'll be able to read about it," she said. The line went dead.

I laughed to myself. It was early to start drinking, but I'd already had one with Javier, so I poured another. "Sharon, activate. Give me anything you can find about people who work at Omicron Propulsion Technologies. Send it to the monitor." Yes, I named my household AI after my ex-wife. Dr. Baqri had a field day with that one. I'd promised the doc that I'd change it, but I hadn't gotten around to it yet.

I sat down and read some news about Omicron.
Puff pieces, mostly. Their CEO, Ellen Haverty, was
somewhat of an icon, known as much for what she did
outside the boardroom as in it. She piloted her own
luxury space cruiser and funded several race teams.
She wrote it all off as research and development for
new engines. She could afford it, since Omicron Propulsion drove half the ships in the military fleet and at
least a third of civilian space traffic as well. They had
their hands in everything that required science and
made massive amounts of money.

I read a few business-related pieces, some naming
public-affairs personnel or a VP or two but nothing
that jumped out at me as useful. I swiped through
a few pages trusting that I'd know what I wanted
when I found it. I opened the page that Dernier
had created and looked at what he'd put in there.
He'd been busy. On top of the list of names I re-
quested he'd dropped in a dozen articles, each with
brief notes.

The third article caught my attention, though the
piece itself didn't give a lot of information, and Dernier's mundane notes didn't add much. The source was
a second-tier science journal reporting on a potential
breakthrough in some medical technology called the
Phoenix Project, which I didn't understand. But I recognized a name: Warren Gylika, a retired general.
We didn't know each other personally, but with senior
officers there was almost always only one degree of
separation. A friend of a friend. I could reach out to

some of my contacts and find somebody who knew him and set up a meeting. I didn't know what I hoped to get out of him, but when you don't know what to do, you move forward and see what happens. It beats standing still.

# CHAPTER FOUR

IT DIDN'T TAKE me long the next day to find the connection. I did a little research on Gylika, found out where he'd been stationed in the past and then called the people I knew who had been in those places. Gylika had been high-enough profile that most everyone had known him, but it wasn't until my third call that I found someone who kept in touch. She agreed to set up the meeting for later in the week.

Since that left me with time on my hands, I tried another angle while I waited. Dernier had continued to pile things up in the computer file, but I wanted to avoid him for a little bit so I ignored them. Instead, I sent an email to the information technology department, and twenty minutes later Ganos knocked on the frame of my open door and walked in to my office.

"You called, sir?" Ganos looked much like she had two years ago on Cappa, small and fidgety, except now she sported blue hair. She'd married her fellow soldier, Parker, and she needed a job while she waited for him to finish up his stint in the military. I'd convinced VPC to hire her when she finished her tour of duty, because there's no point in having power if you don't use it to help out good people. It didn't hurt that she was a computer genius, either. And I *did* work in the security department, after all.

"How's it going, Ganos? Heard from Parker lately?"

"Every day, sir. He's on Aranna 5, and you know us techies always have a good comms link."

Newlyweds. "That's good. I've got kind of an off-the-wall question."

"That's very surprising to me, sir." She said it with a straight face, but a slight hint of mocking crept into her tone.

"I think I liked you better when you were shy and scared of me," I said.

"I'm not sure we remember that the same way. What can I do for you, sir?"

"I want you to break into Omicron's computer network."

She paused and looked at me as if assessing my sanity, but to her credit she didn't overreact. "I can do that, sir," she said, after maybe half a minute of thinking.

"Really? I thought you were going to tell me it's impossible."

"Nothing's impossible with computers, sir. I'm going to need full-time access to three LMR-2800 supercomputers and eighteen months."

I chuckled. "Seriously?" Even I knew that an LMR

was a top-of-the-line machine that cost millions. A high-end research facility might have *one*, and the time on it would be booked out in small increments a year in advance.

"It's not impossible, sir. But it's pretty close."

"Okay," I said. "On a scale of one to ten, where ten is high-end military security, where would you rate the security of a company like Omicron?"

"Eleven," she said, without thinking about it.

"Really?"

"Without a doubt, sir. Our security here in the high-end corporate world is better than we were running on Cappa. It's not close."

"Well that's a little bit frightening." What was more frightening was that somebody had potentially cracked it.

"Yes, sir."

"So then hypothetically, if I wanted to learn something from inside Omicron's system, how would I go about that?"

She thought about it, bouncing her weight from one foot to the other. "You'd get a job at Omicron."

"That makes sense. But even then, I might not have access."

"You might not, sir, but you'd be in a better position to break in. Most of the security faces outward. It's much, much easier to break into internal stuff once you're on the inside."

"So all I need to do is get onto an Omicron terminal," I said.

She laughed. "No, sir. All you need to do is get somebody like me onto an Omicron terminal. You'd be next to useless. Sir . . . I have to ask: Are we really trying to break into another company?"

I debated quickly how much to tell her, and decided on most of the truth. "We're not trying to break in. But there's a rumor that somebody else already did. I wanted to get an idea of how it might happen, so that we can better protect ourselves from a similar attack."

She nodded slowly. "That's a hell of a hack, if somebody did it. I'll keep my sensors up in the tech community and see if I hear anything. If this is real, people might be talking about it. Or they *won't* be talking about it. Either way, it might give us a clue where to start looking."

"That would help a lot. Thanks, Ganos. And if you would, I'd appreciate if you kept this between you and me for now."

She looked at me like I had a dick growing out of my forehead, offended. She wouldn't dream of breaking trust. Somehow, though, her "Of course, sir," came out with relative politeness.

**THE MEETING WITH** Gylika happened faster than I expected. I hadn't been sure he'd contact me at all, and when he did he surprised me by setting something up for lunch the next day. We agreed to meet at an out-of-the-way place that I picked. I went there because they knew me and did a good job helping me maintain some semblance of privacy on the few occasions when

I ventured out into the real world. They catered mostly to locals and didn't get much tourist traffic. They had a decent menu, but nothing special—it was all about the location.

"General Gylika," I said, as I walked up to his table in the back corner of the dimly lit space.

He stood, pushing his heavy fake-wood chair back. "Please. Call me Warren. It's good to meet you, Carl."

"I was surprised you set this up so quickly."

"How could I pass up an opportunity to have lunch with a celebrity?" He gave me a lopsided smile that lit his entire face.

"Right. I forget about that sometimes."

"I'm just busting your balls. It was curiosity, more than anything. Gets me away from the office, which the Mother knows I need to do more often. What are you up to these days?"

I was sure he knew my job situation and was only making conversation, but I obliged him. "I'm with VPC. I work in the security department."

"Sounds like a nice gig," he said.

"It's not bad. Pays well, and the hours are pretty good. Nothing as exciting as what you've got going with the Phoenix Project."

He glanced down at the table for a split second, then met my eyes again, hiding the moment of discomfort. "I really can't talk about that. I hope that's not what you wanted to meet for."

"Not at all," I said. "I just saw it in the news with your name attached to it."

The waiter showed up and took our order. I chose a grilled-chicken sandwich without looking at the menu. Gylika dithered for a moment before breaking down and ordering a burger. The whole interchange gave us a moment for the slight awkwardness I'd created to pass. I also ordered a whiskey on the rocks. If Gylika had a problem with me drinking at lunch, he did a good job of hiding it, though for his part he stuck to water.

"So what's going on?" he asked, once the waiter had moved away. I liked him. He knew I didn't call him on a whim, and he got right to the point.

"It's about security," I said. "There's a pretty strong rumor going around that Omicron had a significant breach. I know you can't tell me everything, but I'm hoping you can tell me something. The non-classified parts. My boss wants to make sure we're not vulnerable to the same kind of attack." Truth be told, I wanted the classified parts too, but it wouldn't do to say so. He'd either tell me or he wouldn't, but asking would have been bad form.

"I've heard about it, but I don't know much." He said it casually, keeping eye contact. He seemed totally at ease, and his lack of reaction made me believe him.

"That's too bad," I said.

"I'm sure I can find out," he added. I listened for a hint that he wanted something in return, something I should offer, but it didn't feel like that kind of thing. I didn't want to flat out ask, either, so I waited for him to speak again. "I'll ask around, and give you a call if I find anything useful."

"Great," I said. "Thanks."

"Anything for a war hero." He smiled again.

I smiled back, genuinely amused. "Let me know if I can ever do anything for you."

"You can pick up the check," he said.

"Absolutely."

I DECIDED NOT to go back to work, mostly because I didn't want to. I'd only had the one drink, and it seemed like a good opportunity to hit the gym on company time, so I crossed the street and caught a two-thirds-full transport. I really do hate public transportation—mostly the public part—but it wasn't practical to have a car in the city, and the 150 percent tax on them was prohibitive, even if I wanted one.

I kept my head down, as usual, but I still felt the eyes on me as I worked my way to a seat in the middle of the vehicle. At least nobody said anything. I pulled out my device and once again hid my face in it to dissuade people from bothering me. I'm not sure what personality flaw made some people want to talk to other people on buses. Maybe I was too judgmental. I reached my stop without incident and made my way to the door. A dark-skinned woman with short hair in the front seat glanced up from her reader and met my eyes for a split second.

I froze.

She had large pupils, too dilated for the well-lit vehicle, and they were oval.

Like a Cappan's.

Sweat started to pour from my body, and my hands shook. I couldn't take another step.

"Excuse me," said a man from behind me. "If you're not going to get off, can you let me past?"

"What?" I stood there another second, then got control of myself and started moving. The woman smiled at me, her eyes normal. My mind was playing tricks on me. I knew it, but even knowing, I couldn't stop shaking.

I nearly ran from the stop to my door, fumbled with the security system for a moment before I could make it work, and stumbled through into the entryway. I grabbed a half-full bottle of whiskey off the counter and slumped to the floor. I sat there on the tile. I should have gotten up to get myself a glass, but I couldn't, so I made do without and drank straight from the bottle.

## CHAPTER FIVE

**I DON'T UNDERSTAND WHAT** you're telling me about the eyes," said Dr. Baqri. It wasn't my normal appointment, but I figured that a total panic attack made a good reason for an emergency session.

"They weren't human," I said.

"I understood that part, but I'm not sure what it signifies. Was there an alien with you on public transportation?"

I sighed. "No. Maybe. I don't know." I debated the value of sharing the story about hybrid Cappan-human combinations and how their eyes looked. I could tell her, if I wanted to. As my doctor, she couldn't repeat anything I said. But she could also legally have me committed to a facility, and it would sound insane if I tried to explain it. "It triggered a flashback."

"Hmm. Is this the first time you've had a flashback while you've been awake?"

"Yeah. Is that bad?" I asked.

"Not bad. But it's a change, so I do want to make note of it. It's not uncommon for triggers in everyday life to set something off. Loud noises, shiny objects . . . lots of things can remind somebody of their time in combat."

"You think that's what this was?"

"What do you think?" she asked.

Under normal circumstances I hated it when she turned a question around on me like that, but this time I gave it real consideration. It had been a quick thing on the bus. When I thought about it after the fact, it seemed more real than not, but not so much that I would swear to what I saw. "It could have been a trick of the light. A glare could have caught her eyes, maybe." As I said it, the explanation took hold and I started to convince myself. It couldn't have been a Cappan hybrid. Why would a hybrid be riding random public transportation? The woman on the bus hadn't given any indication of being aware of me, other than a quick look.

"We do need to consider that this could be a worsening of your condition. I know you're against medication, but if you continue to have hallucinations—"

"I hear you, Doc."

WHEN I REACHED my office, Jacques Dernier was waiting outside my door, sharply dressed, his mouth in a tight frown that he flattened into a neutral look when he saw me.

"Sorry," I said. "I had a doctor's appointment. I didn't know you were waiting or I'd have called."

"Totally okay," he lied. "We just hadn't talked about the assignment since the initial meeting, and I wanted to make sure we were synched."

"I've been reading the stuff you sent me." I entered the office, gesturing for him to follow. "I've picked up a few leads from that, but I'm still assessing things."

"What kinds of leads?" he asked.

"Nothing solid," I said. "A couple names."

"I've been instructed to give this my full attention." *And I have to tell my boss something,* he didn't add.

"Yeah. Okay." I sat. "One of your articles had a name I knew, Warren Gylika. We had lunch. He's well positioned over at Omicron, so I thought maybe he might know something."

"Did he?"

"No."

"So that's it?" he asked.

I hadn't trusted him at first out of principle, but now I started to genuinely dislike him. I didn't know why I felt that way, but I trusted my gut. "He's going to look around. But yeah, that's it. These things take time. You never know what might lead to something important."

"What can I do to help?" he asked.

"Right now, nothing. We'll see if this lead pans out, and meanwhile I'll keep looking to see if I can come up with anything else. If you find anything, let me know."

"Sure," he said. "You too?"

"Sure." I looked at him until he finally took the hint and left my office.

I didn't have a great explanation for being an asshole. Maybe the woman on the bus with the eyes had me spooked and that had me off my game. Either way, I didn't feel the need to apologize.

**AFTER AN HOUR** or so in my office pretending to look for leads, I got up and walked around the building. I took a random path, checking behind me at regular intervals to make sure Dernier wasn't watching. Silly, I know, but I wouldn't have put it past him. After I assuaged my fear, I made my way down to the IT floor to see if Ganos had learned anything by asking around the hacker community. The elevator opened into a rat maze of cubicles that somehow seemed to suck the light out of the low-ceilinged room. Music played from somewhere, though not too loud, and I could swear that I smelled popcorn. I looked around for some sort of directory to tell me where to find Ganos but found nothing other than bare wall.

"Can I help you?" A young man, maybe twenty, walked toward the elevator.

"I'm looking for Ganos," I said.

He looked at me blankly.

"Smallish woman, spiky blue hair."

"Oh! You mean Maria. Right. She's back toward that corner." He gestured vaguely to the back and right of the room.

"Thanks." I headed in the direction he'd indicated.

"No problem." He raised his voice. "Suit on the floor!"

The music cut off instantly, and it might have been my imagination, but it seemed to get a little brighter. Heads popped up from cubicles in a few places. I'd never been called a suit before, but it had a distinct "Officer on deck!" feel to it. After a minute I found Ganos standing at a raised desk that had three monitors on it, two of them open to confusing computer things that I didn't understand. The other played a video of some sort of animal chasing its tail.

"How's it going, sir?"

"Not bad. Should I call you Maria?" It felt wrong, but that's what the other techie had called her.

She scrunched her face up in a way that suggested she thought I might have lost my mind. "No, sir. That would be weird."

"I thought so too. Did you find anything on that thing we were talking about?" I asked.

"It's strange, sir. I didn't find anything."

"How is that strange?"

"Because I should have," she said. "At least *something*. When I say I found nothing, it's like nobody knows it happened. Are you sure it did?"

That brought me up short. I was pretty sure, but I didn't have any actual facts other than what Javier had provided. Gylika hadn't denied it, but he hadn't really confirmed it, either. If he brought me in and had a different motive . . . I suppose Javier could have been planting a false flag to get me to look for vulnerabilities at Omicron, but I doubted that. "Pretty sure. Like eighty-five percent."

She shrugged. "I'd take a harder look at your sources. The other possibility seems unlikely."

"What's that?" I asked. In my experience, unlikely never seemed to be quite as unlikely as I hoped.

She paused. "No way does somebody in my world pull a miracle hack like that with zero noise. There's too much credibility on the line. Even if the actual perpetrator didn't claim it, *somebody* would. Which would be followed by a bunch of people telling them they're full of shit. There's an evolution with these things."

"Could they have covered it up? Or what if it wasn't anybody from the community?"

"Right," she said. "That's where it gets scary. The only people who could do this and keep it totally quiet . . . like I said, it seems unlikely."

"Go ahead. Finish that thought," I prompted. "Who could do it?"

"The government could," she said.

**GANOS'S INFORMATION WEIGHED** heavy on my mind and I couldn't concentrate on anything else. It had just passed two in the afternoon and I was debating knocking off for the day when my comm buzzed. I pressed the button. "Butler."

"Carl. This is Warren Gylika."

"Hey! I didn't expect to hear from you so soon."

"We should get together." He paused. "I've got something interesting."

I didn't need to check my calendar, which was empty. I'd have cleared it for this, regardless. Something in the tone of his voice triggered my instinct, and I suddenly found myself very alert. "Sure. Same place?"

"That works. I'll be there in forty-five minutes. Three o'clock."

"I'll meet you there." I got up, grabbed my jacket and headed immediately for the elevator. It would take me twenty minutes to get there if I hit the transportation right, but I couldn't tolerate sitting at my desk and waiting.

I ARRIVED AT the restaurant twenty minutes early and made my way between the empty tables to the same place we'd sat the previous day. The same waiter took his time coming over, despite not having any other customers as it was the dead space between lunch and dinner.

"What can I get you?" he asked.

I debated a drink, but decided against it. "Coffee." I glanced at my device, discovering that one minute had passed since the last time I'd checked. After three repetitions of that, I opened a news site and tried to skim the headlines. None of it registered. Finally three o'clock rolled around and the chime on the door sounded. I looked up to see a couple of university-age women, one with fair skin and pink hair, another who had darker skin and black hair shot through with purple highlights. I found myself looking at their eyes, but then forced myself to look past them for Gylika. He didn't seem like the type to be late, though with city traffic and sometimes unpredictable transportation delays, it wasn't anything to worry about.

At fifteen past I started to worry. It began as almost a tickle in the back of my mind and grew from there. I called Gylika's office, but it went straight to his message. It should have forwarded to his device if he was on the way. Maybe he was on the comm, and that was what was holding him up. Maybe his boss had called him in, and he hadn't had time to send me a note.

At three thirty I got up and started to pace around, and not just because I had to pee from drinking all that coffee. I tried his office again but got the same response. I went outside and walked a hundred meters or so in each direction, looking for something. *Anything.* I didn't know what, but I couldn't sit there. Finding nothing, I forced myself to go back inside. I drank another cup of coffee and waited until four before I finally gave up and left.

It was a pleasant day, so I slung my jacket over my shoulder and walked the four kilometers home to avoid transportation. People still recognized me on the street, but usually I passed them before they had time to react. There hadn't been any demonstrations against the destruction of Cappa in more than a year, so that didn't worry me. At least not on this planet. I walked briskly, dodging in and out of the light afternoon crowd, some of whom had their faces hidden behind devices. I passed a shop that sold high-tech toys, and I paused for a moment to look at the merchandise in the window. I didn't buy a lot of things, but I liked to see the coolest new gadgets.

As I stopped, something caught my attention from the corner of my eye, back from the direction I'd come. Somebody else stopped at the exact same time, two stores back. It probably wasn't anything, but Gylika not showing had me on alert. I risked a glance back for a split second. The person wore a light beige jacket with the hood up, which seemed out of place on a warm, sunny day. The jacket fit loosely enough where I couldn't tell if it was a man or a woman, and while I thought I saw dark skin, I couldn't be sure. My pulse started to pick up, but I took three deep breaths to calm myself. I couldn't risk another episode like the previous day.

I pretended to go back to looking at the merchandise in the display, then, without warning, I started walking. A light turned, and I darted across the six lanes of traffic just before the vehicles started moving, drawing a blaring horn from a private car. I stood on the far side of the road, scanning for the tan jacket. He—or she—had disappeared. They couldn't have followed me across the road, and there weren't so many people that I should have lost sight of Beige Coat. I stood there for a moment, unsure what to make of it, then I started for home again, paying too much attention to people behind me and almost bumping into someone twice. I took some random turns and walked a few blocks in the wrong direction to be safe. I pretended I could use the extra exercise, but it's hard to lie to yourself.

I waited several moments in the lobby of my building, watching the door. When nobody showed, I went upstairs, deactivated my security, and went inside.

# CHAPTER SIX

THE BUZZER AT my door sounded, waking me from a restless sleep. Light streamed through the rectangular windows and my side of the building faced east, so I knew it was morning. I checked my device beside my bed: 7:30. Maybe I'd imagined it. I levered myself up out of my puddle of drool to a sitting position and stayed there a minute. The buzzer rang again.

"Hold on," I shouted and instantly regretted it, my hangover just bad enough to hurt. I didn't expect anybody. I never expected anybody, and damn sure not at seven thirty in the morning. As far as I knew, nobody actually knew where I lived. I'd even lied to my employer about that, which is a necessary precaution for the infamous. On the way to the door I checked my desk drawer for the pistol I kept there. I didn't take it out. Talca 4 law made guns illegal for private citizens, but I considered myself an unusual circumstance as half the galaxy hated me. That probably wouldn't hold up in court, but I liked having it there. Not like someone could shoot me through the door. Not unless they brought a cannon. The door was bulletproof, pulse proof, and pretty much any other kind of proof money could buy. I'd even had the wall to the hallway reinforced. You can't ever be too safe.

"Video," I said, activating the screen by the door so I could see my visitor in the hall. Two professional-looking people in cheap suits stood there, a dark-skinned, slightly overweight male standing about two paces behind a blonde woman with her hair up in a bun. "Yes?"

"Colonel Butler?"

"Who?" I asked. "Who is Butler?"

"Colonel Butler, I'm Lieutenant Mallory. This is Sergeant Burke. We'd like to have a few words with you."

"Could you identify, please."

Mallory held her ID up to the scanner, then pressed her thumb on the pad. The screen on my side of the door gave me two green circles. "That good?"

My system boasted voice-pattern recognition advertised to be able to detect a lie and state-of-the-art identification programming. It claimed a 100-percent accuracy rate. But I'd been seeing things I didn't trust, so I hesitated. "What do you want to talk about?"

Mallory looked around, as if checking for anybody in the hallway. "Can we come in? It's rather important."

I paused a moment longer, then hit the authenticate button that deactivated the system. Mallory came in first, trailed by Burke.

"Thank you," she said. "I recognize you from the news, but for clerical purposes, please put your thumb here." She held out a slim device, and I obliged. Half a second later it flashed green.

"What's this about?" I asked. Burke meandered a little bit, looking around, checking out my apartment while trying not to be too obvious. "Do you mind?" He shrugged—I decided I didn't like him.

"Colonel Butler, where were you yesterday?"

"I was at work. I left between two and two thirty for a late lunch."

"What restaurant?" she asked.

"A place called Gerard's."

She glanced at her partner, who nodded as if he knew the restaurant, then looked back to me. "Do you know Warren Gylika?"

My heart sped up until I could feel it in my neck. "Yes. He was supposed to meet me yesterday afternoon. Is he okay?"

"At your late lunch?"

"That's right," I said.

"That wasn't on his calendar," added Burke.

"No," said Mallory. "Did you also meet with him the day before yesterday?"

I glanced at Burke, then back at Mallory. "Yes. We had lunch. What's this about?"

"Was it a planned meeting or something spur of the moment?"

"Why?"

She fixed me with a stare for a few seconds. "It's a simple question."

"Spur of the moment," I said. "He called me that morning."

She looked to her partner, who nodded. I got the impression that he'd checked the phone record or something similar. "What did he say he wanted to meet about?"

"He didn't." I felt like short, direct answers served me best. Something was off. "Again: what's this about?"

She paused for several seconds, as if deciding whether to tell me or not. "We found Mr. Gylika's body last evening. He's dead."

I couldn't form words for a moment. "He's . . . what happened?"

"We're hoping you can tell us," said Mallory.

I stared at her. "Wait, you think I know something?"

She gave me a flat smile that didn't touch her eyes, but she didn't respond. My brain finally dialed in. She kept her silence in order to get me to fill the void. Classic interrogation.

"Do you think I had something to do with his death?" I asked. Classic reverse interrogation. Ask a question instead of answering one.

"It wouldn't be like it's your first time," said Burke.

I didn't react for several seconds. He was trying to bait me. I dropped my voice and spoke calmly. "That's out of line. Tell you what, I'd like you to leave. You're welcome to contact my attorney." I made a show out of fumbling with my device, pulling up information to send them. I didn't have a lawyer. I didn't think they'd call my bluff.

"We apologize, Colonel Butler," said Mallory. "You're right. That was out of line. Sergeant Burke didn't mean anything by it. Tell him you're sorry, Burke."

"I'm sorry," said Burke. He wasn't sorry.

"Don't worry about it," I said. I didn't forgive him.

"Are you sure you don't have anything you can tell us that might help?" asked Mallory.

"I'm taking it that it wasn't a natural death?" I asked.

Mallory thought about it, again deciding what to share. "No. It wasn't natural."

"He was supposed to meet me at three yesterday afternoon. Like I said, at Gerard's. It's off of Vine Street and Latten."

Burke cut in. "I think I know the place. A lot of fake wood?" He acted casual, but he'd probably been there already. They knew we met for lunch two days prior, so they'd almost certainly checked it out.

"Yeah, that's it," I said. "We had lunch there the day before yesterday, too."

"What was your meeting about then?" asked Mallory.

"A mutual friend put us in touch. Another soldier. She knows I don't have a lot of friends in town, so she thought it might be good for me." I didn't feel the need to share the whole truth, especially when I didn't know if they considered me a witness or a suspect.

She tapped something into her device. "And you hit it off so well that you decided to get back together yesterday at three?"

I gave her a fake smile. "I told you already, I have no idea what that was about. He called me a little after two and asked me to come. I wasn't doing anything, so I said, 'Why not?' I figured they'd have his phone records and see the call, so it made sense to give that info to them. Working for Omicron, he'd probably have had high-end encryption stuff like I did, but for a murder—assuming that's what it was—the police might be able to trace it. "When he didn't show up, I called his office a couple times, but it went straight to message."

"Did you report it?" she asked.

"Report what? A guy missing a meeting?"

Burke looked like he wanted to ask me something, but Mallory gave the slightest shake of her head to wave him off. She turned to me and smiled. "Colonel Butler, I'm sorry to have brought you this kind of news so early in the day. If you think of anything that might help us, give me a call. My number's in your security system from where I scanned my credentials."

"Sure." I followed them toward the door, Burke still looking around the apartment like he might spot a bloody knife.

Mallory turned after she passed through the door, talking almost over her shoulder. "Oh, and Colonel Butler? Please don't leave the planet."

**"TELL ME YOU** have something good for me," I said, when Plazz answered my call. I waited maybe half an hour after the police left, hoping I'd be in a better frame of mind. It didn't work.

"Nice to hear from you, Carl. I'm doing great, how are you?"

"Well I was questioned by the police for what I assume is the murder of a mid-level executive at Omicron, so—"

"Holy shit."

"Yeah. So my side of things is pretty much at a standstill, and I don't know where to go next. So I hope you've got something."

"Who's dead?"

"I don't want to talk about it," I said. "What did you learn about the breach?"

"No way. You don't get to drop a *there's a dead guy* and then say you don't want to talk about it," she said.

"Yeah, that's fair." I filled her in on Gylika and the police visit.

"Thanks, Carl."

"For what?"

"For actually sharing your information with me."

I shook my head and grinned in spite of myself. "You're an ass."

"Assholes get things done."

"Truth," I said. "So tell me about the breach."

"Their official response to my inquiry is ignorance."

I grunted. "Great."

"It's not that surprising. It's not public news, and they don't want it to be. Think of how their share-holders would react if they found out they had a hole in their security that might have been exploited."

I sighed. "I guess. But that doesn't really help us."

"There are other ways to get information beyond official channels. You know that."

"So you got something." I could hear it in her voice.

"I *might* have something. I can say with pretty strong conviction that there was a breach, and that a few people at Omicron are pretty excited about it. Not in a good way."

"That's something," I said.

"It is, but I can't get close to what it might have been."

"Shit. How about how it happened?" I asked.

"No chance. Not from the source I've got now, and I don't think anybody in the know is going to talk to me. It's a pretty tight circle, from what I gather."

"I hear you. And I think there's a chance that the circle got smaller by one today. We're on a secure line, right?" I should have thought about that first. In the military I'd never had to ask.

"Absolutely. You think your guy knew?" she asked.

"Is there another way to see it? When he called me, it sounded like he had something to share. Now he's dead."

"Let me look into his death," she said. "Omicron can clam up and lock me out, but the police can't.

There are too many leaks there. I'll let you know what I find."

"Thanks," I said.

"You see how that works? You share information with me, and I get answers for you. It's almost like we're working together."

"Yeah, yeah. Talk to you later."

# CHAPTER SEVEN

**WANTED TO AVOID** Dernier when I got to work. I'd have to tell him about Gylika, and he'd push me for information, and in my mental state I didn't want to deal with that. He'd find out, but I wanted to wait. Despite my desire not to share, I didn't think I could get away with shutting out Javier, so after I had my first coffee I headed up to his office.

I had a secondary agenda. I'd tell him about Gylika, but I wanted an opportunity to ask about his original military source. I didn't have any other leads now, and that might give me a new way to look at things. His secretary offered me another coffee, which I accepted, then she ushered me into his office.

Javier spoke without looking up from his screen. "Carl. You've been avoiding the attorney I assigned you."

"What? No. I've just been busy." *But it's good to confirm you're getting reports from him.*

"You're a poor liar, Carl."

*I am when I want to be caught.* "Okay. I didn't have anything, so I was avoiding him."

"But you have something now."

I breathed out audibly. "No."

"But . . ." he shut his screen down and looked at me.

I shrugged. "I thought I had something, then a guy turned up dead."

He hesitated for a moment. He hadn't known. Good. "Oh, shit. What do you mean?"

I took a moment to catch him up on Gylika's death, the events of the previous day, and everything else that had happened. I didn't mention Plazz or Ganos. He didn't need to know my sources, just the general information and why I was stuck.

"So . . . crap. What do we do? We need to get away from this, right?" He stood up and began to pace. "The police are involved. That could look bad for us."

"I don't think so," I said. "I didn't do it. The optic might not be great, but in the end all I did was have lunch with the guy. He didn't tell me anything, and a mutual friend set up the meeting. Just two ex-military guys getting together."

"But people won't see it that way," said Javier.

"I can drop it if you want," I said. "But you gave me this job because you were worried about the security breach. To me, this makes it more worrisome, not less. What if the people who were responsible for the breach in Omicron's network were also responsible for Gylika?" I surprised myself with that one. I hadn't intended to push to continue the job, but when I said it, it instantly felt right. Gylika might have died because of something I set in motion, and I wanted answers.

"You think that's likely?" he asked. "Never mind . . . that's not the issue. The point is that this is a police matter now. We have no business in it."

"But we do. VPC is potentially at risk. It's our obligation to act to protect the company the best we can."

He paused, considering. Then, nodding: "I guess. Okay, stay on it. But you've got to take a very measured approach. What's your plan?"

"I could find another contact at Omicron, but until the police figure out what happened to Gylika, I think that would be pretty irresponsible."

"Right," he said. "That's definitely not the way to go."

"I do have another way," I said, setting the hook.

"What's that?"

"Who was your original source in the military? If I knew that, there's a good chance I could get to him . . . or her . . . and get a new start there." I tried not to hold my breath. Javier held my sole lead, and I found myself heavily invested in the outcome.

He inhaled deeply through his nose, and then walked to the far side of the room to stare out the window. I followed him but didn't get too close.

"I'm not sure I can do that," he said, after at least a minute of silence. He'd either legitimately been thinking about it or pretending to. I decided it was probably the former. If I had a way to push him, I think he'd have given me the information. Instead I backed off. He seemed hesitant about continuing at all, and I didn't want him to tell me to drop it altogether.

I let the silence hang as long as I dared. "I'll find another way."

He thought for a few more seconds. "Yes. You're right. We have to do something. Find another angle." He stared at me with that alpha-male stare that some leaders get, as if daring me to contradict him.

"Can do." I had cards left I could have played. I left unsaid the fact that somebody had died and that his holding back information put us at more risk. He already knew that, and had to have reasons for not offering up his contact. He had more to think about than I did. As the boss, anything that fell on the company would fall on him. I'd find another way. I always did.

"SIR, WHERE ARE we going?"

"It's called lunch, Ganos. People eat it." I navigated my way through the people crowding the city sidewalk at the busiest time of day, with Ganos trailing along in my wake.

"Right. Sir, you don't go out for lunch."

"Sure I do."

"Let me rephrase that. *I* don't go out for lunch."

"Exactly. We're changing that."

"We're outside. I work in IT. I'm not dressed for lunch." She wore purple yoga pants and a hooded gray sweatshirt. She had a point.

"We'll go somewhere casual."

"Since I'm assuming you want something from me, you're buying. Let's go somewhere with good fries."

"You've got it." I checked behind us to make sure nobody was following us. I'd started to believe that my paranoia might be a good thing. Of course that in itself was paranoid, but better safe than sorry.

I passed two places before finally choosing a spot a bit down a side street. I hadn't told Ganos, but I didn't want anyone from the company—especially Dernier—to see us eating together, which meant I needed to get away from the building.

"We could have stopped at one of the other ones that were closer," she continued, once we sat down. "Wait . . . Oh, Mother . . . you're ashamed to be seen with the little people of the company, aren't you?"

"Have you been here before?"

"I have not." She laughed. "I'm getting a milk-shake, too."

"Get whatever you want."

"Sir . . . what's going on? You're acting really strange. This is about that thing I looked into, isn't it?"

"Yeah." *Of course she'd figured it out.* "It's been a rough week. Look, I'm going to ask you to do something. You can say no." That was bullshit, of course. I knew she wouldn't refuse. I hated myself for being such an asshole. Okay, I didn't, but I pretended I did so I didn't feel as bad about it.

We paused as the waitress showed up to take our order. True to her word, Ganos ordered the least healthy things on the menu. I ordered chicken salad. I made small talk until our food arrived, watching the door to see who came in. Nobody seemed suspicious. Once I was as comfortable as I could get, I got to the point.

"I want you to hack into Javier Sanchez's computer."

I'd waited until Ganos had a mouth full of milkshake before I said it. Like I said, asshole. To her credit, she didn't spit it out.

"I'm going to go out on a limb and say that's not a great idea."

"So you can't do it?" I asked.

"Please," she said. "Who are you talking to? I *can* do it. The question is if I *should* do it. Mr. Sanchez doesn't know who I am. I prefer to keep it that way."

I basically lived by the same principle until he put this on my desk. I could respect it.

But I pushed anyway.

"What if I said he approved it?"

"He approved hacking his own account." She didn't roll her eyes, but I think that was only out of respect.

"I work security," I said. "It's my job to look for vulnerabilities, especially after the Omicron thing I told you about. He wants solutions. He gave me the go-ahead to find unique ways of looking at the potential problem."

She met my eyes for a few seconds. She didn't buy it. Smart woman. And yet, there was a spark there, gears turning. I had her.

"Hypothetically—and I do mean *hypothetically*—if I were to do this . . . what would I be looking for?"

"Nothing sensitive. We just need something to prove we were in there. Let's say . . . his list of contacts."

"His list of contacts. That's it?"

"Yes. That would give me definitive proof that he could be compromised."

She took a moment to think while she ate some fries. "What's the catch?"

"The catch is it would be better if he doesn't catch us."

She laughed. "Sir, what are you up to?"

I met her eyes. "It's better if you don't know. Can you do it without getting caught?"

"If I do it, no way are they catching me." She took a sip of her milkshake to give herself more time to think. "Okay. I'm in. Give me a day."

"Really?"

"Sure, why not? I like to screw with the security folks anyway. It'll be fun."

"Thanks, Ganos."

"I'm guessing, since we went out of our way to avoid being seen having lunch together, that I shouldn't tell anybody in my department what I'm doing," she said.

I almost choked on my water. I thought I'd been slick, but I hadn't fooled her for a minute. "That would be best, yeah."

IT TURNED OUT to be a good precaution that I sent Ganos ahead of me back to work, because I ran into Dernier in the lobby. His heels clacked against the polished floor, like even they were uptight. "I heard about the new development," he said.

"Which development?" I asked.

"Warren Gylika. The dead man."

"Oh, that. Yeah."

"You asked what development. Were there others?" he asked.

"No, not really."

"Would you tell me if there were?"

I thought about how to answer. He already knew, so it seemed pointless to deny it. "Probably not."

"I don't know what I did to turn you against me. Why won't you let me help?"

I didn't have a great answer. Right after I'd told him about a lead I had, the guy ended up dead. I didn't blame Dernier for it—at least the rational part of me didn't—but I couldn't dismiss it, either. I couldn't share that, so I made up an excuse. "It's nothing personal. I just feel like anything I tell you you're going to tell your boss."

"Of course I'm going to tell my boss. Why wouldn't I? We're the legal department. It's our job to keep the company out of trouble."

"I think you and I see things differently in that regard. Because I see that as *my* job."

He stopped walking, which forced me to either leave him or stop as well. I considered leaving him there but thought better of it. "This is going to be a problem," he said. "I don't want to, but I'll take it to Mr. Sanchez if needed. I'm not getting fired because you can't be bothered to cooperate."

He had me there. His look and tone told me that he

wasn't bluffing, and I couldn't afford to have him go to Javier again. After our last meeting, I knew that the CEO would pull me off the project with the slightest nudge from legal. "Fine. Let's go."

"Where are we going?" he asked.

"To work."

A few minutes later we were seated in my office, looking at each other across my elegant but not-too-fancy corporate-issued desk.

"What do you see as your role in this process?" I asked.

"For starters, protect the company from liability."

"Speaking of that, I may need a lawyer. The police questioned me about Gylika's death."

"I'm not that kind of lawyer. And you're changing the subject," he said.

"You asked what would help. I could probably use some legal advice, though I had nothing to do with his death."

"Sorry."

I sighed. Fine, I'd try another tack. "How can I help you do your job?"

"I need to know the plan. What are you going to do next? Where are we going?"

"I told you, I usually don't know until I get there."

"I can't work with that. I have to give my boss something. Can we at least draft some potential courses of action?" he asked.

I started to snap back at him, but held it for a moment. I was acting too defensive, and that would make him dig in rather than back off. At the same time, I couldn't tell him my real plan, because that involved hacking into the CEO's account, and I had to believe legal would frown on that. So instead I made up some bullshit. "Look, I visualize things from different directions than other people. It's not better or worse, it's just how I operate. Sometimes, if I'm being overanalyzed by my boss, he might not see the big picture from the fragments. I might not have put it together yet myself."

He appeared to be receptive, so I continued. "You and I want two different things. We both want what's right for the company, but you want to brief your boss, and I want to control the information so that I don't get questions from higher until I have some answers. I don't want to make them nervous. We have to get past that fundamental difference."

"Why can't we do both? What's wrong with a few questions, if you're doing the right thing?" he asked.

I almost laughed at that naivete. How did this guy become a corporate lawyer with that attitude? "Because if I'm trying to answer questions from the boss, I'm busy chasing things that might not help me get the real answers. I like to keep things controlled until I have something worthwhile to share, then present a complete picture."

He thought about it for a moment, without dropping his gaze. "Okay. I get it. Maybe we can work out a system where you share what you get, but you let me know what I can pass on and what I should keep to myself. But you've got to work with me. You have to give me something to feed the beast."

That sounded totally reasonable, to the point where I started to wonder if maybe I should have been less of an asshole from the start. I could never rule that out. "I can work with that."

"As for the legal advice, I'd recommend that you don't talk to the police again without a lawyer present. That's pretty much true in any situation."

"Thanks. I guess I'll need to find somebody."

"I can get you some good recommendations," he said.

**THE WHITE ROOM** smelled of antiseptic, and the mechanical beeps of a dozen machines provided a soundtrack. I pulled at my arms, but straps held them to a narrow bed, one of eight identical ones in the room. I was alone, but had the uncomfortable feeling that someone would join me soon. I jerked my right hand back and forth, finally loosening whatever fastener held me in place. I freed my other arm and swung my bare feet over onto the cold tile. I glanced at the door, expecting someone to come through at any minute, then dashed across the room to a control board.

The panel didn't fit the rest of the scene. This was a medical facility, but the controls looked like something that belonged on a ship. A targeting computer. I pushed the thought aside and let my fingers fly over the keys the way they had so many times before. Muscle memory. I had to destroy the base. We had plenty of firepower in orbit to do it.

I paused.

I was on the base. The planet. If I finished the firing solution, I'd be signing my own death warrant. The scene blurred, changed as I tried to work through the problem. I searched my brain for an answer, but the harder I tried to find it, the more it slipped away. I punched in the coordinates and authenticated the command. A timer came onto the screen, counting down. It didn't belong. No system in the military had a timer like that. It looked more like something from a poorly written holo-vid.

*Beep. Beep. Beep* . . .

I sat dead up in bed, gasping for air, the clothes that I'd passed out in soaked through with sweat. It took me a moment to get my bearings in the room, dark from the blackout curtains. I took a deep breath and then another, trying to slow my pounding heart. I sank back down into my pillow and closed my eyes. I needed to sleep, but it eluded me for the rest of the night.

# CHAPTER EIGHT

SINCE I COULDN'T rest, I did what I always do in that situation. I went to the gym. While I worked out, I recorded all the things that came to mind. Once I made a physical list, it got easier to deal with, became less overwhelming. By the time I'd showered and had coffee, I had some semblance of a plan, and that always relaxed me. Taking charge and moving forward always beat sitting still and waiting for others to act. When others acted, I had to react, which immediately put me behind.

I couldn't control when Ganos would get back to me with the information from Javier's account so I pressed on to other tasks. With the investigation stalled, I focused in on the rest of my life. I had to deal with my paranoia about somebody following me. I couldn't rule it out, and I knew myself well enough to know that if I didn't find a way to empirically prove my suspicion wrong, I'd keep thinking about it. That would lead to me seated back in the psychiatrist's office, talking about things I thought I saw. I spent enough time with her without adding weeks of a new topic to discuss.

I headed out to do some shopping. The wind blew with a bite, and the sparse early-morning crowd on a weekend meant fewer places to hide in the throng, but also fewer eyes to avoid. I took three transfers to get to the west side of town. The streets grew progressively narrower, the signs on shops less elaborate. I wouldn't visit this part of the city alone at night, and even during the day it made me a bit more uptight than usual. I walked about three blocks from the transportation stop and found the store I wanted. The digital sign had some pixels out, making it barely readable, and the thick plexiglass windows obscured the view of the inside, but I'd visited before and knew I had the right place.

A thin, light-skinned woman stood behind the counter, alone. She wore her black hair long on one side, shaved on the other, and she had three studs through her bottom lip on one side. She looked me over with a glance that said I didn't belong here, though she inclined her head slightly, acknowledging me. "What can I do for you?"

"I'm looking for some surveillance equipment."

"You're not from the west side. You came all the way over here for that? You looking for something to take pictures at a distance?"

"What I'm looking for isn't available everywhere," I said.

She assessed me more thoroughly, now. "What do you need?"

"Programmable drone," I said.

"It's illegal to fly a drone in the city."

"I have a place out in the country." I smiled.

She snorted. "Right. So this . . . country place. I assume you want something that won't be easily seen?"

"Right," I said. "You know . . . so it doesn't scare away the animals."

"I've got just the thing. Animals won't know it's there. Flies at about fifty meters up, quiet enough that it won't be heard five meters away."

"Streaming link?" I asked.

"No," she said. "Downloadable only. That's the only way to keep it as small as you want. And to minimize the electronic signature." She paused. "You know. In case the animals have electronic detection."

I chuckled. "Yeah. Smart animals. How does it work?"

"Passive sensors. You put the sensor on the . . . animal you want it to look at, the drone's camera stays on it. After a set time, it returns to a preprogrammed base."

"How big is it?" I asked.

She showed me something about the size of half a walnut.

"Sounds like exactly what I need."

"It's not cheap," she said. "Cash only."

"I've got cash."

"Hope you have a lot."

I SPENT THE rest of the morning flipping through news on my terminal, looking for everything and anything I could find on Gylika's death. Something like that couldn't stay quiet for long, even if the police wanted to keep it that way. The man probably had a family—people who loved him. Somebody had to be talking about it, because even in a city of 15 million people, a murder made the news.

Except it didn't.

Not exactly. The stock article that all the sources carried said that he'd been "found dead" in the parking structure beneath Omicron headquarters, but nowhere did it mention foul play or a cause of death. Nobody published pictures, save for a photo provided by the family for the obituary. Omicron had published an official statement mourning the loss of one of their own and sending condolences to the family. The family themselves had said nothing; at least nothing that reporters captured. I wondered briefly how much the family knew, but I couldn't contact them to ask. It would be incredibly tasteless, not to mention it might make the police wonder about me more than they already did.

So I did the next best thing. I ignored the legal advice Dernier gave me the day before and called Lieutenant Mallory. I wanted to find out what she knew, but she wouldn't offer it for free, so I decided to play a little game and pretend that I might have something of value in order to see what I could get from her.

"I hope it's okay that I called you on a weekend," I said, after I'd identified myself.

"It's no problem. I'm working anyway. You have something for me?"

"I'm wondering about the status of the case," I said. "Did you find out what happened?"

"Why are you so interested?" she asked.

I'd expected the question. "I'm not allowed to leave the planet until you clear me. I have plans off world."

"What kind of plans?" she asked.

"Meeting an old business associate about work matters."

She grunted. "The case is still open."

"No leads?"

"Look," she said. "I'm a busy woman. Do you have anything for me or not?"

"I might," I said.

"Mr. Butler, I suggest very strongly that you don't fuck with me. You won't like the result. Now tell me what you've got, or I'm hanging up."

"I'd like to come in and talk," I said.

"So come in."

"That's the thing. I think someone's been following me. I don't want to go outside." A partial truth, but close enough.

"I'll send a car. Fifteen minutes." She hung up.

The hover-car arrived as promised, on time, white with the gold symbol of the police on the sides and roof, and it dropped me at the station a few minutes later. A tall woman met me at the front entrance and led me back to a windowless room with a single door. An interrogation room. I sat in a plain, hard-backed chair and waited until Mallory came in a few minutes later and shut the door.

I gestured to the bare room. "Is this really necessary?"

"I figured we wanted privacy. I don't have an office, just a desk in the pit."

"Where's your bad cop? Burke."

"He's out. Let's cut the shit, Butler. What do you have?"

"Other than somebody following me?"

She met my eyes without blinking, but didn't speak.

"I first noticed it the same day I was supposed to meet Gylika. The day he died."

She hesitated for a couple seconds. "Why didn't you tell us about it when we came to your apartment?"

"I wasn't thinking clearly. Maybe I was in a bit of shock to find out that the man who I was supposed to meet was dead."

She didn't call me on it, but her look said "bullshit." She was good at this, and I had to be careful. "This person who was following you. What did he look like?"

"Tan jacket," I said. "I'm not sure if it was a man or a woman."

"So you didn't get a very good look."

"No."

"So how do you know the person was following you?"

"Instinct," I said.

"Instinct," she repeated, with only a hint of sarcasm.

"I've learned to trust it."

"Mr. Butler, you know I can't do anything with that."

"I'm sure enough that I considered calling my old contact at the military security office," I said. "A couple years ago I had a team assigned to me. There were some threats on my life back then."

"Why didn't you call them?"

"Thought I'd give you first shot at it," I said.

She paused, looking more thoughtful now. "Threats on your life. Have there been any recently?"

"None that I've received," I answered. "You'd have to check with the security office to see if they've had any that I don't know about."

"That's not really helpful," she said, but she tapped a short note into her device.

"I'm here," I said. "I'm trying to help." She had me on my back foot, which kept me from pressing her for information.

"You're here, I'll give you that." She stared me down for a few seconds. "Why are you here?"

"Because nothing in the news says what happened to the guy. I knew him, if only briefly, and I want to know."

"Mr. Butler, do you know how many people confess to crimes they don't commit in this city?"

"I have no idea."

"More than a few. So if we publicize how a death happened, all of a sudden we've got half a dozen false leads. We don't need that. Usually we can't control it. This time, Omicron security had it contained by the time we arrived, and the company and the family agreed to keep it quiet. Military family, you know. Good people."

I finally got my opening. Mallory had already confirmed that Omicron had contained the situation. Time to get what I came for. "So how *did* it happen?"

She looked at me like a teacher looks at a particularly difficult student. "Really?"

"Are you sure he was murdered?"

"Officially? We're not sure of anything."

"But . . ." I offered, hoping for a consolation prize.

"We're sure, yes."

"So he died in the Omicron building. Are you considering the potential that somebody from the company did him in?"

"Did him in?" she asked. "Is this a bad detective holo-vid?"

"You know what I mean."

"We've considered everything. Now if you don't have anything else to offer, I have crimes to solve."

"Sure. I can see myself out."

"You need a ride home?" she asked.

"I'm good."

"So the person who was following you . . ."

"That's real," I said. "I might have exaggerated about how scared I was."

She gave me a flat look. "You're taking a car."

# CHAPTER NINE

SPENT THE REST of the weekend fiddling with my drone and sending it out on surveillance of the surrounding area. I didn't find anything, but I had a lot of fun playing with it and learned how to get it to do what I wanted it to do without crashing into buildings. Most of the time.

The next morning Dernier met me at my office about fifteen minutes after I arrived, which I appreciated as it allowed me to get coffee before diving back into the dead ends of my investigation. "I found something that I thought you might want to see."

I flipped off my screen so it wouldn't distract me and I could give him my full attention. "What've you got?"

"I'm not sure it's anything, but you mentioned that you sometimes don't know where your leads will come from, so you like lots of information. I almost just posted it to the page, but I'm not sure how far you've gotten on that—"

"Dernier," I said, keeping my voice pleasant as I interrupted, "tell me what you've got."

"I thought about Mr. Gylika this weekend, and

what happened to him. And I started to think about how we got his name in the first place."

It interested me that he'd been thinking about Gylika, because I subconsciously still wondered if he had an inadvertent hand in his death, but I pushed that thought aside. I needed to trust him. He had nothing to gain from subterfuge . . . and I had nothing better to go on. "What about him?"

"It was from that article you sent me. The Phoenix Project," he said. "I started doing some digging on that. It's all very hush-hush in corporate releases and the news, even in the business journals. But I kept at it, and I stumbled across an obscure reference. I found an unpublished research paper by some young doctor at a medical school on Ferra Three."

"How'd you find it?" I asked.

"Brute force. Word search across the entire net, then an AI program to help sort through the entries until I found ones that fit enough of my criteria to search them manually."

"That had to have returned a lot of results."

"After the AI was done? Two thousand two hundred and forty-seven." He said it casually, but he meant it to impress. And it did. It certainly beat my contribution of flying a drone around.

"That's a lot of reading."

"I stopped at around seven hundred when I found something that held promise."

I sat forward on my chair, my cooling coffee forgotten. "Okay. You've definitely got my attention."

"The paper discussed the nature of advancing medical technology and vaguely mentioned the Phoenix Project as one of a few things with potential. It wasn't much."

"What was his field? The guy who wrote the paper."

"Ortho-robotics," he said.

It's a good thing I wasn't drinking my coffee because I'd have spit it out. It couldn't be. But the coincidence loomed like an asteroid hurtling at a space station. I couldn't avoid it.

"What?" he asked. "What is it? You just went pale."

I fumbled for an answer, still reeling. "I lost a foot during the war. I've spent a lot of unpleasant time around ortho-robotics departments."

"Oh, I'm so sorry." His face reflected genuine concern. "I didn't—"

"You couldn't know. And it's a good piece of information that you worked hard to find. When we pair it with other stuff, it might mean something." I was genuinely happy I had opened up even a little with him. But my newly developed plan to trust him didn't extend as far as telling him about my history with ortho-robotics on Cappa. I could always let him in on my true suspicion later, if this developed into something real.

I was lying to myself, of course. I believed it was real the minute I heard it.

"Okay. But I really didn't mean to—"

"Think nothing of it," I said. "It's been a long time, and I'm mostly over it."

He didn't believe me, but he nodded and started backing away. People do that when soldiers bring up old war demons. "I'll check back in with you tomorrow if neither of us finds anything else before then."

"Sounds good," I said. I emptied my coffee in the trash then stood to get a fresh cup. I needed to be doing something. Anything.

I COULDN'T FOCUS, so I called Dr. Baqri to see if she could work me into her schedule, and she told me to come over.

"You sounded distressed when you called," she said after I'd settled in.

"Thanks for seeing me." I was sitting in my normal spot and stared down at the expensive rug that covered the faux-stone floor.

"What's on your mind?"

"Coincidences," I said.

"You've told me before that you don't believe in coincidences."

"I don't. But that's the thing." I thought about it for a moment, and she gave me time. "At what point does that become paranoia? Like if I see every little thing as connected . . . what if I'm overthinking things?"

"You've always been a confident person, right?"

I shrugged. "Sure."

"So what's different, now?"

"I guess it's a different world."

She gave me a doctor look. "Is the world different, or are you just looking at it differently?"

"Since I became a civilian?"

"Sure, that. But more than that, too."

"Ah," I said. "Since I did what I did. So you're saying since I have regrets about what I did on Cappa, I've started to question my thoughts on other things."

She smiled. "I didn't say that."

I liked her. Sometimes I wanted her to just tell me the answers, because she had them. But it worked like this, and as much as I didn't want to go see her, I always ended up in a better place than when I arrived. "So how do I get past it? The self-doubt?"

"Well you might have to accept that as your new normal. Doubt isn't a bad thing."

"But it's not me."

"Maybe it is you. Or maybe it's something to work on."

I nodded. It clicked with me, what she said. I had to believe in myself. If I saw something, I had to trust it, no matter how it made me feel.

I GOT BACK to my office and sat there through lunch. Despite the calming influence of Dr. Baqri, I couldn't sit still. It seemed impossible, now, that I'd been sitting in this office every day for the better part of a year doing nothing. It would have been smart to let the whole thing go; the investigation, or even the job. I could make some sort of excuse and get out of it. Javier would pull the plug on it in a hurry if I asked.

But I didn't want to.

Some part of me—a big part—wanted to figure things out. I wanted to take all the coincidences and break them to my will, shape them into an answer. It made me feel somehow more alive. It made me feel relevant again—and in charge of my own fate—for the first time since I left Cappa.

I still had to run a fine line with Dernier and the legal folks. I'd started to like the man after my initial misgivings, but I had to keep him a little bit in the dark. The minute he thought I'd started in a direction that might bring any kind of negative attention to the company, he'd report it. No connection between him and I would change that.

In the meantime I headed to the IT floor and found Ganos. Ten minutes later we were outside, headed away from the building.

"It's past lunchtime," she said.

"I couldn't take another meal of fries."

"It's going to look weird, us leaving together."

"Nah. People will just think you're having an affair," I joked.

"Ew."

I clutched my hands to my chest. "Ouch."

"Don't get me wrong, sir. It would be a good deal for you. Younger woman, brilliant, all that. But I'd be the girl sleeping with the old dude."

I laughed, and as I did I realized how much I needed it. "We can head back. I didn't want to talk in the building. Too many VPC eyes. Did you get it?"

"Sir. Who are you talking to? Of course I got it."
She fished a few pieces of paper out of her pocket,
folded over several times. "Dude has a lot of contacts.
I didn't copy them electronically anywhere because
that would have—"

"You don't have to explain," I said. "I'll assume it's
computer magic."

"Right. Magic. Magic I don't want to get caught
doing." She handed me the folded paper square and I
took it without looking and shoved it into my jacket
pocket.

"Thanks, Ganos. It's a big help." I paused. "Hey, if
anybody finds out about this and asks you—"

"They won't," she said. "Not unless you tell them."

"But anything you can do, somebody can trace,
right?"

"In theory? Sure. In this case . . . I buried that shit
so deep that if they knew what they were looking
for *exactly*—like they knew I did something, when
I did it, and what I was trying to do—if they knew
that, they'd find it. So sure. There's a one in a million
chance."

"Still."

"It's okay—I wouldn't even get fired for it, sir. It's
not really sensitive information. Hell, if I did get fired,
I'd play it off as a prank, say I was messing with the
boss. I'd have another job in six hours."

"Great," I said. She'd have another job in six hours.
I had to wonder if I'd be able to say the same thing if
Javier caught on to what I'd done. He'd wanted to pro-

tect his contact, and now I'd potentially taken that out
of his hands. Yeah, he'd definitely fire me.

I RESISTED OPENING the paper Ganos had given
me while riding transportation. I didn't know what
I expected to find in it, or if what I found would do
me any good. Perhaps I'd find a military contact and
have no way to do anything with it. Perhaps there
wouldn't be one. I kept my head up more than usual.
People glanced at me while pretending that they
weren't, and at least one person whispered the word
"scourge," though not loud enough that I could tell
if it was in revulsion or merely pointing me out to
her companion. A well-built man with black hair and
golden skin stared longer than most, longer than was
strictly polite. I didn't usually seek conflict, but for
some reason it pissed me off, so I stared back at
him. He kept my gaze for a few seconds without
really meeting it, then glanced away as if he'd never
seen me . . .

I froze.

As he glanced away, his eyes shifted in shape, and
for a split second I thought they were Cappan ovals. I
started to sweat, cold and clammy, and I looked down
at the floor between my feet. The transport lurched to
a halt, one stop short of my normal debarkation, but
I got up and stumbled to the door. If I had stayed on
the transport, I feared I would take root there, unable
to function. I had to get away. I walked quickly and
didn't look back until I'd put twenty meters between

me and the door. The transport lumbered away and the people who'd gotten off scattered, but the dark-haired man wasn't among them.

I took several deep breaths and tried to focus. I put my hand into my jacket pocket and touched the paper, reassuring myself of its presence. I hadn't seen anything but a trick of the shifting light on a moving vehicle. I had a mission, a purpose, and I couldn't devolve into another panic attack. I shut off my brain and walked the last half kilometer to my apartment, my hand in my pocket the whole way, holding the list like a talisman.

Clearing my security system, I glanced at the bottle on the side table but decided against it. I unfolded the sheets of paper, nearly tearing them in my haste. Three pages of handwritten names stared back at me in green ink. Ganos's letters were blocky and utilitarian but easy to read. I recognized most of the names on page one, because I worked with them. I'd almost reached the bottom of the second page before one jumped out at me.

Serata.

Shit.

# CHAPTER TEN

GENERAL SERATA HAD retired from the military right about the same time I did, for the same reasons, though his happened much more quietly. I had something to do with that, dominating the headlines at the time. Nobody ever came out and said why he stepped down, and as far as I knew, nobody ever asked publicly. I always assumed it was political. Some rumors suggested that he stepped down voluntarily in exchange for them not prosecuting me. He'd never said as much himself, but I didn't rule it out.

He landed on his feet. Most generals do. He now had a job as a part-time motivational speaker and also worked as a consultant for high-level military exercises. He got paid a lot of money to work a few days a month. I could relate to that, as VPC paid me well. Not as well as Serata, but I couldn't complain. Even though he lived on Talca, the same as me, we never visited. His sparse work schedule allowed him to live outside the city, so we didn't live in close-enough proximity to make it easy. We exchanged communications every few months, and we always talked about getting together but hadn't made it happen.

I didn't blame him. Not about that, at least.

I'd had plenty of time to think about it—how Cappa ended. A lot of those thoughts ended up with me lying awake, drenched in sweat or vomiting my dinner into the waste disposal. But there had been rational times too, when I examined it more objectively. When I didn't think about what I'd done but how I'd come to do it.

The answer was clear: he set me up.

I suspected it back on Cappa, but when I returned home, I think some part of me tried to find another solution. One that let me still see him as my mentor, but one that ultimately didn't exist. Serata had needed someone to do the job he couldn't do himself, and I fit the bill. I don't think he specifically went looking for a scapegoat. Maybe I'm naïve in that. But Serata is a smart man, and he'd have known the likely outcomes. Perhaps somebody above him needed a scapegoat, too, and they'd used him.

Yet, despite knowing how he used me, I didn't hold it against him. He'd had a job to do and he did it. I'd had a job to do and I'd done it too. I had choices, even at the end, and I made them. He didn't push the button. I'd killed a shitload of Cappans, and as a bonus, it destroyed my marriage and turned me into a pariah. And thinking about it that way—how it affected me— made me feel worse because how dare I think about my one little life in comparison to all those others that I'd ended. But I'd been down the road of thinking about the Cappans and how it affected them, and that always ended in an even darker place for me. I had to avoid it for my own mental health.

We did the job. I hate the job that we did, and I wish I'd never been put in position to do it. If I could go back in time, I'd have told Serata no that day standing in his office. After all, he hadn't ordered me to go. He'd asked. Maybe he'd have found somebody else. Maybe if he did, that person would have been smarter than me and found another solution that didn't end in so much loss of life. Maybe that other mythical person would have been blind and missed the conspiracy, and there would be a bunch fewer dead Cappans and an ongoing genetic experimentation project.

I could screw myself into the ground dancing around all the what-ifs.

But I couldn't go back in time. I'd said yes and I'd gone out there, and I did what I did and that was that. Serata sent me, and he did it with a purpose. But like I said, I didn't blame him.

I blamed myself.

And now I needed to talk to him, and that meant I had to find a way to bridge the gap. I couldn't call him up and ask him why he was in Javier's contacts. That wouldn't get me what I needed. I had to see him in person. I needed to get into a room with him, where I could watch his reactions. Three years ago I wouldn't have said that. I'd have asked him over the comm and believed his answer. Not anymore. I don't blame him, but that doesn't mean I trust him. I think maybe I'm bitter about that, more than anything else with Serata. I missed our relationship. I needed somebody to trust, and it should have been him.

I opened a message to him on my device—his private account, not his work—and sent him a note.

> *Sir, I'm going to be out your way for business tomorrow. Would love to get together if you've got time. My schedule is flexible. Drop me a line.*

I kept it open for a moment and reread it a few times. I could have included more, a reason, but that would only make him wonder. This would be enough. I hit send.

I got a response maybe ten minutes later.

> *Carl, good to hear from you, brother. Why don't you come to the house for dinner? Say around 1830.*

Perfect.

I APPROACHED THE door of Serata's house in what passed for the suburbs. The very rich part of the suburbs, with large houses and manicured landscaping and security gates. I stopped short when Serata opened the door. He'd always been a physically imposing man, and I don't know why I expected it to be different. I'd prepared for this mentally, seeing him again, but now that he stood in front of me I locked up a little.

"Carl. You look like shit, brother."

I laughed. I don't know what I expected him to say, but it wasn't that. Suddenly everything was fine. "I haven't been sleeping very well. You look like you're doing okay."

"I'm trying to stay fit. It's hard, though. Getting old sucks." He paused, not quite long enough for it to get awkward. "Come on in," he said. "Lizzie is putting dinner together. It will be a few minutes."

I handed him a bottle of whiskey. "I brought something."

He took it and admired the label. "The good stuff."

"Never show up empty-handed. That's what my mom always said."

"Smart woman." He led the way into a study that looked like it belonged in a holo-vid, all dark wood and rich brown carpet. He opened a cabinet and got out two glasses, poured two fingers into each glass, splashed in a little water, and handed me one. "How are you, Carl?"

"I'm good," I answered.

He shook his head. "No. Really. How are you?"

I took a sip of my liquor, enjoying the warmth of it in my throat. "About the same. Some days are okay, some days not so much."

He nodded. "You seeing anybody?"

"You mean like a woman? No, I haven't really felt like it since Sharon left."

"I mean professionally," he said.

"Ah. Like a shrink. Yeah, I go a couple times a month. It doesn't do much. It's not like there's a support group for guys who destroyed the lives of millions."

"It still helps to talk about it."

"You're probably right," I said. "You trust them? I mean, I start talking about things, it gets out, people start talking about what I say."

He took a sip of his whiskey, then swirled the remainder in his glass. "I think if you find the right one. You have to be careful. Look around if you have to. I worry about you, brother."

I nodded slightly and stared at my drink before taking a sip, savoring the flavor. We drank in silence for a moment. He meant what he said; I had no doubt about that. Not just about worrying about me either.

*Brother.*

I felt pressure behind my eyes, a headache building from holding things in. I took another swallow to get it to go away. Sometimes that helped.

"How about you, sir? How are you doing?"

"I'm okay. There was a job to do, and I did it. People can question it after the fact, but I made the best decision I could with the information I had at the time."

"I'm the one who did it, sir. Really. I know you sent me, but I programmed the targets."

"It's bigger than that, what I did. You . . . your part, that made up a small piece of it. And I'm sorry for that, for what I did to you. But what I did . . . I circumvented the will of the civilian leaders, and while I still think I did the right thing, that's not okay. I thought I had a better answer, and I implemented it. I *did* have a better answer. But that's not really the point."

I finished my drink. I hadn't expected this kind of discussion—really almost a confession—but somehow it made things okay. Not okay for the rest of the galaxy, but between Serata and me, at least.

"You want to sit?" Serata asked.

"Sure." I took a heavy, leather-upholstered chair. Anywhere else I'd have figured it for fake, but I doubted it with Serata.

He walked over and poured me some more booze, added some to his own half-finished glass and then sat as well. "So what's going on? Unless you really expect me to believe you showed up out of the blue."

I laughed. "What? Can't a guy be in town and drop by for dinner?"

He smiled, and his eyes crinkled around the edges. "He absolutely could. But you didn't."

He wasn't upset. More curious. "Yes, sir, you caught me. There's a thing at work. It's a bit strange. I thought maybe you'd know something."

He settled back into his chair a bit. "Shoot."

"I got asked to investigate a potential breach in security."

"Sounds normal," he said.

"It would be, except the suspected breach was at Omicron."

His face scrunched a bit, and he thought about it for a few seconds. "Huh."

I watched him closely for signs while pretending to focus on my drink. I couldn't pick up anything from his reaction so far. "What made it stranger is that I really don't do that kind of work. If I'm being honest, I really don't do much work at all."

"So they gave it to you because you were available?" He didn't sound like he believed that.

"Not likely. Especially since the job came directly from the top."

"From Javier?"

"Yes, sir. You know him?"

"Yeah. We're not friends, but I've met him a few times. We talked about me going to work there when I retired. You sure it came from him?"

"He called me into his office, which has never happened before, and he gave it to me personally."

"Huh." Serata sipped his drink. I didn't read it as a cover, more like he needed a moment to think. "I'm assuming you looked into it."

"I did. I found a contact at Omicron and met with him. A guy named Gylika."

"Warren Gylika?"

"Yes, sir."

"I only know him by reputation, but I've heard he's a good man."

"He was. He's dead."

Serata had been raising his glass to his mouth, but stopped halfway. "Shit. I didn't know that."

He was telling the truth. I'd have bet a lot of money on that. "He called me after we met and asked to meet again. Told me he had something he wanted to share. He never made it."

Serata took a deep breath. "Damn. You think it had something to do with what he was going to tell you?"

"Police say it was a murder. Is there another way to see it?" I asked.

"It's definitely suspicious." He thought for a few more seconds. "So how does this lead to you being here talking to me?"

Now we were getting to the crux of it. If he decided to lie, we'd reached that point. "Once somebody died and the police started asking me questions, I began to take things a little more seriously. I went back to Javier and asked him about his source. I wanted to know how he heard about a breach at Omicron when it didn't appear in the news feeds. It wasn't public at all."

"And you thought I told him?"

"I asked him, and he told me his source was military, but he wouldn't reveal any more than that. I knew he knew you because he recognized your picture in my office, so I figured I'd take a shot and see if I got lucky." I didn't think I should reveal that I'd had Javier's contacts hacked. I still didn't know his relationship with Serata.

"Nope. Wasn't me."

"Did you know about the breach?" I tried to ask it casually. We weren't in the military anymore and I didn't have to defer to him, but I didn't want to piss him off, either. He could still kick my ass.

"Rumors," he said. "More than rumors. Strong rumors. Like something happened, but nobody really said what. I didn't believe them . . . that's not right, it's not that I didn't believe them . . . I never gave them much thought until you brought it up just now."

"It didn't seem important?"

"It didn't. Nobody made a big deal of it, you know? And if something major had gotten out, people *would* have made a big deal of it. No alarm, no fire."

I put my glass to my lips and studied him over the top of it. I believed him. He was capable of lying to me if he thought he needed to, but I didn't sense it. He really didn't know. "Any idea who else Javier might know who would have that information?"

He considered it. "I can't say for sure, but from what I know about Javier I'd say that he's unlikely to do anything without being very deliberate. He doesn't strike me as someone who makes rash decisions."

"I agree," I said.

"I feel like if he called you in and put you on it, he had to know something pretty firm. I don't think a rumor would do it."

"The way he said it, it didn't come across like a thing where I should find out *if* it happened. He wanted to know *what* happened."

"In that case, I don't know anything useful. I'm not as connected as I once was. I could ask around, call in a few favors."

"Thanks, sir. That would be great." It crossed my mind for a fleeting second that Gylika had said something similar just prior to his death, but I'd already shared that info with Serata, so he knew the risks. He could protect himself.

"What are you going to do?" he asked.

I shrugged. "I'll keep on it."

"Carl, I know that look. What are you thinking about?"

"It's nothing, sir. It's . . . I'm wondering if there's a reason that Javier put *me* on this. Some specific thing, tied to me."

"Like you're involved somehow?"

I shook my head. "I don't know. It sounds ridiculous, when I say it out loud."

"Well." He paused. "Sometimes things sound ridiculous and they aren't. Sometimes you're staring at everything, and it points one way, and you still have that feeling that it's something else. You know?"

And sometimes people in power want to use you. I nodded. "I know."

"And we train people to put their feelings aside. We tell them to look at the facts and take emotion out of it. But we both know that's bullshit. You can't do that and be worth anything. It's why we have humans make decisions, not computers."

"So you're saying I should run with it," I said.

"I don't know. Try another angle. What if Javier *did* bring you in for a reason? What would that reason be? Find that, and you'll find your connection, if there is one."

Lizzie called us for dinner then, and we let the conversation drop, transitioning to more pleasant things like remembering old friends and catching each other up on mutual acquaintances and what they'd been up to. I needed that conversation. I hadn't realized how much until I sat there and laughed and found myself comfortable for the first time in a couple of years. I didn't stay long after dinner. I didn't want to go back to the study and discuss deep matters. I wanted to let the good times remain at the forefront for a little while.

"Thanks for having me, sir," I said, as I stood at the door. Serata had a genuine smile plastered to his face. I think our talk was important for him, too.

"I'm glad you came, Carl. It's good to see you."

"It was good to see you, too, sir." I meant it. I should have come to see him sooner. Not about the business with Omicron, but about everything else. Nothing had changed with what I had done, or what he had done, but the shared experience somehow spread the weight of it, made it not quite so heavy.

And I needed that, too.

# CHAPTER ELEVEN

THE TALK WITH General Serata did a lot of good for my well-being but didn't do much to help me with my mission. Still, his words kept coming back to me. He called Javier deliberate, said that he didn't do things without thinking them through. That got me to considering how I came to be at VPC in the first place. Javier had brought me in for my connections. Maybe I could find a way to use that, though I didn't want to dive back into Omicron directly without knowing more about what might be waiting. If Omicron had linked me to Gylika, they could be watching for anyone else who might talk to me.

I came up with two other possible places to look for a source of information: MEDCOM and SPACE-COM. A lot of the MEDCOM people disappeared two years ago when Elliot shot herself and the whole mess became public. Certainly they didn't eliminate everybody who knew, but they got rid of enough where everybody else would stay clear of even a hint of the project. But a file could still exist. If one person leaked it, the brains at Omicron could do the rest. Unfortunately, I didn't have any way to check into MEDCOM, so instead I focused on the other possibility. One that had been haunting me for some time anyway.

Some of the subjects had gotten off of Cappa.

Some of it may have been paranoia—me seeing things—but I couldn't rule out the possibility that Cappan hybrids were actually here. If people who had the treatment survived and escaped, they'd need medical attention. With Elliot dead, they'd have had to search out somebody else who knew the technology and had the facilities to continue treatment. I'd seen what happened to people like Colonel Karakov back on Cappa when they didn't get treatment. So when the theoretical escapees found someone to treat them, it wouldn't take much for that doctor, whether they knew about the program or not, to contact somebody in a position of authority. Once that happened, a link to Omicron became simple.

I'd destroyed all of the Cappan off-planet launch capability with my attack, so they'd have had to get off before that. I'd been ambushed on the space station, so I couldn't rule out that they'd been off planet all along. They also could have blended in with the humans during the evacuation before I launched the strike. Many Cappans—millions—survived. They wouldn't have any way to get off the planet anymore. Even mining operations had shut down. Humans didn't go to Cappa anymore; Cappans didn't leave it. The government embargo ensured that. If they hadn't left before I went planetside—and I didn't think they had—then that left a short window of time for them to have escaped. I knew where to check that window, but I needed help. I sent a note to Serata.

> *Sir, I need to get access to some old files at SPACECOM. Who do we know there who might be able to help?*

His answer came back almost immediately.

> *Stirling is Director of Training Development. You want me to give him a call?*

I laughed.

> *No, sir. Thanks for the lead. I'll take it from here.*

I hadn't seen Stirling since Cappa, and I hadn't realized he lived so close. I knew he'd been promoted to brigadier general, but not his assignment. We didn't keep in touch. Director of training development for Space Command sounds like an impressive job, but it isn't. The promotion probably had more to do with pretending there hadn't been any issues on Cappa than because he truly deserved it. A lot like mine and Serata's "retirements." He landed in a dead-end job where he'd be in charge of some things that didn't matter much and ran mostly on their own, and he'd serve out the rest of his time in obscurity. I knew something about that, because I'd been on the same track a few years back. The difference was that I had accepted it. Unlike me, it would eat Stirling up from the inside. He didn't have the personality to handle that sort of thing.

I looked forward to seeing him.

**I SHOWED MY** retiree ID at the gate of the base and they admitted me without question. Getting an audience with the man I wanted to see presented a bit more of a challenge. One can't just walk up and visit a brigadier general, especially if he didn't want to see you—and he almost certainly didn't want to see me. I could have had Serata set it up, but where was the fun in that? I headed to his office unannounced.

The base directory led me to an ugly one-story building that had to be forty years old. The rocks lining the walkway outside sported a clean coat of paint, and the construction appeared serviceable, but it hadn't been designed to impress visitors. The door had a touch pad and I didn't have authorization, so I waited for somebody else to go in and I followed her. I had prepped a story to talk my way through when she challenged me, but she didn't stop to look. Guess they didn't put a big priority on security, which might have spoken to the importance of what went on in the building.

Finding myself alone in a dim hallway, I fell back into my normal method: I pretended I belonged there. I passed a major in the hall and didn't make eye contact.

I needed a better target. I turned the corner and found a young soldier coming out of a supply closet with a mop.

"Excuse me. I have a meeting with General Stirling. Which way is his office?"

The soldier pointed to his right. "Right down there and take a left, sir."

"Thanks."

I walked into Stirling's outer office as somebody else came out so I wouldn't have to buzz in. I walked directly up to the secretary, a civilian lady about my age with short blonde hair shot through with gray. "Carl Butler here to see Brigadier General Stirling."

She looked at me for a few seconds, appraising. I knew immediately I wouldn't fool her with my bullshit. People didn't stay secretaries to generals without being good at their jobs. "Mr. Butler, I don't see you on the appointment list."

"He'll want to see me."

"He's in a meeting. I don't know when he'll be out." She kept her eyes locked on mine without flinching.

"Tell him my name. We go back."

She stared me down for a few more seconds, and sighed. "Fine. But he's not in acquisitions. Whatever you're selling, you're wasting your time."

I almost cracked. She pegged me for a corporate salesman. Of course. She probably got that a lot, and they'd all be guys like me. Retired officers. "I'm not selling anything. We served together on Cappa."

Her eyes went wide at that. I knew the look, because I got that same look every day. That moment of realization when somebody makes the connection and recognizes me. "Butler. You're *that* Butler?"

"I am."

"The general really is in a meeting," she said. "I wasn't making that up."

"I didn't think you were," I said. "I can wait."

"Have a seat over there on the sofa. I'll let him know you're here at the next break. You want some coffee?"

**"GOOD TO SEE** you, Carl," Stirling lied, still as transparent as clean glass.

"Good to see you too, Aaron." I lied too. But I wanted something from him, so of course I did.

He sat behind a large, modern desk, the polymer surface uncluttered and polished to a shine. "I'm sure you didn't just drop by to catch up."

I chuckled. "No. I need some help."

He hesitated a second too long. "Sure. Anything, of course." He meant that, but mostly because he didn't have much choice. He owed me, and we both knew it. I took the fall for Cappa, and I never mentioned publicly how bad he'd messed things up and how that contributed to what I did. He certainly didn't hold himself as culpable as I did, but I could have made it rough on him and I didn't.

That didn't mean he appreciated my showing up to collect.

I didn't care.

"I need to know if any ships left Cappa. Any non-sanctioned ships. Could have been miners or disguised as them. It would have been right before the end. Within a couple of days."

He considered it a moment. "We had the blockade."

I adjusted my position in the worn, padded chair across from his desk. "Right. Did anything get through?"

"I'd like to say no. But we didn't have enough ships to do the job. So . . . I don't know. I guess I couldn't rule it out."

"Any way we can find out for sure?" I had already worked out the answer, but I wanted him to come to it on his own.

"It's important?"

"I have reason to believe that some Cappans made it off the planet. Or possibly some people working with them. Maybe both. They seem to have taken an interest in me, and I really don't want all that stuff to come up again." I left it unsaid that *he* didn't want it to come up again either. I figured I'd given him enough of the truth to spur him into action.

He thought about it. "They'd be able to access the records from Ops. We store everything somewhere, so if they don't have it immediately, they can pull it."

"Any way we can see it? I figure I need maybe two days of data."

"You still have a clearance?" he asked.

"Yeah. I need it for my job, so the company pays to keep it updated."

"I'll make a call."

"You can do that? With Ops?" I asked. If he could, that would make it easier than I'd hoped. I'd thought I'd need two visits to get what I wanted, but with his help, I could potentially find what I needed in one.

He snorted. "I might be at a dead end, but I'm still a general. Nobody will think twice about something minor like this. You'll need a cover story, though, unless you want to tell everybody the real reason why you want the data."

He had a point. "Sure. Let's say I'm writing my memoirs, and I want to verify some facts about the last days before the attack. They'll be unattributed, of course, and I won't use anything classified. You're just doing a favor for an old comrade."

"That'll work." He picked up his phone and got somebody right away. He had me set up in under a minute.

"Thanks, Aaron," I said.

"Don't mention it."

I MADE THE ten-minute walk to the Ops building, glad that he'd set me up for a meeting the same day. I needed to act quickly, because once Stirling had time to think about it, he'd tell somebody, and depending on who he told, I might lose my access to the information. If the Intelligence folks found out what I suspected, they'd likely want to bring me in for debriefing. I'd rather not have to deal with that.

I entered the same modern wonder of a building

where I'd visited Serata three years before. A female major with dark skin and her black hair in a tight bun met me at the door to the headquarters and led me downstairs, opposite of where I'd gone to meet Serata the last time. Two floors down she led me through a maze of corridors before palming open a door that opened into a low-ceilinged room with no interior walls. About forty workstations lined the sides of the large space, about half of which had operators.

"Wow," I said. "This is quite a setup."

"There are five rooms like this, sir," said the major. "We monitor every distant station in SPACECOM. Not in real time, of course. Jump lag."

"Right," I said. I'd known SPACECOM kept track of many things, but I'd never considered exactly what sort of overhead that required.

She led me over to a tall female sergeant with broad shoulders who stood near two empty terminals, watching us. "Sir, this is Sergeant Kobiaski. She's one of my best techs. If she can't help you, it can't be done."

I extended my hand to Kobiaski. "Good to meet you."

"Good to meet you, too, sir." She glanced down for a split second, embarrassed. "It's an honor, sir, if I might say so."

"Thanks. The honor's mine. I really appreciate you doing this." Nobody had given her a choice in the matter, but it never hurt to thank soldiers, even when they were just doing their jobs.

"I'll leave you to it, sir, if that's okay?" said the major.

"Quite all right. If it's acceptable to you, the good sergeant here can escort me out when we're done. That way you don't have to hang around."

"If you're sure it's okay, sir." The major had already started edging away. The last thing she needed was to waste an hour of a busy day babysitting a retired colonel. That fit my needs as well. I had no illusions. I wasn't invisible. If I found something of interest today, it would make it up the chain almost immediately. But I had a better chance of controlling the spread of information with the sergeant than I did with the major.

"Totally okay. Thanks. Sergeant K, you want to get started?"

"Yes, sir. You can sit here. I need a little info from you. Dates, locations. Anything that you can give me that will narrow the search parameters."

I had the dates readily available, seared into my brain. I gave them to her, and she hunched over her terminal, clacking at keys so fast that I couldn't follow.

"It will take a few seconds to come up, sir. We're pulling data from a distant server."

"Sure," I said. "How hard is it?"

"Not hard at all. It's an unusual request, but not unprecedented. I've pulled stuff from further back than this."

"How far back do we keep it?" I asked. Showing interest in her work was smart business, but I found myself genuinely curious as well.

"Forever, I think, sir. I've never looked, but I've

also never gone searching for something and had it not be there."

I got chills at that, remembering other data that should have been there in the past but wasn't. "I appreciate the effort."

"Here we go, sir." A computerized image of the outline of a planet that I assumed was Cappa popped up on the screen, surrounded by blue dots that represented friendly ships. Two green ships showed as well. Green represented neutral, such as contractors or mining company ships. "We've got sixty hours of data. How do you want to look at it?"

"Let me tell you what I'm looking for, and then I'll defer to you on how we find it. You're the expert." She nodded at that, so I continued.

"I'm looking for any ships that might have gotten through the blockade. Anything that got off the planet without being searched."

She thought about it a minute. "Should be easy enough, given where the blue ships are flying. It's a pretty high orbit. The ships you're looking for have to take off from the planet?"

"Yes."

"So call it ten minutes from launch to reach the blockade. We can look at six data points an hour and we'll catch everything. We'll make it seven to be on the safe side. That's just over four hundred images to check. Where we see a green track, we flag it, then come back and follow it to see if blue intercepted it."

I breathed out through pursed lips. "That's a lot of data."

"I figure we can work through it in three hours or so."

I checked the time. "Three hours puts us past the end of the duty day."

"I get paid to be a soldier twenty-four seven, sir. I'm game if you are."

I smiled. "You're a good soldier, Kobiaski. You're really helping me out."

Her face lit up. "Let's get to it, sir." She punched some keys and the screen jumped forward in time. She flicked her cursor over the one green track on the screen and tagged it, then jumped the screen forward again.

Two and a half hours later I felt like somebody had taken sandpaper to my eyes. We'd been through four hundred twenty screens and tagged nineteen ships leaving the planet. Mother bless the techs who stared at screens like this every day. After a short break for coffee, we sat back down and followed each of the tracks as it left Cappa's atmosphere. Kobiaski ran the display at four times normal speed, but with space being so huge, we could easily follow them. One after another, each ship creeped across the screen, and one after another they rendezvoused with a blue track.

When the nineteenth ship linked up with friendly searchers, I sighed. "Well, that's that."

Kobiaski didn't respond. She stared at the monitor, running the last track backward in time. She zoomed out and zoomed back in. She grunted. I didn't interrupt her. When a tech got deep into her machine, you let her go with it. "What the fuck is that?" she asked, almost under her breath.

"What have you got?" I peered at the screen, trying to gauge what she had seen.

"Do you see that?" she asked.

I didn't see anything but blue tracks intercepting green. "Where?"

"Over here." She moved her cursor to the far side of the planet, well away from the green track, highlighting a blank part of the screen.

"I'm sorry, I don't see—"

"Hold on, sir . . . there." She paused the display.

I couldn't be sure I'd seen it, but for a split second it looked like a green dot blinked on and then off again. "I think I saw it. What was it?"

She shook her head. "No idea, sir. But it's not right."

"Can we zoom in?"

She fiddled with her keyboard. "Not really, sir. The display doesn't have as much fidelity on that side of the planet."

"That makes sense," I said. "There's nothing inhabiting the other hemisphere on Cappa. It's all ocean and dead continents."

She scrunched her face up a bit. "Shouldn't matter, sir. We get our feed from satellites that orbit the planet . . ." Her voice trailed off, then she punched some more keys, and several gold symbols popped up in orbit. "Holy shit."

"What?" I asked.

"Sorry, sir." She blushed slightly.

"No, don't be. 'Holy shit' is fine. What happened?"

"The satellites. We use a network of both geosynchronous and orbital platforms."

"Sure," I said.

"At this exact moment, the two orbital platforms that should pick up departing space traffic are both on this side of the planet."

"That seems pretty ill considered," I said.

"Not really, sir. We're not in a space war, and all the traffic leaving the planet is considered friendly. It takes a satellite ninety minutes to orbit, give or take. We're talking about maybe a ten- or fifteen-minute window. It shouldn't matter."

The hairs stood up on my arm. "It shouldn't matter unless someone knew the time window and snuck off the opposite side of the planet."

She nodded. "Can't rule it out, sir."

"That's impossible, right? There are no launch facilities over there."

She thought about it. "I don't know, sir. How much of a conspiracy-theory guy are you?"

"In this case? A pretty fucking big one."

"Our system only handles high-altitude tracks. I assume that ground-based systems monitor the lower atmosphere."

"That's right," I said, remembering that from my time on Cappa. "The Cappans had their own air control inside the atmosphere."

"So if you really wanted to get off the back side of

the planet, all you'd have to do would be to fly low and avoid our ground-based systems, and you could get to the opposite side unseen."

"And all our ground-based stuff was heading back spaceside at that time."

"Even easier," she said.

"Is there any way to check this?"

She looked at me for a moment. "The satellites run on set patterns. We can look at that."

"So if we look every time they're partially obscured . . ."

"It's worth a shot, sir. I'll back it up the length of the satellite orbit around the planet. That's . . . eighty-eight minutes and twenty-seven seconds."

"Give it a window," I said. She knew that, but I couldn't help myself.

"Yes, sir. I'll give it four minutes on either side." She tapped at her keyboard, then sat back and watched the screen.

I almost forgot to breathe, staring at the little blips. After a few minutes it stopped moving. "Did it happen? I didn't see anything."

"Me either."

"Back it up again," I said. "Another orbit."

She did. We watched. Nothing.

"Is there any other explanation for what we saw on the first one?" I asked. "Any chance that it's not a ship?"

"Yes . . . yes, sir. It could be . . . I don't know. It could be interference."

"But you don't think so," I said, reading her tone.

"I don't, sir."

"You're the professional. Back it up another orbit and let's see."

She entered the data and started the feed. "There!" She paused the system and scrolled it back. "See it, sir? The same thing as before."

"I see it," I said. "Let's see how many we find."

By the time we finished it was an hour before midnight. We'd found four instances of ships departing the planet, all sequenced at exactly the right time to avoid detection. Almost. They hadn't counted on one brilliant sergeant with a computer. We couldn't get a fix on the type or size of the ships, and we couldn't be sure we'd found all of them. The system didn't have enough fidelity. To get that, I'd need data from the Cappan air-control system, and something told me they wouldn't offer that up, even if I had a way to contact them.

Despite my fatigue, my mind churned out the implications. I had no doubt, based on my previous experience on Cappa, that they had access to satellite information and the ability to manipulate it. Back when I'd been there, I assumed they'd got it from Karakov's people, but given what I'd seen since then, I couldn't rule out the possibility that the Cappans themselves had cracked the system. I didn't want to make assumptions, though, because that would narrow my focus. I might miss something important. But *someone* had the satellite information and purposely used it to get ships off the planet. Those ships could have had Cappans on them, or they could have had special forces troops. Hell, they could have been smugglers loaded down with silver. No assumptions.

Except I had a pretty strong belief that at least a *few* humans from Elliot's experimental procedures got away, since I'd seen one of them on public transportation.

At least I think I had.

Kobiaski walked me to the main exit of the building and I stepped out into the night, immediately wishing I'd brought a heavier jacket. I thanked her for the fifth time. I'd have put her in for an award, but that would mean telling somebody in authority what she'd found. They would find out eventually—I hadn't asked her to keep it quiet, because I didn't want to put her in that position. But I had a head start, and even when they found out, they might not immediately know what it meant. She'd done the impossible for me, and I owed her. I put her on my long mental list of great people who did things they'd never get credit for.

# CHAPTER TWELVE

I HAD THE NEXT day off, but I couldn't sit idle in my apartment. I'd have lost it. The information about the Cappans had left me stunned, and I didn't have anybody I could talk to about it. I trusted Dr. Baqri, but even that had its limits. I decided that since I couldn't do anything with what I knew, I'd try something else. I still didn't know what was going on with Omicron, the police considered me a person of interest in a murder case, and I still believed I had people watching me. Action beat inaction, so I made something up. I programmed my drone to keep an eye on a radio-frequency marker, and launched the machine from my roof. I put the marker in my pocket and headed outside. In theory, if somebody was following me, the drone would capture my tail on camera.

I didn't have much to lose. That was one benefit to taking action in the civilian world over the military. In the army, I'd have had a lot of people helping me, following my orders. There's good and bad to that. It puts a ton of pressure on a leader to get it right. Make a mistake and people who trust you end up getting killed.

Sometimes even when you didn't make a mistake, people who trusted you got killed. I'd made decisions in my career that I still played back in my head over and over, and I couldn't find anything I'd have done differently. But sometimes they still turned to shit.

In the civilian world, if I made a mistake, it only affected me. I could live with that. Not being responsible for the lives of others made it easier to try something that might or might not work.

I didn't have anywhere specific to go, but that helped my plan. The day was cool but not cold, so I could wander around and see what happened. I started off at a good pace, as if I had somewhere important to be. I fought the urge to look up. I wouldn't be able to see the drone anyway. I tried to act natural. If someone *was* following me I didn't want to do anything to make them suspicious. I couldn't kid myself, though. I expected to find someone there.

It didn't take long for that theoretical person who was following me to go from one person to a group in my mind. It stood to reason that if I had a tail, they had a larger purpose, and that purpose implied a larger organization. I tried not to dwell on who the group might be, though deep down it prickled at me. A side benefit to the walking was that it helped clear my head and give me time to sort through my thoughts.

Omicron was the most likely to be watching me. They'd been a victim of a breach, so they'd be wary of anything out of the ordinary. Gylika was dead, and they almost certainly knew that he and I had met. That made me think about the first time I noticed Cappan eyes, and whether it had been before or after I met with Gylika. And that led me further down the rabbit hole, and I found that the link that Dernier discovered between the Phoenix Project and ortho-robotics still gnawed at me. A lot of coincidences pointed toward Omicron.

But I forced myself to consider other options. It could be a tabloid, or even a legit news source. Maybe they were following me in hopes that I'd lead them to a story—not about Omicron, but about anything. I *was* the Scourge, after all, and notoriety drove page clicks. A picture of me doing something seedy would let them drag my name across the net again. That didn't seem likely, though. Everywhere I went, people knew me, and if I did anything like that, it would have already gotten out. Besides, they didn't need to follow me. There were eyes and cameras everywhere. It could even be Plazz. As much as I trusted her, I had no illusions about how far she'd go to get an important story.

It could have been somebody from VPC's legal department, following me to try to keep me out of trouble. Shit, it could even be Sharon's lawyers, trying to get more money out of me.

But in the end, I didn't believe any of that. No matter how much logic I applied to the situation, I kept coming back to the Cappans. I'd seen those eyes. Maybe. Or maybe the new information about them leaving the planet had me believing in ghosts. It's easy to make what you see fit your own assumptions if you're not disciplined with your thinking. I didn't use to have a problem with that. I'd always been an organized thinker, able to compartmentalize and take emotion out of the equation. Lately I wasn't so sure.

I made about a five-kilometer circuit, pausing a few times to look at things that interested me and once to grab a box of water from a local shop where I liked the owner, then made my way back to my apartment. I went inside and triggered the function to return the drone to its base. I retrieved it from the roof, bringing the base with it, and plugged it into my terminal to download the video. Before I started watching, I took the drone back to the roof and programmed it with the standard sequence I'd developed to watch my apartment building. If somebody had followed me on my walk, they'd have to have gone somewhere when I got home. Maybe it could spot them.

I'd paid a lot for the drone, and the clerk hadn't lied about the quality. I could make out faces, signs, and pretty much anything else I wanted. When I zoomed in, I could almost read what somebody had on their device screen. I'd purposely set the observation to a wide lens since it centered on me and I needed to find someone a reasonable distance back. I took still shots at every five-minute mark and sent them to my big video screen. I put eight pictures side by side to see if the same person showed up more than once.

Pretty quickly I found one person who matched in both the first and last photo, but when I examined it

closer she hadn't actually moved. I'd simply walked by
her twice at the same spot, once while leaving, once
when I returned. It didn't rule her out as somebody
watching my place, but she hadn't followed me.

I compared other pictures. It took me thirty minutes
before I found it. A dark-skinned woman in a beige
pullover with a high collar showed up behind me in
picture two and picture seven. It didn't take long to
find her in two other frames, as well. I captured her
face from each angle that I had, then I watched back
through the entire video, focusing on her. Once I knew
what to look for, I tracked her easily. She broke off a
few minutes before I got to my apartment and never re-
appeared, as if she knew my destination and got bored.
Or she had somebody else watching my residence and
didn't need to approach herself. Why had she followed
me on my little stroll but not done anything? She didn't
learn anything, because there was nothing to learn. I
rarely went anywhere outside of the routine. I wondered
how long they'd been following me. And why? It didn't
make sense to just follow. Unless I wasn't the target.
Maybe they wanted me to lead them to something, but
if that were the case, I couldn't imagine where I was
supposed to lead them.

I took each of the pictures and fed them into my
system to see if I could match it to some known image.
A scan of the net came up blank, but all I had access to
were public files, and a competent amateur could scrub
herself from those with a little bit of effort. People did it
all the time as a routine measure to ensure privacy. To

dig deeper, I'd need access to a better system. Something like what the police had, or the military. I filed that away. I didn't think walking into the police station with random pictures would get me very far. I didn't rule it out for the future, though. If they solved the murder and no longer viewed me as a suspect, maybe they'd be in a conciliatory mood. Then again, they might ask where I got the pictures, and I didn't want to admit I had an illegal drone flying over the city to watch my six.

I headed to the roof to retrieve the drone once more and check out the surveillance footage to see if I could spot somebody around my apartment. I got up one flight before the sound of footsteps a few floors below me brought me up short. When I concentrated, I thought I could make out three sets, definitely coming up. My heart started pounding. Nobody walked up the stairs in our building except me. They took the elevator. They definitely didn't walk it in groups of three. I dashed down the steps, hurrying toward my apartment. I got through my security check as the footsteps reached the floor below me. I bolted inside, slammed the door, and rushed to my desk to get my pistol.

Standing there with my weapon in my hand, I felt stupid. I couldn't shoot through the door, they couldn't get in, and there wasn't a chance in the Mother's Galaxy that I was going out there. Yet I didn't put it down. I stood there, straining to hear something through the thick security door. When the buzzer rang, I almost leaped out of my pants. After a second

I calmed down enough to remember my camera system, and activated it.

The woman from the drone surveillance stared at me from the screen, and though I could see her and she couldn't see me, I flinched a little. She had people with her, but I didn't see them in any detail. I couldn't get past the woman's pupils. Ovals.

I froze, my hand halfway to the button that keyed the intercom. I wanted to talk to her, ask her why they were here, why they'd been following me. But I couldn't. I couldn't make myself move.

The buzzer rang again, then again. I don't know how many times. I don't know how long I stood there. Eventually they left.

**DESPITE MY COMPLETE** breakdown, two positives came from the Cappan hybrid visiting. One, I knew now that I hadn't imagined it. They were real. Second, in addition to the drone photos, I had a good picture from my security system. The two people the woman had with her had positioned themselves in a way that my system didn't pick them up—I'd have to fix that—but I had her image clearly.

I hid out the next day in my apartment, afraid they'd be waiting for me outside, but the day after that I had to go to work, so I scanned the hall with my security system, made my way to the roof and launched my drone for a quick scan of the area. I didn't pick up any sign of the woman, and I couldn't discern anyone else watching my place, so I headed out quickly. Still, I constantly looked behind me as I walked and scanned the transport as I entered. The same eyes looked back that watched me every day—some that showed awe, some that showed hate. No ovals. When I arrived at VPC, I headed down to IT and found Ganos talking to a bunch of sweatshirt-wearing programmers. At my approach, they scattered like mice do when the lights come on in the kitchen.

"Sorry to break up your group."

Ganos laughed. "They're not used to suits showing up at random. Seriously, it never happens."

I handed her the picture of my visitor. "How hard is it to run a picture and identify someone? I tried the standard public searches and didn't get anything. I have reason to believe that the person might be trying to hide herself."

She glanced around, then lowered her voice. "Is this hush-hush?"

"No, this is on the record. Company sanctioned. She has something to do with the investigation I'm doing. Nothing illegal, but I'd be happy if we could tap into a better source of information than what's available to me." It wasn't a total lie. The woman *could* be related to my case. I felt justified putting company assets behind it.

"Sure thing, sir. I'll keep it totally legal."

"Thanks," I said.

She smirked. "As far as you know."

I snort-laughed, which made her laugh as well. "I trust your judgment."

"Probably not your best decision, but I do appreciate it. I'll get back to you tomorrow with this. I want to work on it from home."

## CHAPTER THIRTEEN

TRUE TO HER word, Ganos was waiting for me in my office the next morning, her feet up on my desk. "Must be nice to be an executive and make your own hours," she said.

I laughed. "It's not bad, I'll tell you that."

She swung her feet down. "I ran that picture you gave me. You're not going to believe this, sir."

"I don't know. I'd believe a lot right now."

"So this woman, she doesn't exist, right? Not anywhere a normal person should exist. No social media, no basic licenses, no pictures in the open net anywhere. Not *too* out of the ordinary, but definitely somebody who made an effort to stay hidden."

"So how'd you find something?"

"Let's not ask questions you really don't want the answers to, sir."

"Got it."

"On a developed planet like Talca, it's pretty much impossible to get down from space without going through security. So I took a shot that maybe she wasn't born and raised on planet, and got a hit through Immigration."

"You have access to Immigration?"

"Remember when we said we weren't going to ask those kinds of questions, sir? Anyway, she came to Talca about nine months ago." Ganos held out a sheet of paper that had a cheap-looking immigration photo, along with a name, Jane Cantella, and an on-planet address that was probably fake.

"This is great work," I said, my mind already whirling. If she'd come to the planet nine months ago, why then? And why had I become aware of her only recently? Any number of answers fit, and I'd need to sort through them.

"There's more," said Ganos. "I figured if she came to the planet, she came from somewhere. So I played a hunch. Something about the picture gave me a military vibe, and nobody keeps better records than the army."

"So you hacked into a military database."

"Sir . . . please. That would be illegal. Anyway, she's ex-military. Started out as infantry, then later she transferred to—"

"Special Ops," I said, interrupting her.

"That's right, sir. How'd you know?"

"Remember that thing we had about not asking questions? Trust me, you don't want to know."

"You got it, sir. She was Special Ops, so I couldn't dig up too much on her record. They keep that stuff tight, and there are places on the net that even I'm not dumb enough to dig into. I did find one thing, though. The reason she left service."

I had a guess, but I decided not to share it. "What was it?"

"MIA, sir. Missing in action. How does that happen? When you're MIA, that's like military code for being dead, but nobody can find your body to prove it."

"Pretty much," I said.

"What kind of shit are you involved with, sir?"

"The same kind I always seem to be in." I shook my head. "Honestly, I really don't know. It keeps getting stranger and stranger."

"I know it's got something to do with Omicron. I want in," she said.

"What do you mean?"

"Get me inside their system, sir. Let me poke around."

"I'm not sure how I'd do that."

"Figure it out."

"I miss when you were just my subordinate."

"No, you don't."

No, I didn't.

SITTING AROUND MY apartment after work, I tried *not* to think about it. But I might as well have tried to sprout wings and fly. I drank some, and I got madder, so I drank some more. Somewhere in that process, I decided I'd had enough hiding. I was going after the Cappan hybrids who had been watching me. At least that would be *something*. Wisely, I decided to wait until I sobered up. The light of morning might show me how ridiculous my nighttime idea had been.

If anything, I woke up madder. That never happens. I'd actually slept, though I had ridiculous dreams, all of which featured somebody chasing me in different environments, most of which jerked me out of sleep for a moment. But all things considered, I still felt rested. I grabbed a quick shower, checked the weather and news, and grabbed my pistol and tucked it into the oversized pocket of my jacket. The weight of it pulled uncomfortably, but it would have to do. I considered doing a quick search with the drone, but that might have led to indecision. The sun had started to lighten the sky and the streets hadn't filled yet, so if somebody was out there, I'd likely see them. Besides, I wanted a confrontation, and if I found somebody watching my place, I'd get it.

I reached the ground floor and the small, empty lobby of my building where the smell of some sort of cleaner assaulted my nose. I looked through the window, and when I didn't see anybody, I pushed the button to open the door. I turned left and had got fifteen or twenty meters when I sensed somebody watching me. A woman stood on the other side of the street, half hidden by a shadow, which was probably why I hadn't seen her from the door. I turned and walked across the street toward her, increasing my pace, but not running.

I'd almost reached her side of the street when she bolted.

Without thinking, I ran after her, my pistol bouncing painfully against my hip bone. She called out something I couldn't understand, either into a communication device or to someone nearby. That wasn't good. If she had backup, my odds got a lot worse.

She pulled away from me and turned down a side street. If she really was a Cappan hybrid, I didn't have much chance of catching her, but I kept up the pursuit anyway. I took the corner fast, almost losing my balance, then caught sight of her, almost to the next corner already. I slowed to a fast jog to conserve my breath, but kept following. Maybe she'd make a mistake, and I'd get lucky. I made two more turns, each time barely keeping sight of her, and we worked our way down narrow side streets and alleys. I passed a spectator or two, but they barely glanced my way, intent on wherever their early-morning travels took them.

About thirty meters from the next corner, the woman from outside my door stepped out in front of me. I almost tripped trying to stop. As I regained my balance, a golden-skinned man wearing a dark, lightweight jacket joined her.

"Colonel Butler," said the woman. "We don't mean you any harm. We just want to talk to you."

Well, shit. That changed quickly. They didn't have weapons out, but then again, neither did I. I resisted patting my pistol. No need to give them any extra information. "Why'd you run away then?"

"You chased me," she said.

"You know what I'm talking about. You were outside my apartment. Why have you been following me?"

She raised her hands slightly, in what might have been intended as a placating gesture. "Like I said, we want to talk to you."

I didn't feel placated. I casually slipped my hand into the pocket with the pistol. "Not buying it. You could have approached me at any time. You didn't."

"We came to your apartment but you didn't answer the door." She took a step forward, though we were still fifteen meters apart. "Now here we are."

"Now that I chased you down." I pulled the pistol from my pocket. I didn't level it at them, but I didn't point it away from them, either. If it made them nervous, they didn't show it.

The woman took two more steps, slowly, hands partially raised, leaving her partner behind. "Hear us out and we'll leave you alone. We need your help."

"Who are you?"

"I'm—"

A gunshot cracked, cutting her off. Projectile, not pulse. The sound echoed off the sides of the buildings, and it took me a second to realize the shot came from behind me. As I turned to find the shooter, shots erupted from the hybrids—now behind me—as well. I dove for cover without thinking, my body reacting by instinct. I scanned for the people who started the shooting, but from my position down low, pinned up against a building, I couldn't find them. From the angle of the fire I calculated that they had a higher position, potentially shooting from a building window or a fire escape. It gave them a serious advantage in the narrow alley. After another second I marked two different origins, one on either side of the street. Instinctively I identified the weapons from their sounds. Pistols, not rifles. Thank the Mother for small blessings.

I pushed myself up off the ground, looking to get off a shot. Something punched me in the leg, hard, slamming me back down, bruising my knees and scraping me through my pants. My pistol clattered away and I went after it until a bullet smacked the pavement in front of me, kicking up sparks. I whipped my head first to one side, then the other, where I caught a glimpse of the hybrid woman as she retreated around the corner, moving inhumanly fast.

I tried to rise again and collapsed. My leg burned and ached at the same time, just above the knee. I reached down and my hand came away sticky and wet.

Shit.

I didn't know who shot me, or if they'd done it intentionally, but it didn't matter. Shots continued from both directions as I huddled in a heap, starting to shiver. My original pursuers fired back at whoever had ambushed us, but the initial attackers returned twice as much. After a few seconds, all the gunfire tailed off, like the last kernels of popcorn in a heater bag. I scanned the upper stories for the ambush team, but my vision blurred. I assumed that while they'd ceased firing, they still had me under observation. I didn't know if that helped or hurt. They'd fired at the Cappan hybrids, but that might not make them friends to me. They definitely weren't friends of my leg.

It throbbed, now, and I pressed my hand against the wound to try to slow the bleeding. It poured through my fingers anyway. Arterial blood. The shooters didn't matter. I was going to bleed out in the street.

I fumbled with my shirt, trying to get it off because I needed to make a tourniquet. My fingers tripped over the buttons, my hands not working right. I tried again, somehow sensing it meant life or death, even through the growing fog in my brain. A siren blared in the distance, getting closer, though it almost sounded like it was underwater. Something whirred in the air overhead. Police drone, I thought, though I don't know why that perception came through when other reasoning had stopped.

It didn't matter.

I passed out.

# CHAPTER FOURTEEN

**I CAME DEAD AWAKE** and tried to sit, squinting in the bright light. My head spun, and dropped back down onto a white pillow. A hospital bed. I had no feeling in my right leg whatsoever. My vision narrowed and the edges went dark. My stomach lurched. I reached down, dreading that the leg wouldn't be there. I let out a breath when my hand found my thigh, though I couldn't feel the pressure of my own touch.

"You're awake," said a nurse. I don't know if he entered or he'd already been in the room. "Good. The blood replacement has taken."

"I can't feel—"

"You've got a nerve block in your leg, that's why you can't feel it."

My eyes focused quickly and my thoughts came clearly, which probably meant they hadn't drugged me much. I took that as a good sign that the leg injury might be my only damage. With the nerve block, I didn't need painkillers, at least until it wore off. "Is it going to be okay?"

"Good as new," said the nurse. "Bullet hit your artery, but we gave you a new one. The doctor says you should recover fully in a day or two, once she gets the advanced growth cells in place, which should happen soon."

"Great." I slumped back a bit into the pillow.

"There are some people who want to speak to you."

My heart slammed into my rib cage. I glanced around the room, looking for my weapon, which I didn't find. They'd followed me to the hospital. Of course they had. "I need to get out of here."

The nurse looked at me, his face scrunched in confusion. Before he could talk, two people entered. Mallory and Burke. The police.

"Colonel Butler. We meet again, and again it's under unusual circumstances," said Mallory. Burke motioned the nurse out of the room, and the man complied, making himself small to slide around them.

"I didn't do anything," I said.

"You got shot. Almost died," she said.

"That's not a crime."

"Didn't say it was." Mallory pulled up a rolling stool and sat on it so our eyes were at the same level. "Have to say, though, you've been in some odd situations recently."

"Lunch isn't an odd situation."

"It is when that guy ends up dead trying to meet you the next day."

She was trying to goad me on purpose. I said a silent thanks for the lack of drugs in my system. I needed to focus, find out how much they already knew. It wouldn't do to lie and get caught, but I also didn't want to give anything away that I didn't have to.

"We've got your illegal weapon," said Burke.

"That's not mine," I said.

"It has your prints on it," he said.

"Those could be planted."

"We have you on video with it in your hand," said Burke.

Video. Right. There had been a drone, along with whatever video surveillance covered the street normally. "People fake video all the time."

"Let's put the gun aside for a moment," said Mallory. "It's a minor charge. Nothing we're really interested in for now. You tell us what happened, we'll see what we can do."

Sure. Burke mentioned finding my pistol, then Mallory dismissed it to build goodwill, hoping I'd feel grateful and tell her something. "A woman was watching my house. I went out to confront her, she ran, and I chased her." They'd have seen that much on camera, so I didn't lose anything by sharing it.

"Is that when you shot at her?" Mallory asked.

"Nice try," I said. If they'd checked my weapon— and they absolutely had—they'd know that it hadn't been fired. I never got off a shot. "I didn't shoot at anybody."

"So who did?" she asked.

"You're the ones with the camera footage," I said. "Did the drones pick anything up?"

"I have to say, you're pretty calm for a man who's been shot."

"What can I say? Not my first time." I noticed that she didn't answer my question. Not that I had expected her to. I hadn't answered hers, either.

"So what happened?" she asked.

I decided to push the issue. "If I had something to look at, maybe it would jog my memory. Video, or something."

She considered it. "We got some video of people fleeing the scene, but nothing very useful. Bad angles and not enough light. We're checking other cameras in the area, but we're not optimistic. It's like they knew where the video equipment was." Mallory surprised me with her honesty, or at least partial honesty.

"Interesting," I said, more because I felt like she wanted me to speak than because I actually believed it. I had a few cards I could play. I could talk about the Cappan hybrids, or the fact that Ganos had a clean picture of one of them. I definitely didn't want to bring her name up, but I could work out some sort of transfer of information if it would help my cause with the police. But I couldn't see any profit in giving away my leverage. I only wanted to share information if I thought I could get something in return, and so far Mallory hadn't offered anything of value.

"Your turn," she said, as if reading the intent in my silence. "Since we're in a sharing mood, how about you share something with us?"

"I chased the woman when she ran, like I said. She

was faster than me, but I kept up. I came around the corner and there she was, with a partner. I stopped, and before we could do much else, the shooting started."

"Did you shoot first?" she asked.

"You know I didn't," I said. She was repeating the same question, trying to trip me up. Even though it was a standard technique, it pissed me off.

"How would we know that?"

*Nice try.* She wanted me to mention my pistol not being fired so they could pin the pistol on me cleanly. "You have video."

"It's not clear who fired when," she said.

"Like I told you, I didn't fire a weapon."

She frowned. I might have frustrated her. I have that effect on people. "You're making this harder than it needs to be. Let me be blunt. Either you start talking, or we have you transferred to a confinement room until you're well enough for jail."

I thought about it for a moment, trying to figure out how little I could tell them while still maintaining my freedom. I could have called for a lawyer as Dernier had suggested, but I still held out hope that they'd give me some information if I played along. I needed that more than I needed to stay out of jail, at least for the moment. Besides, I read her for a bluff. They weren't going to take an injured veteran into custody.

"There were two groups of people. The woman I chased and her partner were in the street, in front of me. They didn't have weapons out initially, and I didn't see when they drew them, but I think I heard them fire. I couldn't swear to it, as I'd lost sight of them by that point. Another group—one I didn't see—started shooting. I don't know if they fired at me or at the other two, because they opened up from behind me, but I'm pretty sure they fired from an elevated position. It sounded like pistols, and since they were firing from what might have been thirty-five meters away, that might explain why they missed the first shot. It happened fast. One minute the woman was talking, the next minute everything exploded—including my leg. You see I'm wounded, right? I can't believe you don't have any clues." She had tried to goad me, so I returned the favor.

"Nothing except the body," said Mallory.

I didn't flinch. My dig at her had struck home, and she wanted to rattle me, so my natural reaction was to not let her. It did pique my curiosity, though. "You found a body?"

"That seems to happen a lot with you," said Burke.

I didn't acknowledge him, keeping my eyes on Mallory. Burke had gotten to me the first time we met, but this time I was prepared for it. "I can describe the two people who I saw, if that helps identify the corpse."

"We think it was from the second group," said Mallory. "It appeared to have fallen from a height, which would coincide with your information that they fired from above. The two people you confronted fled, though one of them may have been injured."

"You saw them on video?" I asked.

"That's right."

"Did you notice anything unusual about them? The way they moved?"

Mallory paused, flicking a quick glance toward her partner, then back to me. "There may have been some anomalies."

I chuckled. "Anomalies. That's a good way to put it."

"You saw something?" she asked.

"I may have noticed some anomalies," I said.

Burke interrupted before his partner could continue. "Right. You're in the middle of a gunfight and you *notice some anomalies*. Bullshit."

"Excuse me?" I turned slowly to face him, partially making a show of it and a little bit because it's difficult to move with one dead leg. I kept a flat expression on my face.

"Bullets flying all around, you diving for cover, and you expect me to believe you were tracking other people and their movements? Why are you lying to us?"

"What the fuck is your problem, Burke?"

He took a couple steps toward my bed, fists clenched.

I didn't back down. "Come on, take a swing at me. Hit the guy who's already in a hospital bed."

Mallory put herself between us before things went any further. "Okay, let's calm down. Both of you."

"I'm just lying here," I said, in a passive-aggressive tone designed to piss Burke off. Part of me wanted him to hit me. It would suck, but it would give me some leverage. Mallory was okay, though, so I addressed my comments to her. "Look. I'm not your typical witness, okay? Bullets start flying and most people lock up. It happens all the time, I know, I've seen it. But once you've been there a few times, things start to slow down. Your body reacts, and your brain doesn't shut down quite as much. So yes. I saw the two people retreat, and they moved really, really fast."

"Care to tell us what you think about that?" asked Mallory.

"About what?"

"The people. How they moved. Do you have thoughts?"

"That depends," I said. "Are you going to clear me of all charges, including whatever you're pretending to have about Gylika, so I can leave the planet if I want to? I'm starting to feel like it might not be very safe around here."

"This isn't a negotiation," she said.

I smiled. "Of course it is."

"We could leave," said Burke. "The shooting has been in the news, and you're a celebrity, so by now people know you're here. Maybe we don't leave a security team."

"Your partner isn't going to leave me here to get murdered, asshole. Besides, I'll have military security here in thirty minutes." I was bluffing. At least partly. If I called in favors and said I was in danger, they *might* send someone.

"Will you two fucking stop it?" Mallory glared at Burke, then at me. "This is complicated enough without you two pissing on everything to mark your territory."

I pretended to be chastised because that's what she wanted to see. I didn't care, though. If they weren't going to clear me of Gylika's death, I didn't owe them anything. Giving them more information wouldn't help. If I told them that there were Cappan-human hybrids running around the city, at best they'd take a note. More likely they'd lock me up in a psych ward. "All I can tell you is that they moved unusually fast. One of them leaped exceptionally high."

"That's all you've got?"

"That's all I've got while I'm still restricted to this planet. Yes."

"Mr. Butler, you're making this hard on yourself," she said.

"Probably," I agreed. "That would certainly be consistent with my nature."

She almost smiled, but shook her head. "I'm afraid you're too close to things for us to release you at this time, especially in light of this new situation and the pending gun charge. Consider yourself restricted to this room until further notice. We'll leave a protection team here."

"I really can get the military," I said.

"Do what you want," she said, "but you're not free to go."

"You get anything from the body you found?" I asked. She had no reason to tell me, but I had nothing to lose by asking.

"Not much. Ex-military, we think, based on the body art."

"I could look at the art, see if I recognize anything."

"No thanks. You've helped enough." She pushed herself up off the stool, kicked it back under the low desk, and headed for the door. "Call us if you remember anything actually useful. Oh, and we're keeping your pistol."

Shit. I played it back in my head after they left. I could have done it better. Perhaps I should have come clean with what I knew about the Cappan hybrids. Cappan hybrids went insane without treatment. The two who I'd confronted hadn't seemed irrational, but then neither did Mallot at first. Karakov had, though. They could be dangerous, not just to me, but to others.

Nothing about the Cappan hybrids explained the other shooters, though. Ex-military, Mallory had said. That didn't help much. You couldn't enter an elevator in this city without an ex-soldier being there. The area attracted them. Attracted *us*. Former soldiers served not only in the industrial-military complex, but as police, private security, and pretty much any other job that had people carrying weapons. Apparently, some served as an extra-judicial hit squad.

They hadn't wanted to kill me, or they botched the job badly if they did. I still didn't know which side shot me, and I didn't know if they'd done it intentionally. It had been a narrow alley, and bullets ricocheted. Replaying the sequence in my mind, I'd definitely dived to my left, putting my right side toward the hybrids and my left side toward the other guys, but I'd turned around after that. The bullet hit my right leg, which would have been toward the non-hybrids, but that wasn't enough to say for sure. There was a chance that the ambush team missed on purpose, but I couldn't figure why they would.

The only thing I could say with absolute certainty was that I'd completely failed in my efforts to clear myself of Gylika's murder, and I couldn't blame anyone but myself. If anything, I'd made it harder. Mallory knew I had nothing to do with that, but she wouldn't let it go because it kept her leverage over me. And now she had the gun charge. She'd hang on to that to get me to tell her what I knew about other things. She probably suspected I was hiding something, which was fair, since I was. I could still talk, but I knew her type. If I told her something now, she'd still keep her hooks in tight to get me to share more. It didn't help her to let me go, so she wouldn't, no matter what I gave her.

I'd have to come up with a way to reverse that and turn her into an asset.

## CHAPTER FIFTEEN

ONE OF THE worst things about being in the hospital is that everybody knows where to find you. Sometimes they feel obligated to stop by even when they'd rather not. I got a pretty good night of sleep, thanks to the drugs they gave me after the block wore off, and the next morning found myself in an awkward conversation with Javier Sanchez. He stood just inside the doorway wearing a tailored gray suit, as if coming in further might expose him to something. I almost told him that bullets through the leg weren't contagious.

"Did the police give you any kind of information on why this might have happened?" he asked.

"They weren't very forthcoming. I think they might have arrested me."

"What? Wait . . . how would you not know that for sure?"

"They told me not to leave my room," I said. "They have people outside. But nobody actually said I was arrested."

"Is there a specific charge?"

"I had a pistol."

Javier frowned for half a second, then schooled his face back to neutral. "Why did you have a gun?"

I shrugged. "Old soldier habit. And a lot of people have wished me ill over the last couple years. It makes me feel safer."

"I'll get legal on it." His face said he had more questions, but he held them in.

"I appreciate it, but it's not a big deal. I'm sure it will all work itself out." I *wasn't* sure of that at all, but I didn't want VPC's legal team poking into what actually happened. I'd probably get out of my trouble with the police. VPC, on the other hand, might fire me if they knew the full truth. They had to protect the bottom line, and I had no illusions what would happen to me if I became a liability. If I hadn't already crossed that line.

"So what are you going to do?" he asked.

"I wasn't leaving my room, anyway." I needed to move him in a different direction. "There's a police team here, but I think they're for my protection, not to incarcerate me."

"Do they think you're still in danger?"

"I'm not sure I *ever* was in danger. I might have just been in the wrong place at the wrong time."

He considered it for a moment, but I don't think he believed me. He wasn't stupid. "You don't . . . you don't think it has anything to do with work, do you?" he asked.

I almost laughed but managed to hide it. Nothing

like wanting to cover the company's ass to bring out the best in the boss. I could work with that. "I don't see how it could, do you?"

"No, no. Of course not. I want you to know, if there's anything we can do for you while you're in here, all you have to do is say the word. At VPC we look out for our people."

"I appreciate that," I said. "I should only be here a couple of days. It was a pretty clean wound." An uncomfortable silence set in for a few seconds before I couldn't take it. "You look like you've got something else on your mind, boss."

"It's . . . no, never mind. Everything is good."

"Javier. I'm fine. I've been shot before. I'll survive. What is it?"

"I think . . ." he paused. "Maybe we should reconsider what you're doing for the company."

"Like move to a different department?"

"No, not like that," he said. "It might be time to let this specific mission go, that's all."

"So you *do* think there's a connection," I couldn't fault him for thinking that, since I thought it myself.

"I'm not sure. You've been through a lot, obviously. Anyway, we don't have to decide now. Come see me when you get back to work, and we'll talk about it."

"Will do," I said.

AN ORDERLY SLUNK inside the door and looked around, as if to see if anyone noticed. The blue of her hair was only a shade off of the scrubs she wore, though a bit brighter. "Ganos, why are you dressed like an orderly?" I asked.

"People are watching this place," she said. "I figured it was best if they didn't know I was coming to see you."

I did my best not to react, which was hard, given how amusingly deranged she sounded. "It's the police watching."

"Sure, that we know of." I didn't point out that her blue hair wasn't inconspicuous, and anyone watching would have seen me with her before. She reached into a canvas tote bag she'd brought in with her and pulled out a tablet. "I brought you something to pass the time."

"Thanks. But they gave me back my own device."

"Don't use that. You don't know what people did to it while you were out. They could be tracking it. If you give it to me, I'll run a scan. Meanwhile, I loaded up all kinds of entertainment on this one. Plus it isn't registered. You can look stuff up and, at least for a while, people won't know it's you."

"Ganos . . . what do you think is going on here?"

She glanced behind her to make sure nobody was near, then came closer to my bed, lowering her voice. "What am I supposed to think? It's all related, right? One day we discover that an ex-Special Ops person has been following you, and the next day you get shot. Doesn't seem like a coincidence."

"It could be random," I said.

The sarcasm conveyed in her look was so impressive I wondered if she practiced in a mirror.

"It *could* have been," I repeated.

"But it wasn't, was it? Was it her? The Special Ops lady?"

"She was there," I admitted.

"She the one who did this?" She gestured to my leg.

"I really don't know. Bullets started flying, and I went down."

"I'm going to track her down," said Ganos.

"How?"

"I've got her picture. There are like a million cameras in this city, and they all run off of computers. I'll find her."

Part of me wanted to hug her, but the smarter part of me wanted to smack her. I had no doubt that she'd do it. She didn't see the danger, wrapped as she was in the imaginary, invincible armor of youth. But I didn't want her putting herself into that kind of situation on my behalf. These people had guns. And I didn't. Even if I did, I wouldn't be much good stuck in a hospital room. Besides, even if Ganos located her, we couldn't do much other than turn the information over to the police, which would lead to some awkward questions about how we got it. It might do me more harm than good with the authorities. "Promise me you won't do that," I said.

"Why not, sir? She needs to pay."

"We're not in a spot to make anybody pay," I said. I wasn't sure she *did* need to pay, but that wasn't a conversation I wanted to have where people might hear me. "There are some dangerous people out there, and until I know what they're up to, I think it's better to sit back for a while."

"So what *can* we do?" asked Ganos.

I thought about it. While I didn't want to involve Ganos any further, I didn't have any other assets. I justified it by telling myself that I had to give her something to do, or she'd strike out on her own. This had gone beyond getting answers about the breach at Omicron. This involved me personally, and telling Ganos to stay out would offend her. We'd served together. That meant something to both of us, not just me. "Remember when you told me that I should get you inside the Omicron network?"

"Yes. How are we going to do that?"

"Slow down," I said. "It's just a thought right now. I need to think it through. This isn't the place to talk about it."

She nodded, her whole body almost bobbing with the action. "When you figure it out, let me know. I'm in."

"I will. But Ganos . . . promise me you'll be careful until you hear from me."

She snorted. "Of course, sir. Who are you talking to?"

That's exactly what I was worried about.

NOBODY ELSE CAME by to see me, which made me happy. I half expected Dernier to stop in, which would have forced me to make up some more stuff to keep him away from the reality of the hybrids.

Plazz didn't visit, but she did call. "You're all over the news. It's amazing how much trouble you'll go through to avoid me."

I liked her. No BS about my health or "oh, it was so horrible." Straight to business. "Yeah. Can you do something about calling off the media? Those are your people."

She laughed. "Sure. I'll tell everybody to stop covering it when we all get together for our media agenda meeting."

"You mean it doesn't work that way? What if I get somebody to dress a kitten up like a robot?"

"Don't worry. Give it another day and it will blow over. This thing doesn't have any legs. You're a famous person caught up in a shooting, that's all."

"That's good. I'd hate to have to sneak out of the hospital."

"Of course it could run longer, if you told me what it was really about." She kept her voice light, joking, but left a sliver of a real question.

"Like you said. Just a semi-famous guy caught up in a random shooting."

"You know I don't believe you, Carl."

"I'm hurt. I thought we had a trust thing going."

"Ha! I don't know anything about what happened in this situation, but I do know you. If you're involved, it's anything but random."

I tried to decide if I'd been complimented or insulted. "Don't force me to lie to you. I don't have the energy to make things up right now."

"I hear you," she said. "I had to try."

"I understand."

"You know how I knew you were lying?" she asked.

"How's that?"

"Because the last time we talked you asked me to get information about the Gylika case and you didn't call me back. That means you're probably hiding something."

Huh. I hadn't thought about that. She was right in that I'd avoided calling her, though Gylika had shifted to a somewhat lower priority. "You know, I forgot all about that."

"You forgot about a murder."

"A bullet in the leg will do that," I said.

"That's fair. Hey, if you *do* decide you're going to talk about it, call me first, okay?"

"Of course."

**GUNFIRE POPPED AGAINST** the wall above my head, throwing shards of concrete off that ticked against my faceplate. My heads-up display showed one soldier down, another seriously wounded. The extraction bird was four minutes out, but we didn't have four minutes. We didn't have one.

"Rockets," I shouted, though my transmitter would have picked up a whisper. My ears rang from all the explosions and I had a hard time controlling my voice.

"Rockets, roger." At least five separate voices acknowledged my order. Good. Using all our remaining rockets would leave us woefully low on firepower, but not using them would leave us low on breathing. Easy choice. We had to make them count, though, which meant somebody had to designate targets. That was me.

"Stand by for targets." I kept my voice quieter, this time. I took two deep breaths, then leaped to my feet, pushing my head up over the wall that gave me cover. The targeting array in my helmet sought out the enemy. I needed three seconds to make sure I had accurate data. I probably had two seconds until they saw me and started shooting me in the face.

I counted in my head. Halfway between two and three I transmitted the firing solution. A split second later my faceplate shattered—

I couldn't breathe. I woke, gasping, clawing at the covers. A mechanical chime brought me back to reality. I glanced at it—my heart-rate monitor. One hundred sixty-two. Medical devices created a slight glow in the room, augmented by a bit of light streamed in through the cracked-open door, allowing me to quickly figure out where I was, which calmed me some.

It hadn't been bad, as far as my dreams go. A real memory. A battle with a group of insurrectionists, a long time ago. One of my first. My faceplate saved my life, and I got off with a slightly fractured neck from the kinetic energy that snapped my head back. It had landed me in a place much like the one where I lay now. I like to think that the younger me hadn't had the same sense of dread, the same worry about what waited outside his door. Maybe I was too young to know better back then.

I DIDN'T WANT to drag Ganos into whatever mess I'd found, but the more I thought about it, the more I suspected a connection between the Cappan hybrids and the breach at Omicron. The Phoenix Project, whatever it was, established too much of a coincidence; I couldn't let it go. And if I went back to work and talked to Javier, he would probably pull me from the case, and I'd lose that connection forever. I could let go of Omicron—that was business.

The hybrids . . . they made it personal.

I spent the day scanning through the huge pile of data that Dernier had put in our shared folder, trying to find another way. In under two hours I wanted to slam my face through my screen. I kept realizing that I'd read multiple screens of information, unable to recall any of it, and having to scroll back. My brain was full, and if there had been something in Dernier's files, I'm not sure I'd have found it. The answers that always seemed to resolve for me when I did something mindless didn't come. Hopefully, by marking the files read, Dernier would at least feel like I appreciated his efforts. Maybe that would keep him off my back for a bit.

I kept going back to what Ganos had said about getting inside Omicron, then pushing it out of my head. I needed somebody to bounce my ideas off of, but I didn't have anybody I could trust enough. Certainly not Dernier. I thought about Serata, but once I brought him in, I'd lose control of the investigation. He might feel obligated to inform somebody in the military, and that would close off whatever lead I might have into Omicron before I could figure out the connection.

I think if I could have shared my ideas, if somebody could have helped me make sense of them, it would have helped. I think if I'd had that, everything might have turned out different. But two years of isolating myself on purpose, avoiding people and especially close relationships . . . I was paying the price for that. Getting close to people brought them into my world, and nobody needed to live like that.

I called Ganos.

# CHAPTER SIXTEEN

THE CONCEPT WAS simple enough: Get Ganos on to the Omicron network. As an idea, it lacked finesse, but my other choice was to go after the Cappan hybrids again. They'd disappeared, from what I could tell, and if they hadn't, the last time I tried to confront them I got shot. I preferred to avoid that outcome again, and whatever my plan for Omicron lacked, the corporate headquarters probably wouldn't resort to gunfire.

To set things in motion I called Omicron's director of human resources—a man named Turkov—and let him know that I was considering a change in employment. He took the bait and set up a meeting, which I steered toward his office by hinting that I needed to keep things quiet, and oh by the way could he try to make sure I stayed off camera during my visit, because I didn't want word getting back to my employer. The plan had holes, but I didn't have any better ideas.

I gathered Ganos and headed to Omicron's headquarters, taking three separate private cars along the way to make sure nobody followed us. The hybrids concerned me most, but I also couldn't rule out a tail from VPC. Ganos had replaced her blue hair with a businesslike brown, and she wore a gray pantsuit that made her look like any middle-level employee at one of a thousand different companies. Bringing her put her at risk, but I didn't have anybody else I could trust, and she was extremely insistent.

"Nice hair," I said.

"Glad you like it, because you're paying for the dye job."

I laughed. "Fair enough."

The Omicron lobby reminded me of every corporate lobby, with possibly a little bit more fake polished stone, if that was possible. It even smelled the same, all processed air and some chemical that fell in the spectrum between astringent and perfume. Ganos's low-heeled shoes clacked on the floor, and when I looked at her I could hardly keep a straight face. I doubted even Parker would recognize her.

I headed to reception, Ganos trailing a pace behind me. I didn't make eye contact with the gentleman behind the counter until I stood right in front of him.

"Can I help you, sir?" he asked, in a polite corporate tone.

"I have a meeting with Mr. Turkov," I said.

The man sat up straighter hearing the name. Name dropping the VP of human resources would do that. "Yes, sir. He's on the seventeenth floor. Elevators are right over there."

I looked him directly in the eyes and gave him a

fake corporate smile. "Thank you"—I glanced at his nametag—"Aaron." I wanted his attention on me and not Ganos. The fewer people who could identify her, the safer she'd be if things went to crap.

"My pleasure, sir," he said, but I'd already turned away and headed for the elevator.

Disembarking on the seventeenth floor, I continued to play my part as another corporate guy who thought a little too much of himself. It made me nearly invisible. I found Turkov easily enough since he had the biggest office on the floor, and everybody knew him. His fancy outer office came complete with a secretary, a tall man whose eyes jumped to us the moment we entered. He sat alone in the room full of high-grade corporate carpet and dark, fake wood. A second desk sat across from his, used but currently unoccupied.

"Can I help you?" the man asked.

"I'm here to see Mr. Turkov," I said, as flatly as I could manage, trying to appear bored. I didn't look back at Ganos, who I assumed stood a bit behind me.

Before the secretary could respond, an overweight man in a suit a half size too small appeared from the inner office, consuming the doorway. "Colonel Butler. I'm Yergei Turkov. Come in."

"Thanks for seeing me on such short notice," I said, once we'd entered the inner office. Ganos followed me, avoiding the door when Turkov tried to shut it on her. "I know you're a busy man."

"Don't mention it," he said. "Can I get you something? Water, coffee? Whiskey?"

"I'm good, thanks." I appreciated that the man had done his research.

"So what can I do for you?" His eyes settled on Ganos, questioning.

"Excuse me," I said. "This is my assistant, Ms. Gabbert."

"Your . . . assistant," said Turkov.

I looked away, not meeting his eyes, trying to project shame. I glanced at Ganos, who stood there as if we weren't speaking about her. I sighed. "Ms. Gabbert isn't really my assistant."

Turkov sat down in his faux-leather chair and leaned back, hands behind his head. He didn't speak, but his look asked for an explanation.

I glanced at Ganos again, keeping the look longer than I needed to, then back to Turkov. I tried to appear nervous. "Ms. Gabbert is with corporate security at VPC." I gave him a meaningful look, trying to convey that she was more than just security.

"You need security?" asked Turkov, right on cue.

"The company feels that I'm an important asset. They don't want me to . . . they don't want anything to happen to me." I looked at Ganos harder this time, daring her to speak. She stood there implacably, as we'd rehearsed.

Turkov smiled the smile of a man who thought himself clever. "I thought that might be the case."

I smiled back. People never suspected the second lie. They expected you to lie once, but when they caught you, invariably they believed the next thing you told them. Turkov didn't disappoint. "I'd like to talk to you about an . . . opportunity." I glanced at Ganos quickly, then back at Turkov. I wanted him to believe I needed to talk to him alone, but I couldn't say it in front of Ganos.

"Why don't I show you around the facility?" Turkov stood and came around his desk.

I paused. "Yes. That would be great." I looked at Ganos. "I'm sure I'll be completely safe, Ms. Gabbert."

Ganos glanced at Turkov, then back at me, nervous. "Sir . . . I'm really supposed to stay—"

"He'll be fine, Ms. Gabbert," said Turkov.

"I'll be fine, Ms. Gabbert," I said. "I won't need to explain any problems with your work to Mr. Sanchez."

Ganos looked back and forth between us, then down at the floor. "I'll wait here."

Turkov hustled his bulk around his desk and quickly led me out the door. "We'll be out of the office for a few minutes," he told his secretary as we passed by.

"Thanks for understanding." I wanted to look at Ganos, but I didn't. I hoped that her end of the plan worked. More important, I hoped she didn't get caught.

He smiled. "Of course. Did you really want to see the company?"

"Not really, no," I admitted. "I wanted to get away from my corporate minder so I could speak without it getting back to my boss. It's so annoying."

"I'll bet. So what can I do for you?"

"I'm exploring my options. I know you were interested when I first came on the market, and I'm thinking it might be time to make a change, if I found the right situation. Things at VPC . . . well let's say I feel like I could be happier somewhere else."

His face lit up. I had him. "What kind of situation are you looking for?"

I rolled my shoulders, suddenly pretending not to be as interested. I had to play the game the way he expected to make it feel real. "I could be open to a lot of things."

He suppressed a chuckle. "Of course. Any particular job you feel you're qualified for?"

"One that doesn't involve someone from the company following me when I leave the building?"

This time he did laugh. "That I'm sure we can arrange. I can't say exactly what we'd put on the nameplate on your door, but that doesn't really matter much, does it?"

"I'm flexible, as long as it's in the same tier I'm at now. Or higher."

He nodded. "Let me look around. Talk to some people. Brief the boss. But I don't see that being an issue."

"Not an issue is good," I said.

"Come on," he offered. "I'll show you a little bit of the place. That way your . . . assistant . . . won't suspect anything."

"I appreciate your discretion," I said.

GANOS AND I left Omicron without talking and headed to her apartment, making another car change along the way. I'd wanted to go somewhere else, but she had the equipment she needed and I didn't. Ganos's apartment surprised me in its efficiency and cleanliness. I think because she usually dressed without a lot of care, I equated that to how she'd live. Her space rivaled mine in size but seemed larger due to the sparse furniture. She had one comfortable chair and three stools that sat at the bar that surrounded her efficiency kitchen. The tile floor sparkled, and dust didn't seem to exist. The entire far wall of the main living area drew the eye. She had three tables, end to end lengthwise, all buried in high-tech machinery. Five monitors formed a semi-circle on the center table in front of a captain's chair, which looked like it might be the most expensive piece of furniture in the room. Lights danced through towers of processors and Mother knows what other technologies.

Everything stood in perfect order, except a little two-kilogram fuzzy terror, which bounded across the floor, barking at me as if it wasn't the size of my shoe.

"Nice dog," I said.

"Francisco! Sit! He's okay." The fuzzy rat backed off half a meter and stopped barking, but he kept eye contact. "Don't mind Cisco. He's all bark."

"He'd have to be. What else is he going to do? Savage my ankle?"

"He keeps me company," she said.

"Of course. So Omicron . . . what did you find out?"

"Nothing," she said. "Well, I learned that you shouldn't leave yourself logged in when you leave your office. But we knew that already. Not that it would have mattered. I'd have cracked his terminal anyway."

"So you got in?"

"Of course I got in, sir. But I didn't get any information. I didn't have time, and if I did, someone would have seen stuff flowing to Turkov's terminal that probably shouldn't have been, and it would have raised a red flag. Not something we want to do when we're in their building."

"Got it," I said. "But if you didn't get anything, what was the point of me getting you into his office?"

"I left myself a door."

"A door?"

"Right. A tiny hole, really. One that I can exploit from outside."

"Won't they see that?"

"They will. Depending how good their security is, they'll find it somewhere between twelve hours and three days from now. They'll wonder how it got there, and depending on their protocol, they'll either look into it or treat it as routine. Odds are on routine."

"But you said that if you brought information to Turkov's terminal, they'd see it."

"They would, if I did it from there. But since I now have all the time I need, I'm going to be more subtle than that. So they might not notice. And if they do, I'm going to be routed through about a thousand different proxies on the way in."

"So it's untraceable?"

She walked over and flipped a few switches on her system. "Nothing's untraceable. But pretty much, yeah."

"That's quite a setup," I said.

"I enjoy my work," she answered. "So this is where all my money goes, other than spoiling Cisco. You might as well make yourself comfortable. This is going to take a bit to get fired up."

I took the comfortable chair and Ganos moved behind her computerized creation. Fans hummed and more lights danced, and she went to another place, lost, as if I wasn't there. Cisco apparently decided I passed muster, and came and lay down between my feet. I pulled out my device and flipped through the news, checking on whether the police had anything new on the murder of Gylika. They didn't, but one article led to another and I burrowed into some other stories until Ganos interrupted me.

"Sir, what's Project Phoenix?"

"Phoenix. Shit. Something in the medical field that Omicron has working. I don't know exactly what it is, but it's important. What have you got?"

"I think that was the breach. Or, rather, Phoenix didn't make the breach. The breach was *in* Phoenix."

"That doesn't make any sense," I said. "Gylika . . . he was my contact at Omicron. He worked on Phoenix, at least in some capacity. But I met him after the event happened, and he didn't know anything."

"There are a couple of emails here. Medical research . . . blah blah blah . . . revenue estimates. Holy shit, that's a lot of zeroes."

"Does it say anything about ortho-robotics?" I asked.

"Yes, sir. You knew about this stuff? It looks like it's something to do with DNA splicing."

I froze. I don't know how long I sat there, silent. I'd heard it before, but this time it really sunk in deep. I couldn't deny it any longer.

"Sir, your face went pale. What is it?"

I took a deep, slow breath to calm myself. "Can you tell who breached it? Who stole the data?"

"Let me see . . ." Her fingers flew across the keys. "Whoa. It's not medical. It's military. Sort of. Something to do with manipulating DNA. Somehow it's supposed to make people tolerate cybernetics better. I don't understand it, but I think they're trying to make mechanical soldiers. Or partially mechanical. I can't tell—there's not enough here."

"Ganos . . . I want you to close it and get out of there." I'd heard enough. I wanted to know who cracked it, but this information was explosive. I had had suspicions, but this confirmed it. I needed Ganos away from it for her own good.

"Hold on, sir. I'm trying to find out who broke in." She buried her face back behind the monitors.

"Close it," I said.

"I just got in. Let me download some of this stuff to local storage."

I stood up, and in my most "I'm a Colonel" voice said, "Close everything and seal it up. Hide the fact that you were ever there as best you can. Take every precaution. Everything you know how to do."

She met my eyes over one of her monitors. "Sir, you're scaring me. What's wrong?"

"Just do what I say," I said. "I promise, I'll explain everything. But you've got to get out of there right now."

My mind raced while she clacked away at her keyboard. They had never shut down the project. They moved it to a different location and gave it another name, made it corporate instead of military. And now there were Cappan hybrids, probably unstable, chasing me around the city, bent on revenge. I stood and paced the width of the room. Cisco scampered to a spot on the floor between Ganos and me and started growling. Even the dog could sense my anxiety.

I couldn't think clearly, but one thing was sure: I couldn't involve Ganos any further. That would put me in a bind for gathering more information since she'd been my one reliable source so far and the only person I trusted. But I'd put her in enough danger, and I had the thread I needed. I'd find another way to pull on it. I'd played a stupid game where I didn't understand the stakes, and now that they had become fully apparent, I found myself three moves behind.

"Do you have any vacation time saved up?" I asked. "It might be good for you to get out of town for a couple of days."

She paused her typing. "Sir, what the fuck is going on?"

"This is big, Ganos. It's tied to what I did back on Cappa, when I blew up the planet."

She stopped typing, her hands hanging there over the keyboard. "Sir . . . tell me everything."

"Finish, first, and I will."

She did, and so I did. I told her all of it. What happened back on Cappa with Elliot, and everything that had happened since. When I finished, I expected her to say something. To yell at me for getting her involved. *Something*.

Instead, she nodded slowly a few times. "Wow. This is big."

"I think it is. You're sure you hid your entry into the system?"

"Yes, sir. I've plugged the hole the best I can. It would take the best techies alive to trace this shit. I'm not worried."

I wished I shared her confidence.

# CHAPTER SEVENTEEN

HR HAD TOLD me to take some days off after my hospital stay, but I couldn't hang around the apartment stewing over the information Ganos had found. I left my place a little after lunch and took an alternate route to work, checking behind me the entire way, looking for my Cappan-hybrid friends. My newly repaired leg needed the workout anyway. Sirens played a symphony that sat over the normal background noise of the city, but I never got close enough to them to see what brought in the emergency crews.

I had barely reached my office when Ganos bounced in, practically vibrating with excitement. "Sir! You're here."

I frowned. "I thought we discussed you taking a few days off."

"Technically *you* said that. But never mind the semantics. You're not going to believe what happened."

"People keep saying that," I said. "Tell me you didn't go back into the place I told you not to go."

"I didn't. But I pulled that picture of the woman that we had, and I poked around looking for known associates, other pictures, those sorts of things."

"And you found something?" As much as I wanted her away from the situation, I couldn't pass up that kind of information. Besides, if she'd already done the work, my getting it from her wouldn't change anything.

"Yes. No. Sort of." She waved her hands as she spoke.

"Slow down, Ganos. Start from the beginning."

She took a deep breath. "Okay. I was looking for things, searching a bunch of different databases. Kinda deep work, but nothing super technical and not particularly dangerous. Then, all of a sudden, wherever I entered, someone closed the door."

I let my confusion show on my face. "Help me out, here."

"The places I was looking . . . they're not exactly public access, right?"

"Sure. I'm with you so far."

"Every time I got inside, something shut me down. Not once. Every. Time. No matter where I went. I thought it was a fluke the first time. These things happen. The second time I started to wonder. By the fifth time?"

"So the agencies who maintained the databases were onto you?" I asked.

She shook her head. "No way. *All* of them? They're not part of the same system. Each action was independent."

"I don't understand. How did it happen, then?"

"I thought about that for a long time," she said. "Somebody else had to have hacked the same systems and shut them down on me."

"That's possible?"

"It shouldn't be. To do that . . . you'd have to be watching every single system out there. And here's the kicker. It's not happening to anybody else in the community. I'd have heard about it. It specifically targeted *me*."

A chill ran up my spine. I thought about my own situation, and how they'd been following me. "I don't know much about computers, but you said they'd have to be watching everywhere you went. What if instead they were watching you?"

She nodded. "That's the conclusion I came to, too. I searched everything I had. It took me a day, but I found it. Barely. A hint of a track in my system. They hacked me, then they hid it so well I almost couldn't find it. Kind of embarrassing, actually."

"How could they do that?"

She shrugged. "I'm working on it. But it's got me spooked, I'll tell you that."

"Me too." She seemed to be focused on how they did it technically. I was more worried about how they knew to watch her in the first place. I didn't know crap about computers, but it had to be Omicron. I didn't want to say it out loud. "What's the damage?"

"That's just it. There isn't any. Whoever did this could have triggered alarms in the systems while I was inside, and I might have gotten caught. But they didn't. They booted me out and locked the door. That's it. The administrators probably don't know it happened."

"That's—"

"Colonel Butler?" A coworker I recognized but couldn't place poked his head in and interrupted.

"Yes?"

"Sir, I need you to come with me."

"Give me a minute," I said.

He didn't leave the door. "I'm sorry, sir. It has to be right now."

I glared at him, but I couldn't muster any real anger. My brain was still spinning from what Ganos had told me. "I said—"

He cut me off. "Sir, the police are in the lobby, and they insist on seeing you immediately."

I bit back the reply I'd been about to give and looked at Ganos as I walked toward the door. "Get out of town. Better yet, off the planet. You hear me?"

"Yes, sir," she said. I didn't believe her, but I couldn't focus on that at the moment.

IT DIDN'T SURPRISE me when we walked around the corner into the lobby to find Mallory and Burke waiting for me, though they did seem incongruous somehow in that environment: the cops in their cheap suits surrounded by the opulence of VPC's lobby.

"What's going on?" I asked.

"Colonel Butler, we're going to need you to come with us," said Mallory, while her partner skulked behind her.

My mind spun. Having just talked to Ganos, I wondered if somehow somebody tied her semi-legal computer activities to me. But they couldn't have. At the most, it was highly unlikely, since they hadn't asked to see her as well. The legal team had assured me I was cleared to go when I left the hospital, so it couldn't be that. "You want to tell me what this is about?"

"Not really, no," said Mallory.

"What if I say I'm not going?"

"You're going. We can do this the easy way or the hard way." Mallory patted the handcuffs on her belt.

"Please say the hard way," said Burke. "Please."

It sounded like something he had heard in a vid. Asshole. I didn't really consider it, but I hesitated a few seconds to make them think I had. "I think I'll take the easy way, thanks."

"Smart man," said Mallory. "Let's go."

I followed them out the front door, absorbing the stares of a couple dozen people who happened to be transiting through and some who showed up when they heard the news. I'm guessing it probably took ninety seconds to spread through the rest of the building.

Mallory opened the back door of their hover-car, a bulky, armored thing that looked twenty years old but somehow still functional. More classic than out-dated. They avoided all my attempts during the drive to get information out of them, which meant they didn't want me to know what they had. I wondered who died. It took me a couple minutes to reach that conclusion, but it had to be that. Somebody died, and somehow the police tied that person to me. The list of people within their jurisdiction that I legitimately cared about was pretty short. I'd just seen Ganos, so that left Plazz, Sheila Jackson, and Serata, who I considered friends. Jackson worked at VPC, and the other two would have made big news splashes, so if it was any of them I'd have probably heard about it. It didn't resolve the question, though. I almost asked Mallory to tell me who died, but I decided to save that for a moment when I could see their faces and gauge their reactions. Riding in the vehicle, I could only stare at the backs of their heads, which held no answers.

At the station they hustled me in through a side door near the parking area for police vehicles. We walked, Mallory in front of me, Burke behind, through an area of desks and low dividers where at least a dozen officers worked on modern computers, a few talking to civilians, taking statements or some such. A couple people glanced up, but none for more than the briefest moment before going back to work. Whatever they brought me in for, either it wasn't that important or nobody else in the room knew about it.

Mallory led me into the same interrogation room I'd visited the last time I came to see her, but with one small difference. This time I couldn't leave if I wanted to, and that made the space seem smaller and darker. The presence of the perpetually angry Burke didn't do much for the ambiance either.

"So who's dead?" I asked. Burke's long glance at his partner confirmed my guess. She shook her head slightly, as if to silence him. I took that to mean he wanted to ask me how I knew somebody was dead, but she wanted to go in a different direction.

"I need you to tell us where you've been for the last twelve hours," she said.

"I arrived home last night before dark. I stayed in my apartment until I left for work a short time ago."

"What time did you leave for work?"

"I don't know," I said. "Maybe an hour ago? I heard a bunch of sirens as I entered VPC. That might give you an estimate of the time."

This time it was Mallory who glanced at her partner. I couldn't be sure, but I think my mentioning the sirens triggered something. "Did anybody see you at your apartment?"

"Not that I know of," I said.

"You know that we can pull camera feeds from the area—"

Raised voices from the hallway cut Mallory off. "Sir! Sir! You can't go in there!"

The door opened and a tall, dark-skinned man in an exquisite charcoal-colored suit stepped halfway through. He wore his hair short, immaculately trimmed, and he smiled at the officers the way a predator looks at its next meal. "Excuse me, officers. I'd like to confer with my client before you question him any further."

Mallory looked at me. "*This* is your attorney?"

"My client is not going to answer any questions until we've spoken. I'm Mark Gaspard. I've been retained for Colonel Butler's representation."

*Mark Gaspard.* I didn't recognize him, but I knew the name. Everybody knew the name. He was the highest-profile defense attorney in the city, if not on the planet. Somebody like me couldn't get a meeting with him. And somebody like me definitely couldn't afford him.

"Colonel Butler?" asked Mallory. "Despite what this very high-priced gentleman says, you only have the right to consult with him if he *is* your attorney. So I'm afraid you *do* have to answer."

"You only need an attorney if you've got something to hide," said Burke.

"Cut the bullshit, officer," said Gaspard. "It's unbecoming." For a moment Burke almost looked embarrassed. I'd have signed on with Gaspard for that alone.

"Yes. Mr. Gaspard represents me."

"We'll leave you the room." Mallory snapped her device cover closed a little harder than required.

"That won't be necessary," said Gaspard. "It's not that I don't trust you with your listening devices. Call it a precaution. You understand, right?"

"Well, he can't leave . . ."

Gaspard smiled. "Is he under arrest? What's the charge? Look, I'm not trying to be a hard-ass, here. Give me five minutes outside, and we'll come right back. You have my word."

Mallory sighed and looked at Burke, who shrugged. "Fine," she said.

I started to speak as we walked through the station, to figure out where my legal savior had come from, but he waved me off until we reached the street.

"Would they really listen in on us?" I asked.

"Hard to say," said Gaspard. "But why give them the temptation? Mostly I just wanted to fuck with them."

I chuckled. "I assume VPC sent you?"

"I got a call from Javier Sanchez himself. Sorry I didn't get here before you arrived, but your detention was somewhat of a surprise, I understand."

"Very much a surprise. I don't even know what I'm here for."

"I'm not sure either, which probably means we can get you out without any further questioning, if you want."

I smiled. "As much as that sounds like fun, if they've got legit questions and I can help, I don't mind. And I'd really like to get some information from them too, if I can. Something happened, and they have at least some thought that it's associated with me."

"Okay. I'll lead into it, and then I'm going to stay there with you during the questioning. That will likely be enough to keep them in line and prevent them from working you over too hard. Give me a rundown on the situation and then we'll go back in."

"Sounds good," I said. "Out of curiosity, what's something like this cost?"

"You don't want to know. I also have a message for you, directly from Mr. Sanchez."

"Sure, as long as he's footing the bill for this, I'm all ears."

"He said that you're to cease all activity with regard to Omicron Corporation. He said you'd know what that meant."

"I do," I said. I'd think through that order later. First I had to focus on the more pressing matter of the police. I briefed Gaspard on the events of the past week, including Gylika's death and the shooting in the street. I specifically *didn't* mention the hybrids or our incursion into Omicron's system. He was my lawyer, but he was also Javier's.

**MALLORY AND BURKE** were waiting for us when we returned, conversing with each other in low voices.

"My client consents to questioning with me present," said Gaspard.

"That's big of him," Burke said.

"It is, isn't it?" Gaspard smiled.

"Have a seat," said Mallory. I took the chair I'd had before, and Gaspard sat to my left. Mallory took a chair across the polymer table, while Burke paced around the room, per his norm.

"I think you were telling us about where you were this morning," said Mallory.

"I'm going to be completely honest with you," I said. "I have no idea why I'm here. I'm completely open to helping you in any way that I can, but you've got to clue me in on what we're talking about. All I know is this: I didn't do anything except sleep, then flip around on my computer until I got bored and went to work."

Mallory sighed. "The sirens you heard this morning . . . they were responding to an explosion."

That caught me slightly off guard. "What connected that to me?"

"We connected it to you because the people who died in the blast were the same people we suspect had a firefight in your vicinity a few days ago. Somebody shoots you, then that somebody dies. Seems like a hell of a coincidence, doesn't it?"

"That sounds a lot like an accusation," said Gaspard.

A chill went through me, despite the warm room. "It's okay," I said. It definitely wasn't a coincidence. But I didn't know which group died, either. Had it been the hybrids or the other group? I didn't want to ask directly, because that would let them know how much I cared. "Are you sure it was a murder and not a terrorist attack or something?"

She shook her head. "Terrorists go out of their way to cause as much damage as possible. This explosion affected exactly one room, killing the two people inside but doing no damage to the rest of the building."

"Wow," I said.

"Whoever did this knew their way around. Does that tell you anything?"

I shook my head. "That's not really my expertise. I know my explosions, but something like that inside a room, that's not me. That would be more of a . . ." I let my voice trail off. It was more of a Special Ops skill. I had a good guess at who died, and it wasn't the hybrids.

"Finish that thought." Mallory looked at Gaspard, to see if he was going to object to her pushing me.

"My client would be offering this information as an expert in the field, not as a suspect," said Gaspard.

"Sure," said Mallory.

"It's a Special Ops sort of skill," I said. "Taking out a target without collateral damage in a confined space . . . yeah. If it was military, I'd bet good money that some Special Ops folks did it."

"And what would Special Operations soldiers have to do with a firefight in an alley? Assuming the same people were responsible for both actions."

"You don't have to answer that," said Gaspard.

Mallory started to speak, but I cut her off. "It's fine. I'll answer. But the fact is, I don't know." I'd given them one piece of the truth, but drew the line at discussing what I knew about the hybrid woman. It would pull me further in with the police, and they didn't have anything to share with me in return. At least not that I could see. "Maybe if I knew who the dead guys were, I'd be able to shed more light on it."

Mallory considered it. "We don't know. They both had some pretty intricate fake credentials. They're ex-military, almost for sure, but that's about all we have."

"Shit," I said.

"What?" asked Mallory.

"I really want to know who these people are."

"You legitimately don't know?"

"I legitimately don't know."

"Butler . . . what are you caught up in?" she asked.

Gaspard cleared his throat.

"Never mind," said Mallory.

I smiled. It didn't matter if I answered or not. I had no idea.

# CHAPTER EIGHTEEN

THE MOMENT I entered my apartment I sensed something off. I don't know what tipped me, but I dove to the floor, scrambling for cover.

"Good evening, Colonel Butler." A woman's voice. Familiar. "You can get up. We're not going to hurt you. We just want to talk."

My heart pounded. The woman from the street. The Cappan hybrid. The same words she'd said before I got shot. "How did you get in here?" I wanted to keep her talking. Stall for time. I had a taser stashed by my bed. It seemed unlikely I'd be able to get to it, but any chance beat no chance.

"You've got a good security system. State of the art."

"Apparently not," I said.

"No, it is. But we're good at bypassing things like that." The woman sat on my sofa, her partner stood behind her, the same guy who'd been with her previously. Neither appeared to have a weapon. Neither appeared to be particularly worried about that either. They radiated calm. "I'm going to ask you to set your device aside," said the woman. "I don't want you calling the police."

I took my device out of my pocket and set it on the shelf. I had no reason to disobey. If they meant me harm, I'd already be dead. If they still intended it, it would happen well before anybody I called could get to me. I suppose I could have called somebody to come clean up my body. I shook that thought off and tried to focus on something less morbid. "Sure. You're here, we might as well talk."

"You know who we are," said the man. A statement, not a question.

"I know . . . what you are. Who? No, I don't know that."

"My name is Sasha. This is Riku," said the woman.

"Carl Butler. You mind if I sit?" I hadn't given up on getting to my weapon, but I wanted answers more.

"Please do," said Sasha. "You're remarkably calm, given the circumstances."

I didn't agree with that. My heart had been slamming in my chest since I'd walked in, and I had only begun to get it under control. Slowly walking to my chair helped with that. "I try not to overreact to things. How did you get here?" I didn't expect them to answer, but if I could change the tenor of the conversation, get them responding to me, it could only help.

"We answered that," said Riku.

"No, not how did you get into my apartment. How did you get to this planet?"

"As we told you when we met before, we need your help," he said, ignoring my question, which further showed me I was dealing with professionals.

"Yeah. I remember you saying that. Right before people started shooting at me."

"That was unfortunate," said Sasha.

I snorted. "Tell me about it."

"The people who shot you . . . they were trying to hit us," she said.

"How do you know?" I asked.

"It's not the first time they've tried."

"They had a free shot. If they wanted to hit you, they would have."

"Perhaps," she said. "A lot of factors go into something like that."

I paused before changing course. "So you have enemies here. You've struck back. They were found dead today. I assume that was your work."

She glanced over her shoulder at her partner. "We have enemies everywhere."

"And I'm the man who is single-handedly responsible for killing a huge number of Cappans," I said. "So I figure I've got to be pretty high on the list."

"Not necessarily," said Sasha.

"Okay. You lost me. I'm going to fix a drink. You want something?"

"No, thank you," she said. Riku shook his head.

I stood and walked over to the counter and poured myself a double. "How am I not enemy number one?"

"Among some Cappans, you almost assuredly are. But as far as the group we're working with is concerned, you haven't done anything yet to show that."

I almost dropped my drink. "Haven't done anything?"

Sasha considered her words before speaking. "More precisely, what you did was in the past. A one-time thing. They—we—are willing to put it behind us if it helps us today."

"That's remarkably . . . mature of you. And the Cappans. I suppose they're behind your visit?" I took a sip of my drink, not worrying that it was somewhere around eleven in the morning.

"They asked us to make contact with you, yes," said Sasha. "They want to speak to you. But it's not like a Cappan can show up on Talca Four without drawing attention."

"Forgive me if this is a bit hard to believe," I said. I couldn't figure out their plan, and the confusion made me uncomfortable.

"Let me ask you, Colonel Butler," said Sasha. "The last time you dealt with someone like us, would you have described them as mature?"

I flashed back to Mallot, who I'd shot in the face because he was unhinged and likely to kill me, and to Karakov, a decorated officer, losing his mind. "No, that's not the word I'd use."

"What word would you have used?" she asked.

I thought about it, not wanting to offend them or put them on the defensive. "I'd say . . . unstable."

"Exactly," she said.

"So you're suggesting . . ." I took my seat again. "You're saying that you're different from them?"

"Yes," she said.

"Interesting. Care to elaborate?"

"The procedure that spliced Cappan and human DNA didn't work then. Now it does." She met my eyes, unblinking, but somehow not challenging. She believed it, but she didn't necessarily expect me to.

"That simple?" I asked.

She shook her head. "Not simple at all. The science behind it, I'm told, is off-the-charts complicated. Before, the two genetic sets were in conflict with each other. Now they're in harmony."

"I don't understand how that's possible."

"I don't necessarily understand it all, either." She gestured to herself and her partner. "But here we are."

"Here you are," I repeated, more trying to give myself time to think than anything else. "What changed?"

"When you attacked the planet, you destroyed the human medical facilities."

I nodded. "Yes."

"Those of us with Cappan DNA splicing who were stranded on the planet couldn't survive without treatment," she continued. "So we went to the only source we had."

"What source?"

"The Cappans."

I took a drink to cover my surprise. "The Cappans?"

"Their understanding of genetics is quite advanced," she said.

"Genetics. The Cappans." I failed to keep the skepticism out of my voice.

"That was the genesis of the project in the first place. A mutual effort between Cappans and humans. Until the humans took it over for their own purposes."

"Forgive me . . . the Cappans are a backwards people."

She scrunched up her face. "Says who? Humans?"

"Everybody. They didn't have space travel when we arrived."

"Space travel is an arbitrary marker. They had no desire to leave their planet," she replied.

"But they . . ." I stopped, considered it. What did I really know about them? "So you're saying they could have left the planet if they wanted to?"

"The population hadn't begun to deplete the resources of their own world. They're a very efficient people. And admittedly, they didn't have fusion technology before humans arrived."

"Until they stole it," I said, my voice soft.

"How fast did they assimilate it?" she asked.

I stared into the amber liquid in my glass without answering at first. "They understood everything."

"Not at first," she said. "But science is a lot easier when you have something to work from."

I wasn't a scientist, but I had no trouble believing that part. "So you're . . . you two . . . you're stable?"

"As stable as you are," said Riku.

"That's not necessarily a great measuring stick," I said, but they didn't react to the joke. "You're saying that the Cappans did that. Fixed you."

"*Fixed* is kind of an ugly word," he said. "But yes."

I took another sip of my drink. I couldn't process it. "How does this relate to Omicron?" Both of their faces clouded over when I said that name. "There's something wrong with Omicron," I added for effect.

Her extended pause told me I'd hit the mark. It also told me she knew about Omicron. "Omicron is a problem, yes. It's part of why the Cappans want to talk to you."

"We're talking right now." I gave up all thought of trying to get to a weapon. Sasha knew something about Omicron, and since she was sitting in my apartment, I could be pretty sure it had to do with me.

"It's not for us to say. The Cappans will decide how much they want to share," she said.

"I need more than that," I said.

She considered it. "I will tell you this: The people who shot at you—shot at us—they were employed by Omicron."

"You have proof?" I asked. If they did, I could use that with Mallory.

"No."

"But you're sure," I said.

"Yes." She spit the word, almost like an epithet.

"Why would they want to shoot you?"

They looked at each other, and while neither spoke, I got the feeling that something passed between them. "We've delivered our message," she said. "Will you meet with the Cappans or not?"

"We're meeting now," I said, frustration clawing at

my mind. She had answers and she wasn't going to share them.

"We're not the Cappans," said Riku. "We're doing them a favor. They help us, we help them."

"The last time I met with Cappans, they beat me up and tried to do medical experiments on me."

"You seem to think of Cappans as a homogenous group," said Sasha. "I would suggest to you that they're as diverse in their thinking as humans. The Cappans you encountered were likely tied to the resistance to the invasion. It follows that they were on the radical side, much like any freedom fighters. But I understand your position," said Sasha.

I started to respond, but stopped. Thinking about it, I *had* thought of them mostly as one body, but now that Sasha said it, that seemed stupidly simplistic. "And the group you represent?" I asked, finally.

"Scientists, mostly," said Sasha. "Much more progressive. They certainly don't trust humans, but they see the utility—or necessity—of peaceful coexistence."

"I don't blame them for the lack of trust," I said, "so I hope you won't blame me for my lack of trust either. Can you guarantee my safety if I agree to meet with the Cappans?"

"Would you believe us if we said yes?" asked Sasha.

A fair point. "I need time to think about it."

"Unfortunately, we don't have much of that," said Sasha. "The Cappans are on a rather tight timeline. They can't stay on Talca Four for long."

"They're *here*?"

"How else would you meet?" asked Riku.

"I don't know, I was thinking via video or something." I mumbled a little, struggling to process the new information. "They flew off the back side of Cappa, avoiding the satellite surveillance, and they came *here*?"

Sasha gave a meaningful look to her partner. I'd surprised them with what I knew again. Good to know they didn't have all the answers.

After a few seconds I repeated, "I need time to think." I was almost sure I'd meet with the Cappans. How could I not? Sasha wasn't giving me answers, and they could. But by asking for time, I could gauge whether or not I really had a choice, or if the two hybrids would force me. Knowing where I stood was a valuable piece of information.

"We can give you two days," she said. "But you have to promise not to take action to expose the Cappans on Talca. We will be watching."

"I agree to that," I said without pause.

"That includes Ms. Ganos trying to dig up information about us," Sasha said.

It was my turn to be surprised by what *they* knew. I considered bluffing, denying knowledge, but something about how Sasha said it told me I'd be wasting my time. "You know about her?"

"We do, but we won't share that."

The implication being that they could, if I didn't help

them. They were asking nicely, but not really. "Was it you who thwarted her efforts searching the net?"

"Associates of ours," said Sasha. "She's very talented."

It did ease my mind a bit that they had found Ganos, not Omicron. That was probably my subconscious telling me which side I should choose. But I still wasn't sure, so I decided to try a different angle to test them. I was still searching for a reason to say no. "What made you side with the Cappans?"

"We spent a lot of time with them while they treated us, and we saw how humans abused them. It's wrong. We feel like the group we're working with now is taking appropriate action."

"And all of . . . all of the people who have been treated medically by the Cappans feel like you do?"

"Absolutely not," said Riku. "We have free will. In fact, most of the people like us have chosen not to get involved. They can pass for human, so they're integrating back into society. They have no reason to fight."

I'd never considered that. Like the Cappans, I'd thought of the hybrids as one contiguous group. Again, it made sense that they weren't. Why would they be? I had a serious flaw in my thinking.

"How many of the Cappans are aligned with this group? How many think it's a good idea to work with me? How many want me dead?"

Sasha smiled. "Now you're asking the right questions. But the answers aren't mine to give. You should ask that when you meet. Take the two days and think about it. We're not looking to force you into action."

"You broke into my apartment. You've not-so-subtly said you might expose Ganos. You have to see how that makes me skeptical."

"That was necessary," said Riku. "With Ganos, we had to keep tabs on people who could expose *us*. And we broke in because we couldn't risk another interaction like we had on the street the other day."

"I suppose not," I said. "But then if you're not here to force me, why are you here?"

Sasha gave me a flat smile. "To ask you to do the right thing."

Shit. If they'd kidnapped me and dragged me to meet the Cappans I might have resisted, and they'd have done what they were going to do, we'd fight, and that would be that. But they went and appealed to my sense of justice.

Fighting dirty.

"Why do they want me?"

"They're convinced that you're the right person to help them," said Sasha.

I shook my head. "Their confidence in me is flattering. But I think they've got it wrong." I held up my glass. "I'm just a washed-up drunk who's seen one too many battlefields."

"Bullshit," said Sasha with a fierceness that startled me for a second. Then again, I didn't believe it myself, so I understood her sentiment.

"You know I did the wrong thing, right? On Cappa?"

Sasha smiled. "We know. But right and wrong are not absolutes. What is right at one moment might be wrong at another."

"That's crap! There *are* moral absolutes. And what I did—"

"If it's a moral absolute, why did you do it?" asked Riku. "Are you an immoral man?"

I gave him a flat smile, then shook my head. "I don't know. I might be."

They glanced at each other again. The woman spoke this time. "Our allies are willing to believe that you aren't."

"Okay. You said I could have two days. I understand your stipulations about not taking action to harm you in any way. What about actions against Omicron?" It didn't seem prudent to specify that I'd already taken one such action by breaking into their system.

"As long as they don't lead back to us," Sasha said.

"Okay. How do I contact you?"

"Message the word 'decision' to this number." My device vibrated on the shelf where I'd set it.

"Two days," I said.

Once they left, I slumped onto my sofa, finished my drink, and contemplated my ridiculous situation. I'd pretty much already decided to take the meeting. The only thing to figure out was how to best prepare in the two days I had.

# CHAPTER NINETEEN

**I** **WENT TO WORK** early the next day. Sasha had told me that the people who shot me worked for Omicron. It stuck with me, and my gut said that Omicron had something to do with the Cappans wanting to meet with me. There were too many coincidences for them not to be linked, especially given what Ganos had found out about the Phoenix Project. I'd lain awake most of the night, thinking about what Sasha and Riku told me. Damn if I didn't believe them. Damn if I didn't think the Cappans were the good guys. Maybe I'd spent enough time around corporations like Omicron to know their ills. Maybe I figured that after killing so many Cappans I owed them. Either way, I had a meeting with the Cappans in two days, and I wanted to go into it knowing as much as possible.

Walking into Omicron's lobby and demanding answers wouldn't work. I could have gone back at them through their computer network, but I didn't want to further involve Ganos—I still held out hope that she'd take my advice and leave the city for a bit. And Javier had removed any official backing I had to go at them as a VPC employee. With my options limited, I felt like I had only one other avenue.

Make things very unofficial.

It was time to put some pressure on Javier about his contact. He knew things he hadn't shared, and I wanted to know them. All that stood in my way was the small fact that he'd had a very expensive attorney tell me to drop my investigation. But with only two days, I had to take risks. If it meant potential termination of my job, so be it. I was tired of VPC anyway. I grabbed some coffee and headed up to his office to see if I could get on his schedule.

Turned out I didn't need an appointment; Javier greeted me the moment I walked into his outer office. "Carl! Just the man I wanted to talk to. You saved me from having someone call you up."

I tried to hide my surprise. I'd rehearsed several possible approaches in my head, but none of them involved Javier issuing me an invitation. "Sure thing, boss," I said, after what I hoped wasn't too awkward of a pause. I followed him into his inner office.

"I want to talk to you about Omicron." Javier spoke before he got the door closed. I was glad he hadn't been looking at my face when he said it, because he caught me by surprise again.

I pretended to look out his giant windows where red early-morning sunlight played across the city, throwing long shadows. I used the time to gather myself. "I got the message from the attorney to stand down," I said, turning back to look at him.

He was shaking his head. "I'm disappointed, Carl."

My mind raced. What did he know? He couldn't know about the hack we'd done on their network. No way. "I'm a bit lost."

"You didn't think it would get back to me that you were at Omicron looking for employment?" he asked.

*Oh.* Relief washed through me, but only for a moment. I wasn't in trouble for the illegal breach of a rival company's network. Good. But I had to explain to my boss about my cover story, which involved me turning my back on the company that employed me. Bad. And I couldn't tell him that my purpose for visiting Omicron was merely a cover for our operation. Very bad. I pondered my options for about three seconds before deciding on a course: blatant lying. When I spoke, I did my best to sound relaxed. "Oh, that. That was nothing. A cover story." The best lies have an element of the truth in them.

Javier started to speak, but stopped himself twice. He'd probably rehearsed this confrontation, and I'd thrown him. He hadn't expected my answer. "Now I'm lost," he said.

"I was trying to find a new lead at Omicron . . . this was before you sent me the message to cease work on that . . . so I pretended to be on the job market to give me an excuse to get into their building and see if I could *accidentally* run into somebody who might know something."

He walked around behind his desk and sat down, then gestured to a chair for me. I took a few extra seconds getting seated, letting my words sink in, hoping he bought it. *Come on. It's a good story. Buy it!*

"That makes a lot of sense," he said, finally. "You should know that they took your overture seriously. That might cause some problems."

"No problem," I said, warming to the lie. "I'll tell them that you found out about it, confronted me, and made me a better offer."

He almost laughed at that. "That's convenient for you."

"There doesn't have to actually *be* a better offer. They won't know. Or, if there is, it doesn't need to be about money. I can be vague, say something like you gave me new responsibilities that I find challenging."

He thought about it. "I could support that. We could create some sort of internal task force, put your name on it. That way Omicron's sources in our company would confirm it."

"They have spies here?"

"Of course they do," he said.

I had a lot to learn about corporate competition. "And we have them there, which is how you found out about me being there."

"Not in this case. Someone from Omicron told me directly. Courtesy."

I couldn't help wondering if that person was the same one who'd told him initially about the security breach. He'd said it had been military, but I didn't know if I believed that anymore. Before I could press the issue, he stood, forcing me to stand with him.

"I hate to push you out, but I've got a meeting. I trust that I won't hear any more about you looking elsewhere for a job. If you have a problem, you come see me, first. Deal?"

"Deal," I said. The door opened and I found myself ushered outside by a frazzled assistant, then standing dumbly in the outer office, wondering what happened to my plan to push Javier for information.

**AFTER HEADING BACK** to my office for a bit to re-group, I decided to try again, so I headed back up to the top floor. Javier had somebody in his office when I showed up, so I waited twenty minutes for him to finish, passing the time reading news on my device. The lead story involved a shoot-out between unknown people about three blocks from my building. I wondered if I'd known any of the people involved. Odds seemed good. The police had no leads.

Javier came out of his office behind two executives, one man, one woman, both in expensive black suits. I couldn't place the man, though I'd seen him somewhere before. I didn't recognize the woman at all. Javier saw me but ushered the others out without introducing us. Odd. Introducing me to people used to be why he kept me around.

"Carl. What can I do for you? I've only got a minute before my next meeting."

"I have a couple things I want to ask you about Omicron."

"I thought I was clear. That's over."

"It is. And I'm not doing anything to violate that directive. But I have a few leftover thoughts that I want to bounce off of you."

A look passed across his face for a moment, but I couldn't place it. It might have been disappointment, or resignation. Either way, it had been a mistake to come back to him. "Let it go, Carl."

I hesitated for a split second. "Right. Sorry to bother you, boss."

"Don't worry about it," he said. "If you'll excuse me."

"Sure thing."

I left the office unsure what to do next. I had wanted Javier's contact, which I believed was inside Omicron, because I wanted to find a way in there that I could use for my plan with the hybrids. He'd shut the door on that possibility pretty firmly. But something seemed off about it, and his saying to let it go made me want to look into it more. On a hunch, I went back in to the outer office. Javier had gone to his inner office and had the door closed, so I approached his assistant.

"Excuse me," I said. "Mr. Sanchez asked me to follow up with the woman he just met with, and I realized I don't have her contact information. Do you happen to have that?"

"Sure thing, sir," the young man said. He pressed a few keys and my device vibrated. "There you go."

"Thanks," I said. "You're a life saver." I glanced at my device as soon as I reached the hallway. I almost tripped as I read the contact. Sheilla Ranier. *Omicron Industries*. There could have been a plausible explanation for it, I suppose. But Javier had told me that the Omicron thing was over, right after meeting with their representative. It seemed unlikely that they'd be so unrelated that he wouldn't think to mention it. I tried to come up with an innocent reason for his actions. I couldn't.

Too many things overlapped, but none of it fit together. Javier had put me onto the case in the first place, but he'd never been forthcoming. I accepted it at the time, but now I wondered why he sent me off to do something without sharing all the information. I didn't understand it. Perhaps I wasn't supposed to. VPC might have wanted me to drop the investigation, but there was no longer any chance of that.

**BY THE TIME** I made it back to my apartment I needed a drink. After I poured, I called Plazz to check in. She might have found something on Omicron or Gylika. It was a long shot, but in the back of my head I also thought there was a chance I might need her help after I met with the Cappans. It's a shitty reason to call somebody—so that you can use them later—but I also wanted to share something that might help her, and maybe convince her that I wasn't an asshole.

Maybe convince myself of that while I was at it.

"I was wondering when you were going to call me again," said Plazz. She had used the privacy setting on her device so it didn't broadcast a picture. "What do you want?"

"Can't a guy just call to check in?"

"He could. But you don't," she said. "How are you feeling after the shooting? You okay?"

"Yeah. Good as new. How are things in your world?"

"What's going on?" she asked.

"What do you mean?" I asked.

"I'm a reporter. I can sense when you're hiding news. You know something good. Spill it."

"I can't," I said.

"You know that you suck."

"That's a pretty widely held opinion, yeah."

"What *can* you tell me?"

"Nothing yet," I said. "But I might have something soon."

"Give me a hint," she said.

"Okay." I had intended to tell her all along, but I thought it would sound more convincing if I let her work it out of me. I might have been overthinking things. "Javier Sanchez gave me an assignment to look into the breach in security at Omicron. Recently, he told me to cut off all action associated with that. Today, after he reiterated that I should cease work, he met with executives from Omicron at his office."

"Interesting," she said. "What do you think it means?"

"No idea."

"You've got *some* idea," she said. "You wouldn't have mentioned it, otherwise."

"I'm still working through it. I shared it in case you had ideas." In truth, I shared it because I needed to tell someone, and she was the only one I trusted. It was a sorry state of affairs when the most trustworthy person I had was a reporter.

"I could run something about the meeting between Javier and Omicron and see what shakes out from it," she offered. "Is that what you want?"

"That would lead back to me," I said. "Besides, if you did that, you'd run the risk of ruining the bigger story."

"There's a bigger story?"

"There is," I said, "but the last time I had a good lead somebody ended up dead." I stopped talking. I had said it as a joke, but it hit close to home. Somebody had killed Gylika, and they probably did it because he was going to leak something. Or somebody believed he might. They'd do the same to me if they thought I was a threat.

"Okay. I'll hold off for now on the story, and I'll poke around a bit to see if I can find anything without tipping my hand. But get me something soon. I've got to go," said Plazz. "I've got a date."

"Anybody I know?" I asked.

"Absolutely not."

"I know a lot of people," I teased.

She laughed. "Don't wait too long to call back. I want to hear from you this week. You owe me a story."

She disconnected before I could protest.

Now I had two deadlines.

**DR. BAQRI STOOD** and went to the window to adjust the blind, reducing the glare in the room.

"Do you think it's possible that guilt can cause you to make bad decisions?" I asked.

"What do you mean? Like in general?"

"Is it possible to feel so guilty about the past that you blind yourself to a current situation?"

She thought about it for a moment, though probably for effect more than anything else. "I think guilt can do a lot of things. What are you feeling guilty about?"

"What do you think?" I asked.

She nodded. "And what kind of decision do you think it's leading you to?"

I'd prepared for that question, so I had an answer ready that didn't give too much away. "I think I want to do something to help the Cappans."

"So some sort of atonement," she said.

"I don't know that I can ever possibly atone for what I did. But yeah, something like that."

"I think you have to be careful with that sort of thing," she said. "Certainly it's okay to do something to help. But if you go into it hoping that it's going to assuage your guilt, you might be disappointed."

I considered it. I didn't know what the Cappans would ask me for—they were going to ask me for something, I was sure—and I had to consider that my own judgment might be suspect when it came to them. Whatever their interests, they probably wouldn't line up with mine. But that assumed I understood my own interests.

"You with me, Carl?" she asked.

"Sorry. My mind wandered a bit."

"You seem off. Are you planning to harm yourself?"

"Blunt as always, hey doc?" I smiled. "No. I'm not planning to harm myself. I haven't been at that point in more than a year."

"You know I had to ask," she said.

"I understand. I'm okay."

I had another day, but no leads, and I was spinning myself into the ground thinking about what the Cappans might want. I sent the word *decision* to the number in my device before I got all the way out of her office.

# CHAPTER TWENTY

SASHA AND RIKU were waiting for me in my apartment when I arrived home. "Not going to lie," I said. "This whole appearing out of nowhere thing is pretty creepy."

"We can't exactly wait out on the street," said Sasha.

"I understand. I'm ready for the meeting."

"You're early," she said.

"Once I made up my mind, it seemed pointless to delay."

"What led you to the decision?"

"I'm not sure," I said. "There are things going on that I don't understand, and I'm hoping the Cappans can help shed some light on that. Another part of it is probably guilt."

Sasha smiled at me, though it seemed sad. "We don't want your guilt. But we do want results, so if that's what it takes, we'll accept it."

"So what's next?"

"We'll be in touch," said Sasha. "Soon."

**SASHA DIDN'T LIE** about it being soon. She fell in beside me as I got off of transportation to pick up a few things from the grocery store the next morning.

"Slow down a bit," I said. "Bad foot."

"The last time you and I were on the street together, somebody shot at us," she reminded me.

"So why didn't you come back to my apartment?"

"Somebody's watching it."

Shit. "Who?"

"We don't know yet. Professionals."

"I didn't pick them up with my drone."

"They're likely prepared for a measure like that."

"You weren't," I said.

"I *wanted* you to see me," she said.

Shit. I was out of my league on this sort of stuff. "Am I in danger?"

"Omicron saw you talking to us. I think it's safe to say that you're never *not* in danger, anymore. But we'll clear the watchers out before you get home."

It was good to have allies. "Thanks."

"We found something out regarding the police case, with the man who died. Our operatives cracked their system last night. You're not in the file. You were, but your part of the case was closed several days ago. They have no other leads."

I frowned. "Why didn't they tell me?"

"That I don't know."

"Are we heading to the meeting?"

She stopped, as if listening to something. "First we have to get rid of our tail." She paused again, and I got the impression that she had some kind of invisible communication device speaking to her.

"The same people who are watching my apartment?" I had to be more careful. I resisted the urge to look back. "What do we do?"

"Follow my lead." She watched the street as we walked, almost imperceptibly turning her head. A few seconds later a hover-car whipped out of traffic and came to a stop just ahead of us. She grabbed my arm and pulled me through the back door. The car started moving before the door closed behind me. We took a hard turn from the wrong lane at the next intersection, barely avoiding an oncoming truck, and sped through three intersections before turning again and slamming to a stop hard enough that I flew forward into the back of the seat in front of me.

"We get out here," she said, and the door popped open. I half fell out onto the sidewalk as Sasha deftly avoided me and took the lead, walking quickly. I hobbled after her. We turned another corner after a hundred meters or so, which I assume was to check if we still had a tail. Four doors down we entered a small antiques shop.

"Morning," said Sasha.

"Morning," said the one person in the small shop without looking up from his device. He stood behind a counter that doubled as a display case, dozens of small knickknacks inside, all in neat rows. We headed past the counter and into the back room. With the quick travel I hadn't considered until that exact moment the emotional impact of who we were going to meet. To my credit, I only hesitated for a moment at the sight of the full-blooded Cappan seated in a hard-backed chair that fit his small frame on the far side of the window-less room. He had a blue-and-yellow-mottled face, which had a distinct yellow circle around one eye. A loose-fitting gray robe-like garment covered the rest of him. I say him without really knowing the gender of the Cappan. I hadn't learned to distinguish.

Sasha led me to a seat across from the Cappan, sim-ilar in construction to his, but larger, to accommodate human anatomy. She didn't speak, and once I got situ-ated, the Cappan and I looked at each other in silence long enough for it to get a bit awkward. Two other human-looking people besides Sasha stood against the far wall: Riku, and a woman I didn't recognize. I had expected more than one Cappan but didn't see any others.

"I'm sorry," said the Cappan. His voice didn't match the motion on his lips since he spoke through a digital translator. It had a computer-generated, slightly stilted male voice, which furthered my impression that he was male, though it could have been the translation program. "I didn't know what I'd feel, finally sitting here with you. It is a little more overwhelming than I expected."

I stifled a chuckle at that and kept my face impas-sive. I had to believe I was at least as overwhelmed as him. But I understood. For everything that humans thought about me, right and wrong, Cappans had to have a deeper set of opinions. "Take as long as you need," I said.

"Thank you for agreeing to meet with me," he said. It struck me as very formal, but that could have been the translation program too.

"It's the least I could do. I have to admit, I didn't know you were here on planet until recently," I said.

"Yes. We have tried to keep that quiet, for obvious reasons. It is not legal, I am sure you know."

"Right. The embargo law."

He shifted in his chair and moved one of his hands in a circular motion. It looked like some sort of gesture, but the translation software didn't extend to physical cues. "I will come to the point. We have considered our options, and we think you are the best person to help us."

"I gathered that, since you went through so much trouble to meet with me. What I don't know is what I'm supposed to help you do."

"You have had some dealings with a company called Omicron. How much do you know about them?"

"Quite a bit," I said. "I've been studying them."

"Did you know that we were in business together? In secret, of course, since it is against the law."

It all clicked then. Ganos discovered that Omicron was working on ortho-robotic advancements. I'd thought they had Elliot's old research, but they didn't need it. They had the Cappans. "Project Phoenix," I said.

If the Cappan was impressed with my deduction, it didn't come across through the translator. "That was their name for it, yes."

"You were working with them on it," I said. "I assume you're not any longer. Why?"

"Our objectives became incompatible." He paused for several seconds, as if thinking. "We have been working together for a long time. Since before the annihilation."

*The annihilation.* That's what they called it. "You were working with Omicron while the human soldiers still had Cappa occupied?"

"Initially we were working with the military, but that relationship changed when the military's objectives changed."

"But I saw Cappans working with Dr. Elliot."

"Soldiers, yes. Scientists? No. Dr. Elliot paid for Cappan volunteers for her experiments. We had stopped working with that project well before that, and that was her solution."

"How does Omicron factor into it?" I asked.

"They had operatives on the planet, trading technology and sharing ideas. They were not initially involved with the genetic program. That came later."

I sat, stunned for a moment. Omicron had worked with the Cappans from the start. I'd assumed Elliot had given them fusion technology. Perhaps they had had another avenue. "I saw four ships leave the planet. Was that them?"

"Four initially," he said. "More later. Yes. To compound the damage from the annihilation, our planet devolved into civil war. Omicron helped some of us escape that."

"And in return, you helped them with Project Phoenix."

"In part. But we also had other objectives. We learned the economic value of the genetic technology, and we wanted to use it to negotiate our position in the galaxy. To reestablish our working relationship with humans from a new, non-violent, position."

"After what we . . . after what *I* did to you? Why?"

"Why does anybody want to interact with any-body? Trade, technology, resources. The planet you call Cappa is in very poor shape, and we have many needs."

It was a lot to process. But he had no reason to lie to me, so I tried to take it at face value and go from there. After all, he'd set the meeting with me. If he meant me harm, he could have done it in much simpler ways. No, we were here, and he needed something. After a few seconds I made the connection. "Something changed in your relationship with Omicron."

"Indeed. Much like our previous relationship with the military on the project, their objectives changed. Someone at Omicron decided that they could make money without us and that our political needs were too expensive or impractical to pursue."

"So they stole the technology?" I asked.

"They did much more than that. They attacked our operatives. They threatened to expose the new planet to which we relocated. They demanded Cappan test subjects. They have hostages and attempted to force our scientists to labor to continue refining the process."

"If they had the technology, why do they need your scientists?" I asked.

"They have it, but their methods are not as advanced as ours are. They would likely work it out in a couple of years. We have it now. We held some things back. We were trusting, but not stupid."

I nodded, but realized that wouldn't translate. "I understand. So you want me to do what? Help you steal back the technology?"

"We have already done that," he said.

I paused a second before it hit me. "Holy shit. It was you who hacked Omicron."

He didn't answer.

"You did. Wait . . . if you penetrated Omicron, that means . . . you killed Gylika."

"We did no such thing," he said.

"Then your allies did." I gestured to where the hybrids stood, leaning against the wall.

The Cappan made another gesture I didn't understand. Agitation? "Neither us nor anyone involved with us had anything to do with that human's death."

"So who did?" I asked.

"That we do not know. But if you agree to help us, we will do our best to discover that information for you. Logic dictates that it was probably Omicron themselves."

I took a deep breath and blew it out. I don't know

why, but I believed him. "Help you do what, then? You already stole the information back. Wait . . . how can you do that? They must have copies."

"We were very thorough," he said. I might have imagined it, but I'd swear that a hint of pride came through the translation.

"So if you have it back, what is the problem? The hostages?" I asked.

"As I said, they know where our new home is. They have threatened to turn that information over to the military."

It hit me like a punch in the gut. They'd inform the military, and the military would send someone like me to deal with it. "They want to profit off of the medical technology, and they're willing to destroy the Cappan race to do it."

"Yes, that is what we believe."

"What is it that you think I can do?"

"We need to negotiate a solution with Omicron that allows us to reach our previous objectives," he said.

"Wait . . . you'd still work with Omicron after this?"

He paused. "What option do we have? We can put the past behind us if it helps us reach our goals. You being here is evidence of that."

He had a point. "Why me?"

His face shifted in what might have been a Cappan version of a smile. "You are uniquely positioned. You have access to the company we need to influence, and you have the cachet to implement it. Were you to speak about Cappans, it would stand to reason that other humans would listen. We need a solution that is bigger than one company. Something that will stick."

"All that makes sense." I paused, thinking about how to phrase the next part. I had an idea about the answer, but I wanted to hear him say it. "But you should hate me."

"Hate is an emotion for someone who has the luxury of better options."

That seemed wiser than what I could process at the moment. "I want to be clear about why we're here. Make sure we have the same expectations. You told me in general that you want things to go back to how they were, but that may be impossible. What are your specific objectives?"

"Even now, they are working to force us to return what we took."

"What are they doing?" I asked.

"We believe they are mounting a mission to our new planet to try to force us to their will via military means."

"You're sure?" I asked.

"Our intelligence is good, yes."

"How many of you are on the planet?" If Omicron planned physical action, we had to deal with that possibility first.

"Fewer than twenty thousand. We do not know the full intent of their mission," he said. "But we can assume."

"So in the short term we need a solution that keeps them from taking armed action, or from threatening armed action." I'd said *we*. I'd already started thinking about it that way. Theoretically, a corporation shouldn't be able to mount a military mission, but when they made half the weapons and spaceships humans use, it wouldn't be that surprising if they had kept a little something for themselves. Too, it was a big galaxy, and it wasn't like the Cappans could appeal to the authorities for protection. Even if somebody official *did* notice, there were pirates everywhere, and it would be impossible to pin something on a specific organization. "Can we get everyone off the planet?"

"Before we discuss plans, I think it is important to decide your role. Officially."

I glanced around the room at the hybrid people. They all watched intently, but none of them appeared poised to add to the conversation. "I'm in."

The Cappan clasped his hands together. I didn't know if that held the same meaning for them as it did for humans, but it seemed like it might be universal. "This is good. I do not think it is possible to remove ourselves from the planet. First, they are watching, and second, where would we go? There are no humans on the planet, and planets that support life but have no humans are rare."

"How much of your population do you think shares your feelings about working with humans?"

"Impossible to say," he said, "though everyone who traveled with us to the new planet signed on willingly. Many do not know about the technology we are working with, but they support our general philosophy of working with humans. Our group is led by scientists. Intelligent, reasonable people. There are differences of opinion, but not an overabundance of politics involved. With that said, we are not one-hundred-percent a hegemony."

He hadn't fully answered the question, and I couldn't let it slide. I imagined getting volunteers would be easy when the other option was to stay on a war-torn planet. "Is it possible that there are other factions working *with* Omicron? Cappans who might help them for a chance at power? Either with you on the new planet, or maybe some of those left behind on Cappa?"

"We think it unlikely," said the Cappan. "Your attack did not endear humans to most of our population."

I could see how it wouldn't. That made an impossible mission at least a small bit easier. If they had willing Cappans, we'd have no leverage at all. The fact that Omicron needed something from the Cappans left us at least a tiny window. "That's good."

"You have a plan already?"

"I have the start of one. What assets do we have? What you did to Omicron's system was impressive. Can we rely on more things like that if we need them?"

"Hacking back into Omicron is a risk. They are expecting us."

"How big a risk?" I asked.

"Too big," he said. "With their security team looking for us, our odds of success are very small. Too small to be worth it. We achieved what we did before because they were not prepared."

"Okay," I said. My mind flashed back to Ganos's incursion. We'd closed that window too, but the idea that Omicron had been watching for a breach at the time she broke in made me uncomfortable. "Can we attack their system to do damage?"

"Possibly," said the Cappan. "But probably not enough to sway them."

"Okay," I said, catching myself about to nod again. It would have been nice to have a network attack as a threat. But I had another idea of how to threaten Omicron. "I'll need a couple of days to think things through. How can I contact you when I'm ready to go?"

"I am going to leave the planet tonight," said the Cappan. "My operatives are here to help you as needed."

I couldn't help but think he was putting a lot of trust in me. Too much. He certainly had contingency plans, but I had no hope that he'd reveal them to me. From my foxhole, it was me and a few hybrids against the most powerful corporation in the galaxy.

My kind of fight.

# CHAPTER TWENTY-ONE

AFTER I LEFT my meeting with the Cappan, I couldn't stop coming back to the thought that he seemed to believe so firmly that I could get Omicron to make a deal. My second-biggest takeaway was that I was an idiot for taking it on, for assuming that much risk and responsibility. But since I fully intended to do it—and intended to succeed—maybe we were both onto something.

Yes, I fully recognize the circular logic there.

To compound the potential stupidity of my decision to help the Cappans, after a couple car switches to ensure nobody had picked us up, I headed to the police station. Even as I arrived, I knew I'd made a bad choice. But after talking to the Cappan, something had flipped. It felt good. I needed to force Omicron to react to me, so it was time to attack. In order to do that, I needed to know where I stood with Mallory. I had to determine whether I could count on her as an asset going forward or whether she'd work against me, and I had some vague notion about using the police to pressure Omicron and make them more susceptible to my overtures.

"Can I help you, sir?" asked the officer at the front desk.

"I'm here to see Lieutenant Mallory." I didn't stop.

"Sir, you can't go back there without an escort."

I'd passed him by several meters before he came after me. I guess he didn't expect somebody to break into a police station, but I didn't want to give Mallory time to set up a plan with Burke. "Lieutenant Mallory!"

The entire open office turned to look at me. Three officers, one a giant of a man, stood up from behind their desks.

"Mallory!" I had already brought trouble for myself by blowing past the desk. I figured I might as well get my money's worth.

Two of the officers reached me at the same time and I put my hands up and let them grab me without resisting. My desire to not get roughed up outweighed my need to talk to the good lieutenant.

"I can see myself out," I offered, forcing a grin.

They didn't grin back, but they only dragged me a little bit on the way to the exit.

"Butler? What's going on?" Mallory walked in the main door right before we reached it, just arriving.

"This jackass ran past the desk and started yelling for you inside," said one of my captors, a stocky woman.

Mallory shook her head. "If you'd called ahead, you'd have known I wasn't here."

"I see the wisdom in that now."

She tried to hold in a laugh, but mostly failed. "Come on." The two officers released me and I did my best not to look smug as I left them behind and followed Mallory to the interrogation room.

"You want to tell me what this is about?" she asked.

"I'm pissed," I said. I wanted to put her on the defensive. "You're keeping me as an active lead in the Gylika case when you know I've got nothing to do with it."

"Yeah? What makes you say that?"

I hadn't thought it through very well. "I know people who know things."

She considered it for a moment. "Didn't I see you in the hospital the other day? Something about getting shot?"

"That had nothing to do with Gylika."

She raised her eyebrows. "You sure?"

"You know it doesn't."

"I do? Why? How do you know it doesn't? What do you want to tell me?"

I wanted to kick myself. I should have known better than to come after a pro like Mallory with a half-assed plan. She'd turned it around on me without breaking a sweat. "Omicron was behind the ex-military types who shot at me."

"You can prove that?" she asked.

"I can't. But it's true. Push on them a little bit and you'll find it."

She shook her head. "Not how it works. I can't walk into a powerful corporation and start throwing around baseless accusations. You say you can't tell me, but you're hiding things. I'd bet my badge on it."

"So you're going to hold this case over my head to motivate me to give you something."

"I would never do that," she said. "That would be unethical."

I shook my head. "You're a piece of work."

"Yeah, well, likewise. But I've got a dead body and a cold case, so I can live with myself."

"What is it you want from me?" I asked. "I've told you about Omicron's involvement. What's it going to take?"

"I'll know it when I hear it," she said.

"Bullshit. What do you want?"

She glared at me. "Fine. I'll tell you what I want. I want to know what was so important at Omicron that a guy got killed for it."

"I don't know," I said.

"Fuck you, Butler. You're a lousy liar."

I started to speak then cut myself off. I wanted to respond to her comment and defend myself, but that's why she'd made it. The lady was good. I *was* lying. If nothing else, I knew exactly what was so important at Omicron. I took a few seconds to regroup. "I can go get my attorney and we can do this differently."

"You're wasting my time." She stood. It was a bluff, but it was a good one. I couldn't call it. I wanted her to make Omicron uncomfortable. To make them react.

"Okay, wait," I said, then paused while she took her time sitting back down, making a show of it. "You're right, there's something I'm not telling you. I can't prove it, but I've got some pretty good thoughts on why Omicron is involved in Gylika's death. Gylika was working on a project called Phoenix. It's ground-breaking medical technology, and it's worth billions. They had a leak, and I have reason to believe that they suspected Gylika."

"Now you're telling the truth." She had a good read on me, that was for sure. "How sure are you?"

"Very sure," I said.

"But you can't prove it."

"Nope. But it gives you buttons to push."

She considered it. I tried to steady my breath, remain calm, give her time to think. I didn't need her to make arrests. I needed her to ask questions that would make people nervous. Make them more likely to negotiate. They could kill Gylika to silence him, but they couldn't kill Mallory. "That's not enough."

I sighed. "Fine. Then I want a public statement saying that I'm no longer a suspect in Gylika's murder."

"Not going to happen," she said.

I stood and walked to the door, then turned. "You've got twenty-four hours."

"Until what?"

"Until I go to the press and tell them about the rogue police officer who is trying to make a name by harassing a well-known veteran."

"You're full of shit. You don't want to be dragged through the media over this."

"You said I was a lousy liar. Do I look like I'm lying now?" I turned and left before she could respond.

It hadn't gone the way that I'd hoped, but I learned

something. Given my plans for Omicron, I had to know where I stood with Mallory. She'd said that I hadn't given her enough, but the longer she thought about it, the more it would gnaw at her. Hopefully, I'd piqued her interest enough for her to poke around. Like she said, there was a body on her ledger that wasn't looking good to her higher-ups. She needed an answer, and I'd at least provided her the right question.

And if she publicly cleared me, Omicron would see it and it would put them on notice.

WHEN I GOT home, I called Ganos first, to see if she'd taken my advice to leave town, which, as I suspected, she hadn't. I reiterated my advice, suggesting that it would be preferable that she got off the planet. Take some vacation. She'd insisted that she wanted to help me, and it took me almost twenty minutes to convince her that she couldn't, and another ten to get her to acknowledge the danger I'd put her in and agree to do as I said. She'd promised to visit Parker's mother off planet at some point, anyway, so she decided to move that trip forward. With that settled, I turned my attention to Plazz.

I couldn't call her because she'd get too much out of me, and I wasn't ready for that stage yet. But I needed a backup in case things went to shit. My plan left me vulnerable, and I had to account for the possibility that I could be taken off the board at any time. That thought didn't bother me much. Risk was part of any mission. But while I could risk myself, I couldn't risk the information I held in my brain disappearing if I died. I typed everything I knew into an encrypted file, logging every detail, whether known or suspected, documenting things with sources where I could and explaining my thought process where I couldn't. I wrote about the Cappan I'd met and the tracks I'd found for their ships in the database at SPACECOM. I detailed Javier's meeting with Omicron, and my suspicions about Gylika. It took me almost two hours to finish it. Once I was done, I backed it up to a removable drive that I put in my safe, and then formatted an encrypted email to Plazz. I set it to send itself in three days if I didn't stop it.

Finishing that, I called Turkov at Omicron. It took his assistant three minutes to get him on the phone, and it took me five minutes to ream him out for the leak that got back to Javier that got me in trouble. With that established, I told him I still wanted the job, and asked if he could keep it quiet if I came in tomorrow to talk about it. I planned to use him to get a meeting with Ellen Haverty, the CEO, but that part of my plan I kept to myself.

That done, I finally allowed myself a drink. My mind was so keyed up that it took me more than usual to get to sleep. For me, that's saying something. For the first time in a long time I didn't dream.

That said something more.

# CHAPTER TWENTY-TWO

TURKOV MET ME as I entered Omicron's lobby, and I briefly wondered how long he'd been standing there waiting. "Good to see you again, Carl."

"Good to see you, too. You didn't have to come down to meet me."

"Actually, I did. We're not going to my office." He walked toward the executive elevator, and I followed.

"Where are we going?" I asked.

"The CEO wants to meet you."

"Uh . . . sure," I said, tripping over my words. One of the biggest mistakes in any plan is failing to anticipate success. I'd let myself fall into that trap. I'd wanted to meet with someone who could negotiate, but I hadn't expected it to happen that morning.

"Top floor," said Turkov, though the man waiting for us in the elevator had already pressed the button. The door opened some twenty seconds later into a small lobby appointed in dark wood and marble. I didn't check closely, but I assumed it was all real, making the room extremely expensive.

Ellen Haverty walked forward and met us as we disembarked. I should say she met me, as her eyes never released mine. I'd never met her, but I'd seen pictures, of course. She lived up to them in a gray blazer, her hair styled short, a cross between blonde and white. She'd once told a fashion reporter that she kept it short so it took less time to keep it neat, allowing more time for business.

"Colonel Butler, so nice that we can finally meet. I've heard so much about you."

"Call me Carl. It's nice to meet you as well, Ms. Haverty."

"Please. It's Ellen. Can we get you something? Water? Whiskey?" She grasped my hand in hers, applying exactly the right amount of pressure, pumping twice and releasing.

"I'm fine," I said. "I don't want to take up too much of your time."

She waved me off. "It's no bother at all." She was lying, of course, but she really excelled at it. CEOs of major companies didn't have free time by accident. She'd moved something to make this meeting happen. I didn't know what that meant, but it was significant. "Come in, let's chat in my office, away from the noise."

I ignored the fact that it was silent, save for us talking, and followed her to her office. It had the requisite floor-to-ceiling windows on two sides, buildings sprawled out below like soldiers of the queen. The polished hard-wood floor almost glared back at six lights inset into the high ceiling.

"Mr. Turkov tells me you're interested in a job." She said it casually, but I immediately marked it as her opening gambit. Unfortunately, I didn't know what game she was playing, and it had me a bit off balance. I wanted to broach the Cappan topic, but it felt wrong to just throw it out there. Whatever her reason, something in her demeanor told me Ellen Haverty had me in her office, but that I almost certainly didn't understand the reason behind it. She had her own designs.

"Yes. Exploring my possibilities," I said. Nothing to do at that point besides play it out.

"I'm sure a man like you has many options," she said.

"Some. It's a mixed blessing, you know?"

She studied me for a moment. "I'm going to cut to the chase. You know why you're here; I know why you're here. But you don't know why I'm here."

"Fair," I said. I figured she *didn't* know why I was there, but I couldn't call her on it without giving something away.

"I want you to do a job for me."

I hesitated. I hadn't expected that. "I was under the impression that that's why I came today."

"Not that job. Something else."

"I think—"

"Hear me out. All you have to do is listen. Listen first, talk second." She spoke with the assured tone of someone accustomed to getting her way.

"Sure."

"Somebody stole something from me. I want it back. And I want your help getting it."

I wished for a second that I'd taken her up on the water she offered so I'd have something to hide my face behind for a moment while I regained my composure. I'm sure my surprise showed. The Cappans wanted me to broker a deal with Omicron, and it seemed like Omicron wanted me to do the same thing. It couldn't possibly be that easy. "I'm pretty sure we're on the same page."

"Are we now?"

"I think so. Let me ask you this," I said. "Why me?"

"I think you're uniquely suited to get it back."

Hearing almost the same wording that the Cappan had used gave me a chill. "How so?"

"I think you know."

"I don't think I do."

"Please, Carl. Dissembling doesn't become you. I know who broke into my company, I know what they took, and I want it back."

"Let's say I know what you're talking about," I said.

"Yes, let's." She stood about a meter away and hadn't moved since we entered the room. I was a few centimeters taller, but her commanding presence made her height irrelevant.

"Again, why me?"

"Who better to deal with the group in question?"

"I want to hear you say it," I said.

"Say what? That the Cappans infiltrated our systems, somehow obliterated all trace of the ortho-robotics project we call Phoenix, and we can't figure out how that's possible? Is that what you want me to say?"

I paused. I hadn't actually expected her to say it. "Yes."

"I've said it. Can we move on now to the part where you help me get it back?"

"Okay," I said. "I have had some contact with people working with the Cappans." Her face didn't move. Perhaps she was so good as a negotiator that she could hide any sense of surprise, but my gut told me she already knew. She knew I'd met with the Cappans.

"And?" she prompted.

"And I'm willing to negotiate terms," I said. "Be a go-between."

"Terms? The terms are this. They'll return what they stole. After they do, I'll be happy to discuss whatever issues they have and see what we can do to accommodate."

"I don't think they're going to accept your word on good faith," I said.

"Which is why I'm not really negotiating." She finally broke eye contact and walked a few steps toward the window. "There are no terms that they're going to propose that I'm going to accept. Because once I start making deals with them, they no longer have any reason to keep their deal secret."

I struggled to keep my face neutral. Threatening to release the information to the galaxy at large had been part of my plan, though I hadn't completely worked out how I would do that while somehow preventing Omicron from seeking revenge against the Cappans. In fact, that was my problem. *All* my plans failed to solve that piece. I thought I'd have more time to work on it. I hadn't expected to be here this quickly, standing in front of Omicron's CEO. I'd made a bluff and they'd not only called it, they'd known my cards and raised the pot.

"So we're at an impasse," I said.

"I don't think so," she said. "I have a plan that's already in motion. It may require *some* negotiation, but I intend to do that with significant leverage."

"So why involve me?"

"You could make things easier. Get me the information now and save me the trouble of nuking their settlement."

"That's a bluff," I said. "If you nuke the settlement, you still don't have the information."

She smiled, though it didn't reach her eyes. "Maybe. But even if it is a bluff, it comes down to who blinks first."

I wanted to tell her it wouldn't work, but I couldn't be sure what the Cappans would do if faced with that dilemma. They could evacuate the settlement, but Omicron would watch for that. They could shoot down ships leaving the atmosphere easier than firing down on the planet itself. "That's a lot of risk," I said, after a long pause.

"It is. And I'm not happy about that. Which is why I want you to go to the planet with my team."

I started to respond, but stopped. "What?"

"I want you to do the negotiation, but I want you to do it in a place that provides the greatest advantage. I think having you present—a man who has shown a willingness to exterminate their population—will add to our bargaining power. You're not going to get the concessions I want if you negotiate from here."

"So you want me to negotiate with them at gun-point." I was still struggling to catch up, so I stalled.

"I wouldn't have put it that way," she said, "but yes."

I stood silently for a moment, pretending to consider her demand while trying to come up with a way to turn things around. She'd put me on my back foot from the start, and I hadn't even made her break a sweat. "I can arrange the deal without leaving Talca," I said.

She feigned a bored look. "I think I was clear that I'm not doing that. It's not in our best interest."

"But it is," I said. "Because I've left a file at VPC, and if I don't return to it within two days, it goes out to the company directory."

She smiled. "Really. And what's in this file?"

"Enough details about your Cappan hybrid genetic program to make VPC a serious competitor. How many billions do you think that will cost you?"

She was still smiling, which was not what I wanted to see. "Nice move. To be honest, if you'd gone down without a fight, I'd have been disappointed." She walked to her desk and turned a screen around on a swivel mount to face me. Javier stared back at me from the display. "I trust you heard our discussion, Javier?"

"I did," he said.

"And?"

"And we're cooperating with Omicron in every way possible. That includes you, Carl. As to the file, I'll take care of that."

"Thank you, Javier." She powered the screen down. "You see, we're not really all that greedy, Carl. We're more than willing to cut in another company when it makes sense."

I stood there, stunned. What a dumbass I'd been. I'd had my suspicions about Javier and I knew he'd been in contact with Omicron, but I hadn't realized the scope. I wondered at what point he'd started colluding with them, and if it was before or after Gylika died. I couldn't think about that now. I had to focus. But I couldn't let it go. "How long have you been working together?"

"Long enough," she said. "That reminds me. I should thank you for finding our leak."

It hit me like a punch in the gut. Gylika. If I hadn't met with him, he'd still be alive. And the worst part was that he wasn't even a leak. The first time I met him, he didn't know anything. I'd set him into motion. "I need to sit."

She gestured to a cushioned chair. "We think our best option is to go to their new planet and take the information physically."

"You're planning a combat mission," I said. My eyes had to be wide. My heart raced, and I couldn't control it, though more from the implications about Gylika than the Cappans.

"*Combat* is an ugly word. They're not humans. There's no law against killing them, as you surely know. It's more like . . . hunting. You'll have the best equipment and the best team money can buy."

I shook my head. "That's sick."

"I find that a bit disingenuous coming from you."

"Fuck you. It's not even close to the same thing."

"I suppose if I were in your position, I'd say that too." She kept her face neutral, not letting smugness touch it, despite the words. It didn't keep me from wanting to smack her. There wasn't any visible security, and I have to admit that for a second I considered it.

"You're not going to goad me into it," I said.

"I'm not planning on it. You're going to go, you're going to get me that technology back, and that's that."

I stared at her, unable to come up with adequate words. The arrogance of this lady blew me away. But going along might be my best chance to still negotiate something, which is what the Cappans had asked me to do. Assuming there were any Cappans left alive once the Omicron mercenaries got done. "I'll consider it."

"Well your other option is that we prosecute you for breaking into our system."

I flinched but didn't speak.

"What, you didn't think we knew about that? Did you not expect that we'd be paying closer attention after a massive security incident? I'm disappointed."

"I don't care. Prosecute me."

"I figured you might say that. I doubt you'll say the same about your accomplice, Ms. Ganos."

"Who?"

"Please. We have facial recognition in our security system."

"You're going to prosecute her?"

"Oh, no. While my legal people think she'd get six to ten years, she's much too valuable to waste in a cell. At least not a jail cell. No, we'll pick her up and use what we have on her to sell her to the highest bidder. She'll spend the rest of her probably short life working for us, or someone like us, until she's used up. Then we'll turn her in. She won't serve much time, though. She'll turn up dead in her cell. Suicide, probably. Tragic."

"You asshole." It was all I could come up with at the moment. I hoped that Ganos had made it off the planet, but if they went the legal route, that wouldn't help her for very long.

"Indeed. I'll take that as a yes?"

I looked away from her.

"I'm going to need to hear it," she said. "I need a yes."

"Fine. Yes."

# CHAPTER TWENTY-THREE

**W**HILE I DIDN'T know exactly what they expected from me, one thing became readily apparent: They didn't trust me. They confiscated my electronics and bundled me off from the Omicron building via a back exit into a private vehicle. A driver and two guards whisked me away from the arching skyscrapers of the center city to the outskirts, an industrial area with old three- and four-story buildings, all rectangles and straight lines. We stopped outside one without any signs, and they led me up to a set of double doors. The high-tech identification scanner clashed with the worn façade of the building, which had to be at least seventy-five years old.

I stepped through the door and bright light blinded me for a moment until my eyes adjusted. The cement floor in the large room, painted gray in that way of most military facilities, looked clean enough to eat off of and reflected the glare from the lights that hung from the high ceiling. A bank of monitors lined the near wall, all dark save one, which showed the news. I recognized the hardware as military. It reminded me of any number of rooms where I'd observed troops conducting tech training in the past.

A few men and women bustled about, intent on various tasks, and though they weren't in uniform, they carried themselves like soldiers. Their posture, the way they walked, everything about them screamed military. Or ex-military, more likely, though not too far removed in most cases, given the relatively young ages.

"Colonel Butler, welcome to the east campus." A tall man of about thirty-five with a square jaw, almost-short-enough-to-be-military hair, and a lanky build walked across the room to greet me and the two goons who'd escorted me. "I have to say, sir, it's an honor to be working with you." He turned to one of my captors. "I've got him from here. Thanks."

I sized him up. Whoever he was, he had me at a disadvantage, as clearly he'd been briefed about me joining the team and I had no clue about him. Ex-military, of course. Probably Special Ops, if I had to guess. I pegged him as someone who got out of the service as a captain after serving a couple tours. The age would work for that, anyway. I took the easy way out and didn't speak, which forced him to carry the conversation or stand there awkwardly.

"I'm Eric Tanaka." He held out a hand and I took it. "I'm the team lead for the mission."

"Good to know." I was being an asshole, but the crap that had gone down with Haverty entitled me to it. From the little I'd gleaned, we'd be going off planet.

I'd have plenty of time to make it up to Tanaka, if I needed to. I thought about escalating it by challenging him, asking him to prove his bona fides in the classic military alpha-type way, but I decided a softer approach might get me further. "What is this place?"

"The east campus? On paper it's a testing facility. High-tech stuff, weapons. Our team puts Omicron's ideas in the hands of ex-soldiers and gives the developers feedback. But it's also outfitted for training. I do a lot of work here, preparing the team for different missions. We've got a full simulator suite in the back and a full set of firing ranges. It's a great environment for training. I'll show you around in a bit."

He said missions, which I took to mean that he led a standing force. I wondered what the government would think of a corporation having their own army. They probably knew and just as probably didn't care. "How big is the team?"

"It varies with the need. For this mission? About two hundred."

The size surprised me, but I didn't let it show. I'd expected a small team, an infiltration scenario. This was more of an assault force, though maybe not big enough if we ran into serious resistance. "Seems like an odd size."

"We can discuss that later. Our intel is lacking on the enemy disposition, so for the time being I decided not to risk a small team. If we need anything bigger, we can use our space-based assets. Maybe you can help fill in some of the intel gaps."

"Maybe." *Space-based assets.* That was a euphemism for high-yield weapons. "How many of the two hundred fight?"

"Most," he said. "About a hundred and sixty will hit the ground. The rest will crew the ship we take, as well as the smaller assault craft."

I nodded slightly to show approval, though I had no real basis to judge without more information. It felt like he wanted my concurrence, so I gave it. Somewhere in the past minute I'd decided to put the asshole thing to rest and play nice for a bit, see where that got me. I hadn't resigned myself to going on the mission. Sasha and Riku were still out there, they'd know I was missing, and they'd shown themselves to be rather capable. I was behind in the game, but I still had moves. "So tell me—you're the team leader. What's my role in this thing?"

He rubbed his hands together, glanced away. "Well, sir . . . your official title is advisor, but I'm not arrogant enough to tell you what that means. Somebody thinks you can help. I'm sure they're right, and I'm glad to have you. But as far as what you do? I thought I'd leave that up to you. I'm sure you'll know best where you can add value."

I held back a chuckle. That was military speak for "they stuck me with you, and I have no fucking idea." I have to admit, he communicated it kindly. "Sure. Let's play it by ear. Once I see what we're doing and what we're up against, I'll see where I fit. Don't worry, Tanaka. I won't try to take over your show." I said *we* on purpose. It seemed best to let him think I was on board. For now.

"Roger, sir. We'll kit you out for ground operations, just in case. If you decide to stay spaceside, that's fine too, but we want to be prepared. Besides, you're going to love the gear."

TANAKA SPENT THE rest of the afternoon showing me around the facility, which spanned almost half a city block, as far as I could figure. It almost seemed as if he wanted to impress me. I played along—and honestly, I *was* impressed. They had a lot going on, and some things I'd never seen. At any other time, I would have loved the tour and enjoyed playing with some of the tech on display. But my role as a forced guest tempered any excitement I might have felt.

They never left Tanaka and me alone, as two or three people at a time rotated through our little company, providing some piece of information or another about various aspects of the base. I did my best to memorize the layout, but I've never been particularly good with spatial awareness inside a building, especially without windows. I did note that the building had exactly six doors that led outside, three in the front plus two and a loading bay in the back. Most of the doors, both internal and external, had scan pads. Nobody had access cards, which indicated a biometric security system.

At some point a big man with jet-black hair and a brownish complexion joined us and stayed on as part of our group. His easy posture and wary gaze marked him as some sort of security, but I didn't know if he was Tanaka's bodyguard or my jailer. The man didn't speak, and I didn't ask, as the distinction didn't matter much.

We ate a late dinner in a well-appointed dining hall. It seated about a hundred and fifty at long, rectangular tables, though half the seats were unfilled and our table remained empty save for me, Tanaka, and the big corporal. They served a military menu, filling and probably nutritious, but nothing special. At least a few people recognized me, since I got the kinds of looks I'd grown accustomed to in public, but nobody approached. More important, I didn't recognize any of them. It was a long shot, but with enough ex-soldiers in one place, there was always a chance that I'd served with one. That could have proved useful.

After we finished, my two escorts took me to my room, a three meter by three meter square, with one corner cut out for a tiny bathroom, complete with shower, toilet, and sink. A small desk, a chair, a bed, and a wall locker made up the only other features of the room. "Sorry about the sparse accommodations," said Tanaka. "We'll only be here a couple of days."

"I've been in worse," I said. My room looked a bit like a cell, but then so did a lot of military rooms. I didn't ask him about restrictions because I didn't want him to tell me to stay put. That way when I tried to get out, I could always tell him that I didn't know I wasn't allowed to leave. He'd know it for a lie, of course, but we could at least both pretend and save face. That assumed I'd be able to open the door after they left.

"If you need anything, Corporal Matua here is your man." Tanaka indicated the soldier who had been with us all day, and the big man smiled.

After they departed, I gave it maybe thirty minutes before I tested the door. I couldn't wait any longer, alone with nothing but my thoughts. Not a great place for me to be on a good day, let alone after everything I'd absorbed recently. Surely they didn't expect me to sit here in an empty room with nothing to occupy myself. To my surprise, when I placed my hand against the pad by the door, it whooshed open.

I poked my head into the hall, expecting to find Matua or another guard waiting, but it was empty. Barely wide enough for two people to pass without touching, the passage had white walls, a gray floor, and doors at regular intervals along both sides. I expected that they led to more lodging, though I didn't know how much of the force stayed on site and how much commuted. They might also be cells, if this was a detention area. It seemed unlikely. The walls met the floor in metal tracks, which probably meant they could reconfigure the building for other purposes, depending on the mission.

I randomly chose to go left and wandered down the hall that direction. I'd marked some key points in my mind during my earlier tour, and once I found them I could hopefully orient myself in the confusing maze of sameness. I pressed my palm against the pad next to the door of what looked to be a supply closet and then tried one that looked like some sort of workshop. Neither door opened. Two soldiers passed me in the hall, chatting with each other about a beta-ball match they'd apparently just watched. They both acknowledged me with a nod and kept walking. That meant one of two things: I was allowed to be out and about, or not everybody knew my status. Either worked for me. I made my way through a large, open training area that I recognized from my tour. Four soldiers played two-on-two soccer using nets that anchored to the floor in preset tracks. They all wore some sort of high-tech equipment that allowed them to jump and run at superhuman speeds, which led to an impossibly acrobatic goal that drew a whoop from all four players.

I followed a passage that led to the big room that I'd entered through when I first arrived. Two soldiers walked toward me, probably coming from outside.

"Hey, is there somewhere in this place to get a drink?" I asked.

They stopped a few paces from me. "No, sir." The tall woman smiled, as if I'd asked a silly question. "Most of us bring it in."

"I didn't get a chance. I think I'm going to go out and find something."

"Around here, sir?" asked a man, who stood a couple centimeters shorter than his companion. "There's not a bar for at least five klicks in this part of town."

"I can use the exercise. And I really need that drink." I put on as friendly a face as I could. Nothing to see here. Just an old soldier who needs his booze. I didn't really need the drink, but it made a convenient excuse. And, of course, I wouldn't turn one down. "I'm sure I can get a car to bring me back."

If they cared, they didn't let it show, and we all resumed walking in our respective directions. I had no idea if I could get outside, but Omicron had gone to the trouble of keeping me alive, so they probably weren't going to shoot me for testing my limits. I thought about how I could possibly get to a communication device and contact somebody, let them know where I was. I'd lost the contact information I had for Sasha and Riku when they'd confiscated my device, but I felt like they'd be looking for me, so I believed if I got anything out into the world, they'd find me. If not, I still had the message I'd programmed to Plazz that would go out in about two days. Hopefully, I'd still be around for that.

I reached the outside door and put my hand against the pad. Nothing. It didn't surprise me. I called to the two soldiers I'd passed, who hadn't quite cleared the room. "Hey, I just got here and they don't have me in the system yet. Do you mind?"

They came partway back across the room so we wouldn't have to shout, whispering to each other along the way, doubtless deciding what they'd do. The woman spoke. "Sir, we're not allowed to key somebody through a door they don't have access to. They're pretty strict about that here."

"I'm sure I'll have access as soon as they get caught up. I just want to get a drink." I could hear the desperation creeping into my voice, which meant she could, too. I was screwed.

"Sorry, sir."

"No problem," I said. "I wouldn't want you to get in trouble."

I made my way around to all the other external doors on the off chance that one of them would open for me, but had no success. I found another group of three soldiers and tried my sob story on them, but ended with the same result as the first attempt. They appeared genuinely sorry, but they couldn't help me. As I headed back to my room, I worried for a moment that I wouldn't be able to get back in, but I turned the corner to find Corporal Matua waiting for me outside the door. He held a bottle of whiskey in one hand, a glass and a small bucket of ice in the other.

I laughed. "I guess you guys were watching me after all."

He shrugged. "I'm your security. It's my job to pay attention."

"Are you security as in protecting me, or security as in making sure I don't escape?"

He gave me a big smile that lit his whole face. "It's my job to make sure nothing happens to you."

He hadn't answered the question, but at the same time, he pretty much had. I didn't push it. It was the least I could do since he hadn't made a big deal of the fact that I'd tried to escape. Plus he had a bottle. I took it gratefully. It wasn't Ferra Three whiskey by any stretch, but it wasn't swill, either. He left, and I went inside and poured myself three fingers.

# CHAPTER TWENTY-FOUR

AFTER A SHITTY night's sleep made somewhat better by breakfast and coffee with Matua, we went to the armory to get my equipment. Tanaka didn't lie about me loving the gear. It took four hours for two techs to fit me for body armor and a helmet, but once they did, I almost wanted to dance. The full-body suit was like being encased in a robot shell, with every action triggered by my natural movements, except enhanced. They started me out slow, teaching me to walk and how to use my eyes to trigger all the helmet functions, calibrating them to my exact measurements. After about five minutes I got tired of their teaching pace and did a standing front flip, landing on my high-tech boots, which thudded on the cement floor. I let out a whoop, and Matua laughed from his spot leaning against the wall.

"Ha!" I took half a dozen running steps and leaped to test out the leg capability. I got about two meters off the ground, and when I slammed back down onto the hard floor, the suit absorbed most of the impact. "We needed this shit in the infantry."

"The army couldn't afford them," said Tanaka, who'd been standing on the far side of the room. "For the price of four of these you could outfit an entire line battalion with standard equipment."

"Four people in these might be able to take on a battalion," I joked. I had to admit, getting geared up gave me a little bit of the old fire, and I liked it. I wondered if that's why guys like Tanaka did it, why they got out of the military and took the same kind of job in the civilian world. Something about it made me feel more alive than I had in two years. I'm sure it wasn't just me. "Most of your team ex-military?"

"Almost exclusively," said Tanaka. "We recruit pretty heavily in the elite units. We've got a good team."

I looked over to the big corporal. "How'd they convince you?"

"Simple. They pay better. A lot better."

Tanaka jumped in. "Sure, you still put your life on the line when it comes to it, but here it's valued. Plus most of the job is testing equipment, and we have all kinds of cool gear." He gestured toward the equipment that filled every bit of the workshop.

"You do have that," I said. "What about weapons?"

"Go ahead and leave the suit here, and we'll show you." He smiled the big, genuine smile of a proud parent.

"You sure I can't keep it on?" I asked. "This thing could come in handy."

"It'll be on the ship for you."

A few minutes later we passed through a heavy

vault door into a weapons locker. Tanaka took a high-tech pulse rifle off a rack and held it out to me. "This is the top of the line, sir. The PR-21."

"Yeah?" I took it from him.

"It's got better water resistance, longer battery life, and a tighter beam than anything you've ever fired," said Tanaka. "It's the most lethal personal weapon in the galaxy."

I walked past both of them, handing the rifle back before grabbing a projectile rifle out of a rack. It looked a lot like the Bikosky I favored back when I served, except with sleeker lines. "I'll take this one."

"Told you he'd want the Bitch," said Matua, using the soldier's nickname for the Bikosky. "You owe me five marks."

Tanaka snorted. "Yeah, yeah. I know you're familiar with the Bitch, sir. This has the same operating mechanism but with a few more options in projectiles. You've got RF and infrared seekers, and the guided bullet has an extra seven degrees of bend in it. All keyed to your helmet, of course."

"It's got an infrared bullet? A heat seeker?"

"Yes sir. It's not super effective due to the limited range, but it comes in handy once in a while."

I nodded, moving over to the sidearms. I picked out a standard-issue pulse pistol. "This too."

"Sure thing."

"What's your background, Tanaka?" I asked. It was a safer question, now that we'd had a chance to bond over weapons and gear. It wouldn't come across like a challenge.

"Oh, you know, sir. Army captain. Special Ops, mostly. One tour with the infantry before that."

"Where'd you serve?" We compared tours, figuring out that we'd been in a couple of the same places, but never at the same time. If we searched further we'd surely find mutual acquaintances, but not many, given our age and rank difference.

"So how's this work?" I asked, finally. "I'm sure Matua here told you that I tried to walk out last night."

"To get a drink," said Tanaka, confirming my suspicions.

"Sure. To get a drink."

Matua snorted.

"You're not a prisoner, sir," said Tanaka.

"No? So I can leave?" I asked.

He glanced away for a split second.

"That's what I thought. Not your fault. I won't hold it against you." I read the relief in his face. I almost had his number. He hadn't asked for me, I knew that. Somebody had forced me on him, so we were stuck with each other.

No, I'd lied. I *did* hold it against him, a little, but letting him know that didn't serve any purpose. Until I found a way out, I had to coexist with him and his team. If I didn't get out, we were going into something that might be hostile, and everybody had weapons. I needed to make myself useful. Or at a minimum, make myself someone who they didn't want to kill and dump on a distant planet.

**AFTER A MORNING** with the cool stuff, we spent an afternoon with the dull but necessary part of any mission: the background. Tanaka sat next to me in the center of a long, rectangular table while Matua took up a position against the wall behind me. Three briefers stood on the far side, lined up along the wall in military fashion wearing gray fatigues. Theoretically they were briefing Tanaka, but he certainly understood the basics of the mission, so they really prepared it for me. A tall, thin woman with short black hair looked at Tanaka, who nodded. She gestured to someone in the back and a holo lit up in front of us, showing a planet.

"Sir, this is Zeta Four. It circles a one-point-one-four-intensity star at an orbital radius of approximately one hundred seventy five million kilometers, putting it in the temperate zone. It's far enough away from its star so that it's not tidally locked, making it ideal." She looked at Tanaka as she spoke, but glanced at me to make sure I got it. "The planet has both liquid and frozen water, which can sustain life, and with further terraforming could be used to thicken the less-than-ideal atmosphere. Oxygen level is currently sixty-eight percent of standard."

I leaned over to Tanaka. "Zeta Four. That's a deserted mining planet, isn't it?"

He nodded and gestured to the briefer, indicating that she'd cover that.

"Due to the thin atmosphere, temperatures vary greatly across regions and from day to night. While the average temperature lies within the norm for human life, the amount of fluctuation makes it rather uncomfortable."

"So you could live there, but it wouldn't be any fun," I said to the briefer.

"Exactly so, sir. The planet is about zero point nine standard size and about zero point nine standard density. Gravity measures right around point eight. Rotation lasts over twenty hours, and the dual moons have a high relative mass in comparison to the planet, causing somewhat extreme tidal effects."

"How bad?" I asked.

"The coasts are nearly uninhabitable, sir." She went through another dozen visuals and about fifteen minutes of basic facts about the continents, the terrain, and other environmental factors, before concluding. "If there are no questions, I'll be followed by Mr. Sherzinski."

Tanaka glanced at me and I shook my head. "No questions," he said.

Sherzinski started without missing a beat. "As you mentioned, sir, Zeta Four was initially approached as a mining operation. Exploratory missions, mostly."

"Sure," I said. "But they abandoned it. Why?"

"Same reason mining companies abandon anything, sir. Money. There's iron and a bunch of stone, but almost none of the precious metals that make a planet viable for a major operation."

"And with the weather, gravity, and tides, it's not a place for residential settlements," I said.

"Correct, sir. Basically it's good for nothing other than water, and for that purpose it's not close enough to other systems to be viable for export. It does hold some small interest as a sportsman's destination with the surf and a huge series of amazing underground caves. A few companies have small financial stakes, but nobody's developed anything yet."

I made a show of not taking any notes but memorized everything. It didn't register now, but having no idea what the future held, I wanted to be prepared.

"Okay. So we've got a dead planet in the middle of nowhere. I'm guessing that the third briefer is going to tell me about the Cappans?"

"Yes, sir." The third briefer took over the spot. "While Zeta Four has been uninhabited by humans since the last mining company explorers left around sixty years ago, the planet is now occupied. Approximately two years ago a group of Cappans settled the planet."

"Wouldn't somebody have noticed that at the time?" I asked.

He shook his head. "Not really, sir. There's no reason. While the planet isn't far away by galactic standards, it's a dead end. The jump that leads to the Zeta system doesn't go anywhere else."

"So then . . . how did we find out they were there?"

"I don't know, sir."

I glanced at Tanaka, but he kept his eyes trained ahead. I knew the answer to the question—Omicron had helped them escape Cappa in the first place—but I wanted to assess what everybody else knew. I couldn't read Tanaka. I nodded for the briefer to continue.

"Our estimate right now is that the population is between ten and fifteen thousand—"

"Hold on. I'm sorry to keep interrupting, but you said fifteen thousand." I knew their population already from talking to their leader, but it gave me another opening to probe.

"Yes, sir."

"I only know of four ships that escaped Cappa. No way could they carry that many. Not that distance. They'd have to have cryo." A huge troop transport could carry hundreds or thousands, but the ships that left Cappa hadn't been that large. "Were there more ships?"

Everyone in the room stared at me, Tanaka turning in his seat to do so.

"What? Do you think I don't know a few things about what happened on Cappa?" I had given away a little information, but if it helped keep them off balance and guessing at what I knew, I'd happily pay that price.

"I don't know how they got there, sir, but we're pretty sure on the number," the briefer continued. "We have satellite imagery that shows they're mostly living in one settlement. We've seen minimal movement away from that area. Here's a visual." The view changed, showing a village of prefabricated buildings in a flat area surrounded by some sort of dirt cliffs on all sides, almost like a bowl.

"And if we zoom out," he continued, "we see that they're on this large island. It's about fourteen thousand square kilometers."

"Island . . . I thought coast was out," I said.

"It is, sir," said the female briefer from her position over by the wall. "But this island rises to about a thousand meters elevation fairly quickly. A series of cliffs and bluffs protects the island from the effects of the tide."

"What are they doing for subsistence? Are they shipping stuff in, or growing it locally?"

"Mostly local, sir," said the current briefer. "There's some indication that they're farming in the cave systems. They should be rather conducive to growing several kinds of fungi and lichens that fit with Cappan nutritional needs. We haven't seen goods delivered from off planet."

"Okay. I've got a good lay of the land. What's the mission?" I looked at Tanaka.

"That will be all," he said to the briefers. They filed out through a flimsy door, awkwardly silent.

"No more briefers?" I asked.

"Sir . . . about that. I'm really sorry. But we'll brief you on the mission once we're on board."

I stared at him for a few seconds. "Really?"

"Sorry, sir."

From his look I could tell he was legitimately embarrassed. It wasn't his idea to keep me in the dark. I didn't care. It gave me ammunition to mess with him. I had very little leverage, so I'd use whatever I got. "So let's get this straight. You're keeping me imprisoned,

I have no communication, but somehow I still can't be trusted with information on what we're trying to accomplish."

He looked away. "That's correct, sir."

"Which means that it's so fucked up that you're afraid . . . no, amend that, *someone* is afraid that I'll back out."

"I honestly don't know about that, sir. It seems pretty straightforward to me."

"So you know the mission?"

"Yes, sir." I could have let it go right there and taken his word for it, but I wanted to push a little and see what happened.

"Then tell me."

"Sir, I don't have the authority to—"

"You said it's straightforward."

"Sir, I can't—"

"Fine, I'm not going," I said. I made the decision on the spot, but once I said it, I liked the idea. I didn't see a way out of the building, so I needed to create some chaos, see if it opened up any opportunities.

"Excuse me, sir?"

"You have your orders not to tell me the mission. So what do your orders say if I refuse to get on the ship?"

"Sir—"

"Are you going to sedate me? Put me in cryo against my will, haul me off to some dead-end planet and hope I'll do what you need me to do when we get there? Come on, Tanaka, is that it?"

He squirmed in his seat. My outburst made him uncomfortable, because even though he was in charge of
the mission, he had been trained not to piss off senior
officers. "I don't have orders like that, no, sir."

"So you'd have to call somebody."

"Yes, sir."

"So call them."

He hesitated. "Sir, you really want me to—"

"What I really want is to know why somebody
thinks a group of trained professionals needs a
washed-up old colonel along for the ride. And until
somebody tells me the mission, I'm not going to have
an answer to that. Since you're not able to give it to
me, I want to talk to someone who can. Am I missing
the mark? You don't need me for a simple infiltration
mission. There has to be something else."

After a moment, he nodded. "I'll make a call, sir."

I didn't expect anything to come out of my outburst, and though it had been spontaneous, I'd kept
it to a time when it was just Tanaka and Matua present. Matua would keep his mouth shut, or he wouldn't
have been assigned to me. I could apologize to Tanaka
later for being an asshole since nobody else had seen
it. If I'd embarrassed him in front of his troops, that
would have been a different level of problem. Either
way, this probably represented my last play before the
email went out to Plazz. I still didn't love that option,
so I'd defaulted to what I always do: I tried to make
something happen. It would either give me a chance to

improve my position or it wouldn't, but it didn't seem likely to make it worse.

**ELLEN HAVERTY STEPPED** into the east campus conference room with a look on her face reminiscent of someone stepping in a pile of shit. I didn't know if her disdain was for the meager surroundings or for me, though I had a pretty good guess. At least when her eyes met mine, she faked a smile. "Colonel Butler. And here I thought we'd concluded our part of the business."

"Ms. Haverty. I'd have been happy to come to you or to do this over video. I really hate to put you out like this." I returned her "fuck you" smile.

"I find it best not to put things on technology these days. You can't be too cautious, you know."

"Did you learn that from Gylika?"

Her eyes went hard. "I'm here out of respect. The least you could do is act civil."

"Forgive me if I treat you like an extortionist. Not sure where I got that idea." Apparently I didn't feel the need to be civil.

"Look. You wanted to talk to me. I didn't have to come. I suggest you get to whatever it is that you want to discuss before I change my mind."

"Fair enough. I want to know the mission."

She took a seat in the moderately-priced office chair across from me. "Why would you need to know that? I'm told that you don't like to get the details of missions before you fly, as things change while you're in cryo and there's time to figure it out after."

I couldn't help but crack a smile at her, despite her being an evil troll. She'd done her homework, and she was right. She'd pegged my normal thought process. "This is different. When I went on military missions, I at least had an idea of what was expected. What I waited on was the details. I'd expect Mr. Tanaka would give me any changes when we come out of cryo in two or three months."

"One month," she said. "You're not on military transport anymore. Our ships are faster."

I gave a small nod. "I appreciate that. Get it over with quicker."

"Indeed."

"Here's my issue. As I understand it currently, this mission makes no sense. There are thousands of Cappans, and we're going in with two hundred. That's not enough force to make them give something up if they don't want to. It's too small to fight, too big to infiltrate."

"That's why we're sending you. To negotiate."

I'd thought through the possibility of how I'd do that. We'd threaten to blow the planet from space, and use that as leverage. Then it would depend on how well I could get the Cappans to believe that. That didn't take into account that I was also working with the Cappans, which dropped a half dozen twists into an already ridiculous situation. "You don't need me on this mission," I said. "Tanaka will tell you. In fact he'd be a hell of a lot happier without me looking over his shoulder."

"I'm not in the habit of asking my employees for their opinion on my decisions. We pay Mr. Tanaka very well. I don't much care if he's happy, as long as he gets the job done."

"With a military mission, maybe you should . . . you know . . . listen to the military guys."

She smiled at me like a mother humoring her child. "I'll take that under advisement."

"So that's it? You came all the way down here to tell me you're not telling me? You could have done that from your office."

She studied me for a couple seconds. "I found it necessary to see this for myself. Sometimes you need to do that as a leader. I'm sure you understand."

"I need more than that."

"Oh, Carl. You're a smart man. We both know you don't have any leverage here." She stood.

I stood as well, and put both my hands on the table, leaning over. "Fine. I'm not going without more information."

"You don't mean that. I've got a team that has located Ms. Ganos. I'm not bluffing."

Shit. "At least tell me this," I said. "When did Javier start conspiring with you? Was this the plan from the start?"

She thought about it, as if deciding whether to share or not. "He contacted me pretty soon after Mr. Gylika passed. You should thank him, if you ever see him again. I wanted to have you eliminated. It was Javier who convinced me you could be useful."

"I'll be sure to say thanks when I see him."

"Don't be so sad. This is a great opportunity." Something in her condescending tone caused me to snap.

"I'm not doing this." I hadn't planned to call her bluff until that very moment, but the more I thought about it, the more I thought she wouldn't play her Ganos card. If she did, she had no further leverage over me. She understood that.

"Very well, have it your way." She pressed a button on her device and four guards burst through the door in gray uniforms. They had helmets on. Fucking helmets. Like I was some sort of threat. Two of them came around the table from each direction and I put my hands on top of my head.

I locked eyes with Matua, who had pushed away from the wall into a ready position, but hadn't moved to stop the onrushing guards. He shrugged, as if to say, "Sorry."

"Easy, folks," I said, eyeing the stun stick a short, squat man carried. "Don't hit me with the stunner. Neither one of us will like the result."

"I also came for another reason," said Haverty.

"What's that?" I asked.

"I wanted to see your face when I told you that we hacked your email. We haven't broken the encryption to see what you wrote yet, but we did see that it was scheduled to send to a reporter automatically in under two days. I hope that wasn't important."

I started to respond, but a tall female guard reached me first and pressed something against my arm. I felt a sharp burst of pain, then nothing. Auto injector.

"What was that f—"

The world went black.

# CHAPTER TWENTY-FIVE

I WOKE WITH A hangover, vertigo, and the sore throat that comes from stasis during space travel. Those bastards had kept me sedated until we went under for the trip. I took a moment to study my surroundings. People coming out of stasis tended to sit immobile and unaware for a couple of hours, so nobody would suspect I'd come out of it completely.

Five or six people moved around an expensive-looking travel suite. Comfortable-looking black recliners lined one wall, and small, functional tables suited for standing lined the other. At least one more person hadn't come out of stasis and sat in her tube, like me. Three people gathered around a small galley area, and the smell of fresh coffee drifted through the cabin.

"You back, Colonel?" said Tanaka's voice.

"That depends," I said, my voice raspy. "Is there more coffee?"

"There is."

"You assholes drugged me," I said.

"In my defense, I recommended against it. Ms. Haverty doesn't always listen."

"I believe that." He wouldn't have ordered that, knowing he'd have to work with me. I had to work with him, too, so I let it go. Space is a cold place, and not a good one to keep enemies. "How long were we down?"

"A little over a month," said Tanaka. "We're decelerating now at slightly under one g, which is why we're good to be up and about."

"Great," I said.

"Shower's at the back of the compartment, then when you're ready, there are biscuits and gravy."

My stomach smiled. Finally somebody who understood space travel. It made me so happy that I didn't care that they'd probably contacted people who know me to find out my preference for the meal. I assumed that anything I'd ever done, they knew. It made it easier. I didn't have to seek out the roster of soldiers on board. Omicron would have done that and ensured none of them had ever worked for me before. It sounds weird, but it made me comfortable. It's always nice to know you're working with professionals, even if it doesn't work in your favor at the moment.

The shower pulsed with the best water pressure I'd ever experienced on a spaceship, and I treated myself to an extra thirty seconds. I could get used to traveling corporate. I dressed in the fatigues that somebody had provided—they fit perfectly—and walked back out into the main berthing area. I counted eight people plus myself. That would make this the leadership. The rank-and-file soldiers probably traveled in a different bay with something less than our royal accommodations. I bet it still beat a standard military troop ship though.

As I moved through the room toward my prized biscuits, I made a point of meeting the eyes of everyone I passed, giving them a smile. I needed allies, and barring that, with the potential of going into combat together, I at least needed people not to shoot me in the back. A short man with dark skin nodded and returned my smile, so I stopped.

"I'm not sure of the rank insignia," I said, though I'd pretty much figured it out. "Two circles . . . that's . . ."

"Lieutenant, sir. Lieutenant Darce Jackson."

"Good to meet you, Jackson. I'm—"

He laughed. "I know who you are, sir. Everybody in the galaxy knows."

I fake cringed and sucked in my breath. "Yeah. It's not all that it's cracked up to be."

He laughed again. "Probably has its perks, though."

"I don't know. It got me on the same ship as you."

"True," he said. "Don't let me hold you up, sir. Chow is hot."

I smiled again, and touched him on the upper arm. "Thanks."

I grabbed a plastic plate, covered it in biscuits and then slathered it with life-giving sausage gravy. I shoveled several bites in before I made it to a table, and the miserable cryo-hangover began to creep away. The effect might have been psychological, but I didn't care. I set my bounty down on the table where Tanaka stood with one of his lieutenants. I wanted to meet the others, but ignoring the commander would have been bad form. People would notice, and it would appear like me slighting him. That would force people to choose sides, and I didn't pay their salaries. I couldn't afford to force confrontation yet.

Tanaka probably expected me to hit him up for information about the mission, or whine some more about how they'd waylaid me, so I took a different direction. "You bring everybody out early, or only the officers?"

"Just us, for now, sir. We'll get the troopers out of cryo about eight hours before we hit orbit, so they have time to recover."

"Is Matua in that group?" I liked the big corporal, despite his role as my kind-of jailer.

"He is," said Tanaka. "He's going to be your security guy for the mission."

"Good." I gestured to the surrounding opulence, then spoke through a mouth of biscuit. "Nice digs."

"Yes, sir. Sure beats military travel, doesn't it?"

"If we'd traveled like this, I might have stayed in. Faster, too. Though I don't know what day we took off."

Tanaka smiled, taking it for the joke I intended. "It was fast, sir. And you were out less than a day when we took off."

I nodded as I sipped a cup of wonderful coffee.

"This is my exec, Chelsea Larsson."

"Sir." The woman who ate with us stood a head shorter than me, and I'm not tall. She glared at me with a face as hard as a spaceship's hull.

"Do you keep command spaceside when we go down, or are you a fighting XO?" I asked. It wasn't an insult. A second-in-command had two options, making it a legitimate question.

Her face softened briefly, pride radiating from it. "I fight, sir. The Operations officer keeps the ship."

"Good to hear. I prefer it that way." I'd have said the same, no matter which way she answered. I turned to Tanaka. "How are you organized for combat?"

"Four platoons, sir. Forty soldiers each, led by one of the lieutenants. The XO goes planetside, as she said, and of course I do. Ops officer stays spaceside, and the Intel officer can go either way. I'm leaning toward taking her with us on this one."

"I think that makes sense. We're not going to pick up a lot from up here, so you get her down on the planet where the information is. You'll lose a bit in analytical power, but she can funnel stuff to her team spaceside and get that via reachback."

"Yes, sir. Exactly how I was thinking."

I chuckled. "Look at me, trying to take over your mission. You've got this."

He smiled again, and it looked genuine. Good. My approval still meant something to him. I'd need that. "Anything you want to offer sir, I'm open."

"You mind if I walk around and meet the team? The worst part about leaving the service is not having soldiers to talk to."

"By all means, sir. Once everybody is recovered and we've had a chance to process whatever's happened in the last month, we'll sit down and get a mission brief."

"No rush," I said. I gestured with my head for him to step away from his exec for a private word, which he did. "What's my comms situation, send and receive? I don't want to make it a big deal in front of the junior officers, but I need to know."

"I appreciate that, sir," Tanaka said. "Receive is no problem. Whatever feeds we get are yours. No sending."

I nodded. "Okay. People are going to wonder where I am, though."

"Sorry, sir. I have to trust that somebody back in the world had a plan to deal with that."

"Fair enough." I'd known the answer before I asked, but I wanted him to say no out loud so that it weighed on him the next time I asked for something. I also wanted cover for when I checked the news. I needed to see if my disappearance had been reported, or at least find the cover story. If it had blown up somehow, I'd likely hear about it anyway. Possibly when they flushed me out an airlock. Tanaka hadn't received those orders yet. If he wanted me dead, he could have done it when I was in cryo.

"I appreciate your cooperation, sir. You could have made this a lot harder."

"No point in that now," I said. "What story did you

give your people about why I was in cryo so early? That had to have been weird."

"Told them you were superstitious and liked to be the first one down. I made a vague reference to something that happened on a previous mission."

I snorted. "They bought that?"

"Sir, if I told them you could fly, half of them would believe me. You're kind of larger than life to most of the troops."

"As long as they don't toss me off a building to test it," I said.

He laughed. "Right. Sir, if you don't mind, I need to go over the latest intelligence before we brief the rest of the team. If you'll excuse me?"

"By all means. It's your show. I'm going to check the news. A lot happens when you're asleep for a month."

I SCANNED THE headlines of the major feeds from the past month, looking for anything that might give me a clue about where I stood. I wanted to know what Plazz had figured out, and I wanted to know about Gylika, but I didn't want to put in any search terms. They allowed me to use the system, but I had no illusions. They'd be monitoring me. I clicked on some random items as camouflage, and they helped me legitimately catch up with the last month, too. The first thing that really caught my attention was in business news. Omicron and VPC announced a joint venture. The story spanned two paragraphs and lacked detail, but hinted at work with the military on medical technology.

So that was that. It didn't take a genius to figure out the project they'd be working on together. *I* was the joint venture . . . we were . . . our mission. We'd bring back the technology and the two companies who put me here would profit. Haverty said that I should be thankful to Javier, but I didn't feel that charitable. I believed her, though, about when he contacted her. Thinking back on it, he had changed after Gylika's death. Whether Haverty made him an offer and he traded me for corporate profit or whether he sold me out to cover his own ass, I didn't know. I'd probably never know. And I still didn't know what role they intended for me going forward. They had me in a bad spot, for sure, going into a potentially hostile area where both sides might want me dead. But I had some plans of my own. Most of them involved pissing on their schemes in any way possible, though in truth I suppose that was more of a purpose statement than an actual plan of action.

I pulled up the feed for the *Galactic Times*, where Plazz worked, and pretended to read it while skimming for her byline. She had a big piece on a high government official who apparently used his position to funnel clients to his mistress's business, but not a word about Omicron, not a word about me. I believed what Haverty had said about intercepting my message, and I assumed they may have decrypted it, though it would be hard because it was point to point.

I kept scanning. I don't know what I expected to find in my general search. I guess maybe I held out some slim hope that Plazz would have tried to reach me, not found me, and started digging.

Finally, I decided to risk it and search Gylika's name. I'd thrown it in Haverty's face in our last meeting, so it would hardly incriminate me further to check it now. It turned up nothing. The most recent result was from before they'd taken me prisoner. The case had completely disappeared from the public eye. I shook my head.

"What's wrong, sir?" A lieutenant asked from the terminal beside mine. She looked over at me, though her thin hands still flew over the keys.

"Oh, nothing," I said. "A friend of mine died a couple weeks before we flew. I was hoping there'd be something in the news about it."

"Oh, that's sad," she said. "How did he die?"

"Murder," I said. Best to keep to the truth as much as possible.

"That's horrible!"

"The city can be rough. How about you? Any good news from home?" I did want to connect with the officers, but not over the murder.

"Not much, sir. Same old stuff. My boyfriend is hiking a five-thousand-meter mountain next week. I guess that's the big thing."

"Nice. Do you climb too?"

"When I get the chance, sir. Nothing that big, though. Too much space time. Makes it hard to stay in good-enough shape."

"For sure," I said. "Speaking of which, does this crate we're on have a gym?"

"Yes, sir. A small one. But we'll barely be space-side long enough to use it, if everything goes to plan."

"Quick timeline? I haven't been briefed yet."

"A day from here to orbit, then a quick turn down to the planet twelve hours later."

"Huh. Guess we're in a hurry."

"Hard to say with these corporate gigs. Can't beat the pay, though."

"No, you can't." I wondered for a moment if VPC was still paying me. They probably were, for a cover story. I'd enjoy spending their money, if I survived.

I scanned through some more of the news, but bored of it and decided to check out the gym. Or to see if the ship had a bar. Definitely one of those two things. I was weaving my way between the cryo pods toward the back of the ship when Larsson stepped in front of me, blocking my path.

"I see what you're doing, sir." Her voice dripped with ice.

"I'm sorry, have I done something wrong?"

"With the officers. I see what you're doing, being nice to them, trying to ingratiate yourself."

"You'd rather I be an asshole? Because I have that setting." I smiled, hiding my discomfort at the fact that I'd been so obvious. Not that it should have mattered.

"Don't start thinking Captain Tanaka is the only person who knows what's going on with you. He's the commander. He has to be nice. Me? I'm watching you, and I'd just as soon shoot you in the face as carry you home."

"Okay, Larsson. Thanks. Good chat." She glared at me for several more seconds before stepping out of the way. So much for not making enemies.

I TRIED NOT to look at Larsson as the officers gathered in the briefing area to go over the mission, but she stared daggers at me, making it difficult. If anybody else noticed, they didn't say anything. I hoped she and I flew on different drop ships. Tanaka would probably keep me by his side, and the commander and XO wouldn't ever fly together, so I'd probably get my wish.

"We'll go down in four ships to the landing point, here," said Tanaka, gesturing to a holo map. "From there we'll move by platoon along these four routes." Four color-coded paths lit up, traveling over several forested hills. Each route measured between fifteen and twenty kilometers. It looked like a miserable walk, but the low gravity and powered suits would help. I wondered why he had the landing zone so far from the objective. Under normal circumstances I'd have asked, since it seemed like a flawed plan, but I didn't want to draw the attention.

Tanaka lit up the potential enemy in red symbols on the map, and it became clearer. "We're landing outside any known Cappan activity, and we'll infiltrate as close to the expected target site as possible. If we don't have to engage, we don't. Let me make that very clear.

If we recover the stolen data and never fire a shot, I'd consider that a perfect success."

One of the platoon leaders, a big beefy guy I hadn't met yet, snorted. "These are Cappans. There's no way it's peaceful."

"We don't know that," said Tanaka. "They're scientists. And that's why we're landing outside their main living area. So they have plenty of time to get used to the idea that we're coming. I don't want to get into a firefight by accident."

"They're fucking Cappans, sir." Beefy guy glanced at me, but I didn't hold eye contact. He was probably a staunch supporter of what I'd done on Cappa. He was probably also an asshole. But if it came to him or Larsson, I'd take him. Better an asshole who liked me than somebody who might shoot me. Still, I didn't need to encourage him.

Tanaka snapped at him. "Do you understand the order, Jurcovik?"

"Yes, sir," said Beefy.

"Good. When we approach the main settlement, here," he lit up an icon in green. "Three platoons will provide cover from these positions." Three ovals lit up. "Myself, Colonel Butler, and first platoon will engage with the Cappans and attempt to negotiate a peaceful transfer of the required data. Once we've validated that we have the right information . . . a task that will take about thirty-five minutes due to broadcast delays . . . our unit will exfiltrate first, followed by the support-by-fire platoons. The pickup site is here."

He indicated another spot, about five kilometers away from the target. I read that to mean that he expected the departure to be smoother than the landing. Or more likely, he didn't know about the landing. By the time we got ready to leave the planet, we'd know one way or the other what the Cappans thought. If we got into a fight, we'd readjust on the fly and find whatever pickup zone worked.

"The rest of the information, including alternate landing sites, contingency plans, and whatever else you might need is in your device. Any questions?"

I didn't have a data pad, so the others had me at a disadvantage. But unlike the others, to whom "any questions" was rhetorical, I could actually ask one. "What sort of fire support do we have? Air cover, fire from orbit, that sort of thing."

"We've got a two-ship of fast attack birds, sir," said Tanaka. "The ship we're on has missiles, but nothing we'd want to use in close. We're mostly on our own. On the ground we've got the standard rockets-in-a-box and shoulder-launched stuff."

I nodded. It didn't change my thoughts on the mission, but I always liked to know what we had in case things went to shit. Because things usually went to shit. Tanaka didn't specify what types of missiles, but something in how he said that we wouldn't want to use them in close caught my attention. I made a mental note to check what the ship had for armament. Being a non-government ship, it shouldn't have had anything. But then being a non-government ship, it shouldn't have had a hundred and sixty armed-to-the-teeth attack troops, either.

I pulled Tanaka aside after the briefing broke up. "I didn't want to ask any more questions in front of the troops, but I've got one big one. What happens if they don't give us the data? We can't shoot it out of them."

"We're hoping it doesn't come to that, but we've got two data-retrieval specialists as part of the crew. Larsson is one, the other is an enlisted guy asleep in the back."

"Larsson does data retrieval?"

"One of the best," he said. "Why's that a surprise?"

"She didn't strike me as the type. Plus she's the exec. She's got another mission."

"We're all cross-trained," he said. He must have seen something on my face, because he frowned for a second before recovering himself. "Come on, sir. Bar is open. I'll buy you a drink on Omicron's dime."

"I really could get used to this corporate mercenary life," I said.

If only I hadn't been abducted into it.

# CHAPTER TWENTY-SIX

**I** WAITED UNTIL THEY took the troops out of storage before I started snooping. The extra people moving throughout the ship offered me at least a little cover from the prying eyes of Larsson, who had made me her personal project. I made my route seem random, walking through the enlisted bay, shaking hands and taking pictures with soldiers who swarmed around me once they knew who I was. The XO could stare all she liked at that, but what could she do? If it came down to a choice between her and me, I liked my chances with the grunts. And she couldn't have the grunts resent her for denying them this (seemingly) innocent opportunity with a bona fide celebrity. If nothing else, having lots of pictures of me in existence would at least make it harder for Omicron to cover up my death, assuming that's what they had planned.

I found Matua after a bit, hunched over a meal and shoveling food into his face at a terrifying rate. "Hungry?"

"Hey, sir! Yeah. For whatever reason, stasis makes me want to stuff myself afterward."

"It hits me that way too," I said.

"I hope there are no hard feelings about the way things went down back at the facility," he said. I did harbor a bit of a grudge, but that wasn't really fair since he couldn't have done anything about it anyway.

"We're good," I said. "Just make sure the next time somebody comes at me that you treat them like that piece of meat on your plate."

He laughed and the crumbs of a biscuit sputtered from his mouth. "You got it, sir."

I continued my trek around the enlisted area, taking the chance to ask each soldier something personal: where they lived, if they were married, their favorite sports team. I made a special point to ask each one what they did on the mission, making note of those who were staying spaceside—I had questions about the ship, and nobody knew their equipment better than the soldiers who ran it. The troops going down to the planet would be physically closer to me, but the people staying spaceside would have the more critical aspects of the mission.

After speaking to about fifteen troops in the landing party I finally found one who worked in ship operations. Lopez had her black hair done in a buzz cut, a scar just under her left ear. "Must be nice, being on something as advanced as this," I said.

She shrugged. "It's okay, sir. It's almost too pretty, you know?"

"I'll deal with too pretty for the awesome showers," I said.

"You got that right, sir."

"You said you work the targeting system?"

"Yes, sir."

"I know a bit about targeting." I smiled, almost allowing myself a chuckle.

She laughed. "Yes, sir. I guess you do."

"What are we packing?"

"XM-25s, sir. Four of them."

"Holy shit." It slipped out. XM-25s were high-powered fusion weapons. Planet busters. The same things I'd fired at Cappa. "I wouldn't expect a civilian ship to have something like that."

"It's an Omicron ship, sir. Who do you think makes them?"

Shit. I'd never thought about that, but Omicron *did* make the XM-25. Not that it mattered. What mattered was that we had them on this ship, which meant somebody thought they had a purpose here. They didn't load them by accident. A chill ran through me. I wondered if we planned to use them as a last resort or if they constituted the primary plan. Given the small area of the island where the Cappans lived, four XM-25s could lay waste to it with no survivors, if targeted properly.

Lopez was staring at me, and I realized I'd been quiet for too long. "Well let's hope that we don't have to use them."

"Yes, sir. Let's hope."

I excused myself as Lieutenant Danner walked by us. He stood eight or ten centimeters taller than anybody else and had exceptionally dark skin. More important, he was the Operations officer and he'd have control of the ship once we headed planetside. Until Tanaka and his XO made it back spaceside, Danner would hold the trigger on those XM-25s.

"Hey Danner, did you do non-com time in the regular army?" I asked. He looked a bit old for a lieutenant, so it was an educated guess.

"I did, sir. I was a forward air controller."

"I always loved my FACs," I said. "Probably the most important guy on a mission."

He smiled. "I did a couple tours where I—"

"Colonel Butler?" Larsson inserted herself almost between us as she interrupted. "It's time to suit up."

Which meant my time to ingratiate myself with the crew was up.

I HAD MORE than enough time to prepare myself for the trip planetside, thanks to Larsson wanting to keep me away from Danner. By the time we loaded, I'd checked my ammunition three times and gone to the bathroom twice. I never pass up an opportunity at my age. I strapped myself into the drop ship, my back against the front bulkhead, next to Tanaka. In front of us, first platoon sat in four rows of ten, each row facing another across one of the two aisles. Matua sat close by and looked in my direction, making sure I'd managed to secure myself correctly into my seat. I didn't say anything. I'd never suggest to somebody covering my ass that maybe they should take the job less seriously.

The mission smelled as bad as a barracks with a broken shower. Every time I'd tried to corner Tanaka about contingency plans in case our primary went to crap, Larsson had materialized with some matter that needed his immediate attention. I'd played it off, but it left a bad taste in my mouth. We were dropping in to an area filled with ambush sites while packing very little fire support. The plan hinged on hoping for co-operation from Cappans who had no reason to give it. A wise man once told me that hope is not a great planning tool.

With Larsson securely ensconced on another ship and Tanaka buckling in, I finally had him where he couldn't escape. "What are the XM-25s for?" I asked.

"Excuse me, sir?"

"The planet busters. Why do we have them?"

He hesitated a half second too long. "Contingencies, sir. That's all."

Liar. If they got the data and destroyed the Cappans, there'd be nobody left to come after it. There'd be nobody left to tell any story other than the official Omicron version. Nobody but me.

Shit.

I'd suspected it before, but the way Tanaka said it, I'd just become certain. I was going to die on this planet. I knew too much. They couldn't kill me back in civilization. Too many questions. They'd learned that lesson with Gylika, and I'd bring ten times the scrutiny he did. But if I died out here, they could spin it any way they wanted. They could even blame me

for the XM-25s. Personally I'd go with "Maverick
Colonel Couldn't Stay Away from Combat, and It
Finally Caught Up to Him." People would buy that.
Shit, I'd buy it about almost any colonel I'd ever met.
The pull was strong. I don't think I understood quite
how powerful it was until I got the chance to go back.
Your whole life you do big, important things. You
speak and people listen. Then suddenly that's over,
and you're wasting your life doing some bullshit job
that doesn't matter, where nobody cares what you do
as long as you show up for the company functions.

Yeah, I'd buy that story. Because even knowing
everything I did, sitting in a ship headed to a potential
combat zone and my likely demise, I had to admit I
was a little excited.

I almost asked Tanaka how it was going to
happen—how he was going to kill me—but I held my
tongue. I knew what he was going to do, but there
was a chance he didn't know that I knew. No need
to give him that advantage. I didn't have much, but I
had that. I had that, and I had my civilian high-speed
version of a Bitch, complete with a dozen magazines
of ammunition. That was something.

"You think I can get the pilot's feed?" I pointed to
my helmet. "I don't like to fly without knowing what's
going on. Habit."

"Sure." Tanaka keyed something in his helmet,
which opened the feed in mine. "All set. Sir, I want
you to know something, between you and me."

"What's that?" I asked.

"I know you're not stupid. I know how this whole thing has to look. But I don't care what the mission is. I intend to bring you back with us. Alive."

A chill hit me. It was like he read my mind. I considered his words for a moment before speaking. "You know that could put you in a bind with your employer."

"I know. I don't care."

"You're a good man, Tanaka. I appreciate it. I'm not sure your exec feels the same way, though."

"She'll follow my orders, sir."

I put my helmet on and closed my eyes, pretending to doze until takeoff. He could have been lying, but I'm a pretty good judge of people, and something told me he wasn't. I might have actually nodded off for a moment—that kind of half sleep where you don't realize you're out—because I jerked when the pilot spoke through my earpiece. She had a husky voice, like she'd inhaled too much smoke at some point. "Fifteen seconds until takeoff."

I counted it down in my head out of habit. The ship began to vibrate, and then the movement pushed me into my belts. After half a minute or so the ride smoothed and we settled into the comfortable flight of open space.

"Six minutes to atmosphere, twenty-three minutes until destination," said the pilot. Nobody else spoke on the comm. I took that as a good sign. Professional units don't chatter on the command net; they keep it to private channels. A few of the soldiers checked their kit. A few more slept. Veterans. I took the opportunity to open a private channel to Matua.

"I don't want to make this weird," I said, "but if shit starts to go sideways and it's my time to go, don't put yourself in the way of it."

"What are you talking about, sir?"

"Look, I don't know what you already know, and definitely don't share this with anybody else. I'm not likely to come back from this. It's in your employer's best interest that I don't. So if you see that start to go down, get out of the way."

The net stayed silent for several seconds. "Fuck that, sir. My mission is to keep you safe. They want you, they go through me."

I smiled to myself. Despite the shitty situation, soldiers were soldiers, and Tanaka and Matua were good ones. Maybe I had a chance.

The ship jumped as we hit the atmosphere, and everything shook. If I made a thousand of these trips, I'd still never get used to the teeth-rattling vibration of reentry. Or entry, in this case.

"All systems normal," said the pilot. "The shake should calm down in a minute."

We approached the planet several hundred kilometers from our destination, hitting the atmosphere at a precise angle, calculated to multiple decimal places by the ship's computer. That's what they told me, at least. Sitting in the back with no windows, I didn't have any way to check. I'd never blown up on entry before, so I gave them the benefit of the doubt.

"Approaching landing. Two minutes out. Weather looks . . . shit! What was that?"

"Look out!" A different voice. The copilot, probably. The ship jerked to the right, then back to the left in a roll. My body strained against the side of my belts as the ship's motion tried to shove me into Tanaka. Outside, a crack of thunder, followed by a closer, distinctive popping sound.

We'd launched anti-missile countermeasures. People had tried to shoot me down before, and it wasn't a sound I'd forget. Our ship had launched flares and chaff to confuse enemy weapons.

"Four is hit!" said the pilot, a bit of panic seeping into her voice. Not thunder. An explosion.

"What's happening?" Tanaka asked, as the ship leveled off. No answer. He raised his voice. "What's happening?"

I put my hand on his arm to get his attention, and opened a private channel. "Let the pilots fight the fight. There's nothing you can do from back here, and answering you will distract them."

He hesitated a moment, then nodded. He knew that, but I had a feeling he'd been out of the fight longer than he'd care to admit.

It would come back quick, though—it always did.

The ship jerked again, punctuated by another pop of chaff releasing. An earsplitting explosion made me flinch, and the ship lurched sideways in a way that things that fly aren't supposed to move. One of the soldiers vomited between his boots. Luckily we were out of zero gravity. That would have sucked.

Shit. None of the intelligence showed anti-air weapons. I should have known better than to trust what the intel said about Cappans. Even if we made it down, we needed a new plan. "We're out of the upper atmosphere. See if you can raise fourth platoon," I told Tanaka.

He nodded. The ships had comms systems, but we had our own built into our helmets, and it would work now that we'd cleared the interference of the upper atmosphere. Tanaka toggled his frequency and spoke words I couldn't hear. In front of me, soldiers darted their heads back and forth. They stayed off the ship's frequency so I couldn't hear them, but they were chattering now. Panic. The fear of not knowing what the fuck is going on. It's universal. They'd expected an easy mission, and it had become startlingly clear that they wouldn't get it. I hoped that my earlier assessment about veterans held true now that everything had taken a right turn toward shit town.

Tanaka looked at me and shook his head. Bad news.

"Okay. What's the plan? Pull out?" I asked, keeping to our private channel.

He glanced out at his soldiers. "I've got to get the team calmed down."

"You do. But first you need to tell the pilot which way to go." I gestured to the soldiers with my head. "These ones will wait. That won't."

He nodded. "Yes, sir. Pilot, can we still reach the landing area?"

"Roger. The fire seems to have subsided. It was a single salvo of missiles. There could be more, though, so I don't want to spend a lot of time flying around in circles."

"I'm with you on that. Any word on what happened to Ship Four?"

"It didn't look good. I don't see any ejects," said the pilot.

No ejects. No survivors. Tanaka's head dipped and he stared down at the floor. I knew the feeling, and I empathized with him. His intelligence failed him and people died. The trick is learning that you can never predict everything, and that people die, and you need to move past it quickly so that other people don't die. It takes a long time to learn. I'm still hoping to get there one day. But it's easier to see when it's somebody else. I nudged him, and gestured to the rest of the team. Not everybody stared at us, but enough did to make a difference.

"Focus on who you still have," I said over the private channel.

Tanaka snapped back to life and flipped to a ship-wide net. "The enemy had more defenses than we planned. We're through it and continuing on to the landing zone. Currently no change to the plan."

Heads nodded. He'd said it confidently, which was more important than the content of the message. He needed to be confident, because if he didn't sound like he believed, nobody else would. Truth was, we had no idea if we needed to change plans or not. The anti-ship battery could have been a one-off thing, or it could presage an overall increased defense posture. We wouldn't learn that for a while. But he had to pretend he knew, because nothing would destroy a unit like thinking their commander didn't know. After a short hiccup, he had handled it well. They didn't all buy in—they weren't stupid—but the soldiers knew the game too. They wanted to hear it from him, even if they'd see for themselves in a few minutes.

One thing we did know. If we'd expected the Cappans to sit back and wait for us, we'd been wrong.

The ship thumped down hard, bouncing me against my belts. The seat absorbed most of it, as designed, but it still shot pain through my lower back.

"Treat it like a hot landing zone," barked Tanaka.

With that simple order, the chaos formed into military precision, as if all they'd needed was to flip the switch. The platoon leader immediately started broadcasting on the same channel. "First squad, exit left and establish a perimeter, second squad take the right. Third and fourth, hold back until we get an initial report on the situation."

Four voices said "roger" at the same time. The four squad leaders. My heart rate had picked up, drumming in my ears as the net went silent for a moment while the squad leaders broadcast orders to their subordinates on other channels. I expected fear, but that wasn't it. It was excitement. My shrink would have a grand time with that, assuming I made it back. For a minute during the silence I let myself wish that Ship Three had been hit instead of Four. Larsson was riding on Ship Three. That's a fucked-up thing to wish for, but self-preservation will do that. She *had* threatened to kill me, after all.

All that disappeared from my mind as the doors whooshed open on both sides of the craft, and soldiers started to move.

# CHAPTER TWENTY-SEVEN

THE FIRST SQUADS got out quickly, without seeming to hurry. The anxiety had sloughed off the soldiers now that they had a purpose. In the air, we had no control; whatever happened, we were strapped in the back and along for the ride. Here, with our feet on the ground, we could at least shoot back. That made all the difference in the world to infantry.

"Contact. Three personnel in the tree line, three hundred fifty meters." A voice on the comm. One of the squad leaders from outside.

"What are they doing?" Tanaka asked, frustration seeping into his voice. That information should have come in the initial report.

"They're . . . they don't seem to be doing anything. Just observing. Should we engage?"

I could almost hear Tanaka's eyes roll as he said, "Are they targeting us, or is it possible that they're just wondering what three ships are doing landing in a clearing?"

"No visible signs of equipment," said the squad leader, after a few seconds. I imagined him looking around at the other soldiers, polling for opinions. I wanted to roll my eyes too.

I nodded my head toward the exit and Tanaka moved that way. We needed to get out there before somebody did something stupid. We had a ship shot down as we came in, but that didn't mean that everybody down here was against us. The destruction of fourth platoon could have been a single actor with the right weapon system. But the soldiers wouldn't see it that way. Their friends died, and they might want to lash out, regardless of if they had the right target. If they started shooting everything in sight, it could complicate the mission. Having to shoot our way through the entire population was untenable for a force our size, especially when success rested on convincing them to give us information. Tanaka had a backup plan in case they didn't cooperate, but he'd still want to go for the easier way first.

None of that changed the fact that somewhere they *did* have heavy weapons, which they shouldn't have. We'd have to deal with that as it came.

My boots sank into the ground as I stepped off the ramp. The temperature reading on my suit put it at a balmy thirty-one degrees Celsius, and humid, too, but that didn't bother me since my super-high-tech suit had temperature regulation. Another point for the corporate life. A light breeze caused the knee-high grass that resembled green wheat to sway. Forest surrounded us on all sides with strange, tall trees in a brighter green that almost seemed to glow.

I punched the magnification in my screen up to six times and scanned the tree line for our observers. Three Cappans. They looked at each other, not us, as if in conversation. I dropped magnification and glanced at Tanaka. He'd found them, too.

"Ignore them," he announced over the command net, ensuring all three platoon leaders heard him. "It's not like we were sneaking in, anyway. Move out on our pre-planned courses. Third platoon, you've got fourth's support position now in addition to your own. Recon the site and decide if you're splitting in two or occupying one of the original spots en masse. Your call, based on the actual terrain."

I agreed with his order. Maps were great for planning, but nothing ever came out quite the same once you put boots on the ground.

The first platoon leader addressed his platoon. "On me." I had their channel active too, since we were traveling with that unit. Tanaka would be on there as well, keeping an ear on the unit closest to him while still running the company. He might try to listen in on all his platoons, which would keep him abreast instead of them having to send reports on the command net. I wouldn't, but that was more a matter of leadership style than doctrine. I found that it took too much of my attention away from the things happening around me, and though the local platoon leader would lead that fight, I liked to remain aware. The distant leaders could break in and talk to me as they needed.

The four-fifths gravity offset the heavy armor I

wore, and the mechanical assist built into it helped as well. I almost wanted to see how far I could jump in the low gravity. I was sure that as soon as the leaders turned their backs, the soldiers would try it. We kept our helmets sealed due to the low oxygen content in the atmosphere. My heads-up display put it at fourteen point four percent, which would be the equivalent of being around three thousand meters elevation in standard atmosphere. Humans could live in it, but they'd be miserable, especially if they had to do anything physical. Our suits could provide a higher level of oxygen to us indefinitely in this environment, because they pulled in extra from the thin air around us, then regulated the content we breathed as needed. It was nice to know that a suit breach wouldn't kill me, though.

As we walked away from the other platoons and toward the woods I lagged a little, letting myself fall back from Tanaka. He was busy, likely getting two or three times the information I was into his display, so I figured he wouldn't notice. Corporal Matua shadowed me, dropping back as well, his bulk identifying him without requiring me to check my heads-up display for his name. Our platoon formed an arrow, and Tanaka walked about a third of the way back. I dropped to the trailing third.

While I walked, I took it as a chance to make myself seen. Soldiers' names automatically popped up on my display, and it gave me the ability to drop onto their private frequency. I didn't do it, but they'd see my name, too. That's what I wanted. They'd see me humping alongside them, sharing the same hardships, not taking any privileges. That would earn me some points. Points that I might need to cash in at some time in the future if somebody decided to kill me. Soldiers are funny like that. An enemy or an outsider, and they could turn off emotion and do what they needed to do. One of their own? Not so much. I needed to be one of their own.

These were mercenaries, not assassins.

The tall trees formed heavy overhead canopies that choked out sunlight and kept the forest floor relatively clear of undergrowth. We headed generally upward, but slowly, over the first three kilometers. My display said we'd gained sixty-one meters of elevation since we left the drop area, but we did it over a series of small hills, traveling down, then back up.

"Halt," announced the platoon leader. The soldiers dropped to one knee as a single unit, and each one focused on their assigned sector, giving us three hundred sixty degrees of coverage. With the shift of an eye I could bring up each sector on my display, and if anybody detected a hostile, we'd all get a red warning symbol. For now the screen remained clear.

"What have you got?" asked Tanaka.

"First choke point, sir." About five hundred meters to the front rocky cliffs rose out of the forest, perhaps sixty meters high. They stretched in both directions, with a narrow pass-through almost directly to our front.

"Around or through?" asked Tanaka. I pulled my map forward in my display to see how far we'd have to travel to get around it. The platoon leader would have seen it in his map recon and already had his plan. I had a definite thought about which way to go, but I kept it to myself.

"The plan is through, sir. It's a long way to get around it. Cost us an hour," answered the platoon leader.

"Roger," said Tanaka. "I want soldiers up top on both sides. No way do we pass through there without eyes above us."

Not the decision I'd have made.

Something felt off to me about the gap, though I couldn't put my finger on what. I couldn't argue with a decision Tanaka and his platoon leader already made without making them seem weak, so I kept my counsel to myself. But I definitely focused more on my surroundings.

"Roger, sir. I'm not picking up any heat signatures."

"I don't care," said Tanaka. "If you were setting up an ambush, what's the first thing you'd do? You'd make sure there were no visible heat signatures, right?"

"Yes, sir. Got it, sir."

"Get them moving," said Tanaka. "I don't want to lose time." The platoon leader dropped to another frequency and twenty seconds later six soldiers detached from the group and headed off at a mechanically-assisted run toward the cliffs, two groups of three separating as they moved.

"Move out," said the platoon leader. "Half speed. Let's give the scouts time to get up top." A few seconds later, two other soldiers launched fist-sized drones, which hovered for a moment before speeding off through the air toward the cliffs.

I took the opportunity to rejoin Tanaka. "Drones and men on top of the cliffs. You think this is an ambush?"

"I don't know," he said. "Something doesn't feel right."

"I agree. Something is off," I said. "Anything from the other platoons?"

"Nothing. That bothers me too. It's too quiet. We didn't expect anything, but after that fire we took on the way down, I don't know."

"Well, if they're going to hit us, they couldn't pick a better spot," I said. "We landed a good distance out. Their signature looked consolidated from the overhead. But then we saw those three Cappans when we landed, so some of them clearly made it out this way."

He thought about it for a moment. "You hit it, sir. That's what's bothering me. They didn't have time to get out here after they saw us coming. They didn't have a visible vehicle. That means they were probably already out here. If Cappans live out this way, we'd see more. But we haven't. They were here for a reason, even if that reason had nothing to do with us."

"I don't believe in random chance," I said.

"Me either. So what are they doing out here?"

I bit at my lip inside my helmet. "Let's think about the worst case. What would that be?"

"Worst case is . . . they knew we were coming."

"But how?" I asked. I knew the answer, since the Cappans had told me, but it wouldn't do to tell Tanaka that. Best to lead him to it himself.

"I don't know. It seems really unlikely. They could have a spy back on Talca who told them we left. But predicting when we'd get here, given the vagaries of space travel, and knowing where we'd land . . . no chance. Right?"

"It's always best to assume the enemy has more capability than they really do, right?"

"It's improbable, though. Isn't it?" He looked at me, though I couldn't see his face through the faceplate. "I mean . . . at a minimum, it's a stretch."

"Hard to say," I admitted. It *was* a stretch, by any rational analysis. But the Cappans knew we were coming. They'd told me that much. They probably couldn't have known exactly when we'd arrive or what we'd have with us.

We reached the entrance to the pass after a few minutes, slowing further as the scouts struggled to find a way up the cliffs. Even with the assist from their suits it presented a tough climb. We paused to let them clear the position, and the platoon leader reported. "Everything's clean, sir. Drones say there's nothing waiting beyond the cliffs, and scouts say there's nothing up top."

"Roger," said Tanaka. "Move out."

The wedge naturally narrowed into a tighter formation of smaller arrows, four soldiers in each, spread as far as they could in the narrow confines of the terrain. Tanaka and I moved behind the third group of four.

An explosion compressed my chest through my armor, knocking me back a step, followed by a second one less than a second later. I struggled to keep my feet through the concussion.

"Potato mines!" someone yelled over the comm.

Shit. Potato mines were a distinctly Cappan weapon, their low metal content making them almost impossible to detect. We'd found my answer about how the Cappans would respond. They mined the natural avenue of approach.

Tanaka's voice came over the command frequency, broadcasting to the distant platoons. "All units, watch for potato mines. First platoon has contact." His calm impressed me. The natural instinct is to react to the immediate situation, but he kept his overall focus and remembered to inform the entire command.

"Second platoon has contact," came a reply from one of the distant units.

Shit. That sealed it. It made sense that the Cappans defended their position, but it put me in a bad spot, because I'd hoped to link up with them. A mine didn't care who it killed. I wanted to pull up a map and look at the overall situation, assess my options, but I didn't have the time, standing in a minefield. Right now we had a fight, and while it wasn't mine, the fight didn't discriminate. We'd halted, which was standard procedure in a minefield, but that left us stationary and made us easy targets. We had drones, and we had scouts on the cliffs, so the enemy didn't have us covered with direct fire, which took some pressure off. But if they didn't have guns trained on us, that probably meant they had artillery or rockets.

Tanaka and I looked at each other at exactly the same time. We'd both come to the same conclusion. We could either brave the minefield or run away, but we couldn't stay static. "Forward or back?" I asked, on a private channel.

"Forward," he said, without hesitation. "First platoon, move out. Double time. Run!"

I took off running, my first mechanically-assisted step launching me forward. Corporal Matua matched me stride for stride. I wanted to tell him to get clear, as we'd each get caught by a mine the other hit, but I didn't have time. I'd gone maybe six steps when the first rocket whistled in from above. Sometimes it sucks to be right. Dirt churned and bodies flew through the air around me, shrapnel dancing across my vision like a swarm of hot, deadly fireflies. My helmet automatically muted the noise to protect my hearing, which somewhat isolated me, giving the impression of sound coming through a thick wall.

I took long, mechanically-enhanced strides that covered ten meters each, hoping I didn't land on a mine. It was all I could do. The enemy hadn't needed anybody on top of the cliffs. They had a tiny camera somewhere and rockets pre-sighted on the most likely avenue of approach. The next blast threw me sideways, and I thumped hard to the ground, tumbling before I came to a grinding halt. I jumped back to my feet without stopping to assess whether I was hurt or not. Staying put meant death.

I lost track of the explosions. Seven. Maybe eight. I could replay it from my helmet's recording later and figure it out, assuming I made it. Something big slammed into me, lifting me off my feet and slamming me to the ground. A split second later my world erupted in an exploding mass of rock and dirt. I tried to move, but something on top of me held me down.

After a few seconds I calmed down, found some leverage, and I pushed and rolled at the same time. The bulk shifted, and I scooted free. I scrambled to my knees, trying to get to my feet. Anything to get away. It took a moment to register that the thing that had pinned me was an armored body, and another second for my heads-up display to re-synch and tell me it was Matua. I let out a breath in relief as he moved, trying to sit up.

He'd taken a big piece of shrapnel just above the elbow, and it had shredded his armor for around twenty centimeters down toward his wrist, leaving a mush of blood and polymer and bone. I took a knee beside him and put my hand on the shoulder on his good side. He turned his head toward me, and I opened a private channel to him.

"You're going to be okay. We'll get an evacuation bird." The words stuck in my throat a little. Even though he was my captor, I cared what happened to him. "Right now, we've got to get the fuck out of the kill zone. Can you walk?"

"I . . . I don't know." He had the dazed sound of someone who'd been hit hard. I was pretty sure he had put himself between me and that last explosion.

"Try to stand. I'll help you." I took his good arm and pulled, and between us we got him to his feet. He wobbled and almost went back down. "Nope," I said. "I'm going to have to carry you."

"I'm sorry, sir."

"Let's go." I crouched and slung him over both shoulders in a fireman's carry, making sure to get his good arm and leave his damaged one untouched. Without the enhanced strength of my suit I could have never carried the big man. Even wearing it I imagined that I heard the joints creaking as I adjusted his weight. I rocked a little, then started moving. I couldn't run, but I put one foot in front of the other, fearing that if I stopped I'd fall down and never get Matua up again. Another explosion hit behind me, close enough that I felt the compression of the shockwave through my armor. I kept walking, head down.

When I'd gotten clear of the danger area, I set Matua down, leaning his back against a large tree. Sweat poured down my face and neck, and I struggled for breath, despite my temperature-controlled suit.

Combat was for younger men.

"Sir, I'm so sorry."

"What are you talking about, man? You saved my life."

He shook his head almost imperceptibly, seeming to struggle with it. "Not this. The other stuff."

"Don't worry about it. We've all had missions we'd have rather skipped. Right now we've got to get you out of here." I took his med pack from the slot on his good arm and got out the auto-injector. It would slow his metabolism and help him clot. He'd be useless, but it would probably keep him alive until he got to more advanced medical care.

He slurred his words. "You watch your back down here, okay?"

"I always do," I said. Things had gotten harder with Matua out of the fight, but I still had Tanaka and his promise. I still had hope that I'd come out okay, even if I couldn't see the exact path at the moment.

Just like before, all I could do was put one foot ahead of the other and pray something didn't explode.

# CHAPTER TWENTY-EIGHT

CREPT AROUND A smooth-barked tree and scanned for enemies. Our drones had checked the area, but I didn't trust them. I couldn't believe that the Cappans had let us off the hook after the mine ambush. They should have had people here waiting to pick us off while we reorganized after the rockets scattered us, but my display stayed blank—no enemy icons—and an eerie quiet settled in, hanging for several seconds, like a thick blanket. I used the time to check on the points of origin of the rockets. The radar in our suits had tracked a trajectory and back-plotted it to where they'd launched from. All of our suits had the software, and networked together they'd provide an accurate location. My display showed the launch site fifteen kilometers away, meaning they'd fired from the far side of our destination. Somebody had already dispatched one of our drones to the site to get pictures. Flying at one hundred meters per second, it would be there in under three minutes.

Tanaka broke the radio silence with a call over the platoon net. "First platoon, status."

Nobody responded for several seconds, and then an unfamiliar voice came on. "The lieutenant is down. Red Seven is now Red Six. Squad leaders, report." Red Seven. That meant the platoon sergeant, normally second in charge, had taken over the platoon to replace Red Six, the lieutenant, who had been hit. It was Beefy. Each squad reported their casualties, dead, wounded, and the severity of injuries. It took longer than it should have because two of the squad leaders had also been hit, putting their backups in charge. Changing leadership during a mission was a standard procedure, but one that never went one hundred percent smoothly.

"Overall tally: seven dead, eleven wounded. Seven of the wounded need evacuation. One immediately."

"Roger," said Tanaka. "Set up an evacuation point. I'll call in the bird."

A different voice, over the company net this time, brought me back to the big picture. It was one of the other lieutenants. "Sir, this is White Six. Second platoon has casualties."

"Report," said Tanaka.

"Three dead. Fourteen wounded. Minefield, then rockets."

"Roger, White. How many require evac?"

"Twelve, sir."

Tanaka shook his head. I knew what he was thinking. Three dead and twelve evacs from a platoon put them at barely over fifty percent strength and in danger of not being able to complete the mission. All that without reaching what would likely be the hardest

part of the action. To my left, two soldiers had prepared shoulder-fired rockets. They'd be waiting on the
drones to see if there was anything left to shoot at
from the enemy rocket positions.

Tanaka got himself together and contacted third
platoon. "Blue Six, any contact?"

"This is Blue Six. Negative."

"Watch for potato mines. Especially in any choke
points."

"Wilco, sir."

Tanaka went silent for a moment on the net, though
his lips moved under his visor. He was likely calling
in the evacuation ships. Either that or talking to someone on a private channel. Larsson, maybe. It's what I'd
be doing. We'd taken enough casualties where he had
to be considering pulling us out.

After he stopped talking, I keyed a private channel
to him. "What are you thinking?"

"Those rockets were really well coordinated. Accurate, too. They had it dialed in."

"The drone has reached the point of origin," I said.
We both paused to pull up the video feed. Empty rails
sat in a half-meter-deep hole in a clearing. A radar-
scattering tarp lay on the ground. Obviously it had
been covering the rockets right up until they fired. No
signs of life meant that everything had been on remote
control. We had no targets to attack.

"Shit," said Tanaka.

"It was well planned, no doubt," I said. "What now?"

"It's a matter of how much have they got," he said. "If they threw this at us here but don't have anything behind it, it could be that they wanted to try to drive us off. Make us quit."

"Possible," I said. "Would you fight it that way, if you were them?"

"If all I had were some mines and some rockets? Probably. If I could make an attacker believe that this was just the start, I might get him to turn around and run. If I didn't have any ability to fight on the ground . . . yeah, I might play it that way."

He had a good point. It was a coin flip. They either had more surprises or they didn't, and we couldn't know without continuing the mission, unless we got lucky and found something with the drones. "You're right. It could go either way. What's the call?" I asked.

He thought about it for long enough where I almost asked him again, when he answered. "We press on."

"Roger." I had doubts, but I didn't want to share them. He needed his confidence. If that went, we were all fucked. Besides, I had a better chance of escaping if we kept going than I did if we turned back.

We walked for another five minutes when third platoon reported contact.

"Snipers on the high ground," the report came on the company net.

"Roger. How many?" asked Tanaka.

Nobody answered. Good. He shouldn't have asked, though admittedly, it was hard to resist. He wasn't there, so he couldn't help. They had to fight their own fight, and they had a platoon leader plus Larsson to coordinate it. But at the same time, we all held our breath, waiting for a response. Aircraft screamed overhead, our air-support going to help third platoon.

"We should drop some bombs on their living area," said an unidentified soldier over the first platoon net. "That would get them to stop." Nobody responded over the comm, but several heads nodded. I checked the two soldiers with the rocket launchers to make sure they weren't thinking of doing something stupid. Neither appeared ready to fire. Good. There was nothing harder than being shot at with no way to fire back, and nerves were tight.

An explosion sounded a long way off, a faint vibration at our distance. The aircraft had found targets.

"Black six, this is Blue six." The third platoon leader, checking in.

"Go," said Tanaka.

"Three enemy shooters destroyed. Three friendlies dead, one wounded, non-urgent."

"Roger," said Tanaka, and the net went silent.

"Tanaka. I have an idea for an alternate course of action," I said on a private channel.

"I'm all ears," he said.

"This mission is about me negotiating from a position of strength, but we're getting weaker by the minute. If we can work a comms channel with the Cappans from here, we might—"

"Can't do it, sir," he said, cutting me off. "It's outside the mission parameters."

I paused for a moment, discouraged. I'd hoped that if I could get in touch with the Cappans I could tip them off somehow without getting caught. "So change the parameters. You're the commander."

"It's not that simple," he said, frustration in his voice.

"What's the criterion for abort?" I asked.

It took him a moment to respond. "There isn't one."

Shit.

Tanaka didn't mean it literally when he said he had no abort criteria, because at some point we wouldn't have enough combat power to continue and we'd have to quit. But it still made me cringe. He intended to push forward until he couldn't. I'd agreed with him a few minutes ago when we faced mines and rockets, but enemy snipers brought another element. That meant that Cappans had physically entered the fight, and that changed everything. They had fifteen or twenty thousand, and we didn't know how many were armed. Despite our technological advantage, we didn't have close to enough firepower to combat that. But I couldn't argue it with Tanaka, the guy who might be trying to keep me alive. It also fit my desire to get closer to the Cappans. If any of us made it that far.

Still, the deeper implication of his action bothered me. Somebody had enough influence on him to keep him charging forward in a situation where he shouldn't, and his people seemed to follow him without much

grumbling. There must have been a big bonus involved
to keep them moving, given the risk to their own lives.
Maybe it was more than the money. I wasn't a part of
the unit's internal workings, so I couldn't know. Soldiers did things for leaders for reasons that reached
beyond the understanding of outsiders. So many in-
tangible factors played into loyalty that to try to make
sense of it . . . I couldn't. I didn't know the relationships. When Tanaka told us to move out again, I keyed
my comm and said, "Roger."

We left a small detachment of walking wounded
behind to supervise the medical evacuation and moved
out. The soldiers proceeded with even more caution
now, though it would look the same to an untrained
observer. We moved in the same wedge formation
at roughly the same pace, but with a different level
of awareness. One of the soldiers with the shoulder-
launched rockets kept his weapon at the ready. The
next target that presented itself, he'd fire first and ask
questions later. The drones had returned, and they
moved in front of us, flitting across our route about a
kilometer ahead, feeding back sensor readings. I set
my filter to screen out anything except actual enemy
contact, as I found too much data to be overwhelming
during this sort of operation.

Information overload could be a real problem for a
leader. Lieutenants could get so focused on all the systems feeding into their helmets that they missed basic
things going on around them. Everybody drew the
line in a different place, depending on their own capa-

bility and experience. I hoped Tanaka and his officers had it down. It was a weird feeling, rooting for the people who had forced me into this difficult situation, but that's where I found myself. The Cappans weren't really my enemy, and the Omicron soldiers weren't really my friends, but those things became less relevant when the shooting started. The soldiers around me did what they had to do to survive, and I couldn't fault them for that. All the subtleties and politics stopped mattering when you hit the ground humping a rifle. Until I got to a place where I could communicate with Cappans, that wouldn't change.

Even at that moment, with the ambiguous situation hanging over my head, some part of me wanted to be there. A big part. As if somehow risking my life for a dubious cause was a better way to live than sitting comfortably in an air-conditioned corporate building and getting paid. Distantly, I think I recognized the flaw in that thinking, but that sort of self-analysis is better saved for outside of the war zone.

The terrain opened up and flattened, and the trees thinned, making travel easier. We spread out, making ourselves harder targets, and for almost an hour we moved unopposed. Neither of our other units reported contact, either, and I began to give some credence to Tanaka's theory that the Cappans had tried to run us off with an initial defense.

I should have trusted my gut instinct from earlier.

Third platoon reported contact first, and almost before they could finish transmitting, the second platoon leader came up on the feed and reported enemy action as well.

Tanaka didn't ask questions this time, instead waiting for further reports. We had our support aircraft still circling overhead, but without knowing which platoon had it worse, Tanaka didn't direct them. He'd be looking at the feeds generated from each platoon, trying to figure out what we faced at each location and who needed help more.

The head of the soldier in front of me exploded.

"Contact, thirty degrees. Sniper!" I couldn't tell who made the report. I didn't care. I hit the ground as two more shots snapped past before return fire from the soldiers around me drowned them out. Red blips appeared on my heads-up. Enemy. Near me, the *fwoosh* of rockets launching cut through the gunfire. Our man with the rocket launcher didn't hold back.

"Three enemy destroyed." Another unknown voice. The ridiculousness of it all grabbed at me. Disembodied voices telling me things I already knew from my display. Reporting death that had already happened. Thankfully, I didn't have time to think about it, to process. I sighted through my weapon, increasing the magnification, searching for a target. I locked in on a Cappan with a rifle. I pulled the trigger, but the alien jerked just before I fired, already hit.

More muzzle flashes flared from our left, too many for me to count manually, but the feed in my helmet put the number at twenty-three. The enemy had us in a crossfire, hitting us in an L shape. Textbook ambush.

Somehow they had avoided the drones and our sensors in order to surprise us. I lost that thought when the first rockets slammed into our position, throwing up dirt and wood splinters and sending an armored body careening into the air. I scanned for Tanaka while hugging the ground. We needed orders, but the company and platoon net both stayed silent. I found him, forty meters away, on one knee, firing at the new group of targets. I started crawling that direction while opening a private feed.

An explosion rocked the ground in front of Tanaka, flinging him backward five or six meters. His back slammed into a large tree trunk, where he hung for a moment, absurdly pinned to the wood, before crumpling to the ground in a heap. Without thinking I leaped up off my belly and covered the ground to him in a few mechanically-aided steps. Something thwacked against the back of my armor as I reached him, loud, but I barely felt it. My system didn't show any warnings, so I said a quick thanks to good technology and evaluated Tanaka. One of his arms was bent up under him in a way that humans shouldn't bend, but his battered suit sent a signal to mine that said he was alive.

I tried to position myself between him and the bulk of the enemy fire based on what my computer told me about their location. Five red blips remained on my heads-up. They'd had the surprise, but once we found them, our superior weaponry took its toll, though several blue icons had gone dark, too. I pushed everything but the essentials to the background so I could focus on Tanaka. I grabbed the med kit out of the slot on the shoulder armor of his good arm and activated it. The twelve seconds that it required to do a diagnostic scan on him crept by as if measured by a sundial. When the screen finally flashed, I winced at the readout. Broken ribs, the damaged arm that I could see, and at least one cracked vertebra.

I didn't want to move him, but we couldn't remain stationary, either. There were enough red dots still shooting at us to be dangerous, and more joining them. Perhaps twenty meters away lay a mangled soldier, but my eyes passed over him in favor of the rocket launcher lying a few centimeters outside the reach of his dead arms. It looked intact. I sprinted to it, pressed the synchronize button, and waited the three seconds it took to link with my helmet. Bullets skipped off the ground near my feet, and I jumped by instinct, for all the good that would do. I checked the weapon and found it unloaded.

Shit.

I rolled the dead soldier over and fumbled through his pack, finding the last rocket box. I'm not ashamed to admit that I hid behind his body, lying on my back, while I fitted the large cartridge into the launcher. I popped up to my knees and pointed it in the general direction of the largest group of red icons, angling it upward at sixty degrees, and fired. The rocket *whooshed* away with very little recoil, and I couldn't help following its briefly glowing trajectory. When it reached its apex, it popped in a small puff of smoke, and six submunitions streaked downward toward the enemy, homing in on them from the feed in my helmet. The warheads didn't carry much explosive—maybe half a kilogram each—but with precision guidance, they didn't need much. Several more red icons winked out, and the enemy fire slowed to a trickle.

I sprinted back to Tanaka, kneeled beside him, and pressed his med kit against him where his armor had peeled away. It vibrated in my hand as it injected him with stabilizers that would hopefully keep him alive. He was done for this fight, but if I could get him back to the ship, they could put him back together. I got his weight positioned on my shoulders much like I had with Matua and struggled to my feet. Jostling him when he had a cracked vertebra might paralyze him, but it beat death.

Something smashed into my back, spinning me and throwing me forward onto my knees. Tanaka's limp form tumbled away from me, almost seeming like slow motion. It didn't matter. He'd taken the brunt of the pulse blast I'd felt, and it had scorched his armor, leaving a smoking hole. I kneeled there for several seconds, maybe longer. When I finally gathered myself, the shooting had stopped.

"Captain Tanaka is down," I said, first over the first platoon net and then over the company frequency.

"First platoon, what's your status?" The response came after a few seconds. A female voice. Larsson. With Tanaka down, that put her in command. My life had just gotten worse. Not as bad as Tanaka's, though.

Nobody answered. After several seconds, I thought about giving the report myself, but something in my gut told me not to. After a while longer, she asked again, this time on the first platoon net. Smart. All the leaders who were on the company net were probably down, so nobody had heard her when she broadcast there.

"Ma'am . . . this is Sergeant Kapoor. I don't know who's in charge. Red six is down, so is red seven. We've got . . . I don't know. Maybe six of us left. They were everywhere. Estimate a hundred and fifty enemy. Maybe more. We kept shooting them, but they kept coming."

The net stayed silent for a few seconds before she responded. "Is Colonel Butler still with you?"

"I'm here," I said.

"Secure him, and continue on the initial course," she said.

"What the fuck are you talking about?" I couldn't hold my tongue. "We need to abort this miss—"

My transmitter cut off. After a few seconds of silence, it became apparent that she'd shut my receiver down, too. I couldn't talk or hear. The sudden isolation disoriented me for a moment in a way that the combat never had. I recovered my wits quickly and stalked over to Kapoor, who was ostensibly in charge of what was left of our unit. Bodies lay strewn throughout the trees. Somebody moved on the ground to my left, and

I turned that way instead. I needed to think before I acted. I might get only one shot with Kapoor, and I needed to make it count.

Blood seeped down the legs of the soldier's armor—a woman—from a crack at her waist. I pulled her med pack and ran a scan. She had no chance. I worked her helmet off and placed the med pack against her neck, waiting for the pop of the injection. It couldn't save her, but at least she'd be comfortable in her last minutes.

I don't know how I ended up sitting, or how long I'd been there. It . . . there was too much. The death. I remembered it from previous battles, I had the dreams, but here . . . I sat in a daze, unable to move.

I yelled into my dead microphone and the sound rattled inside my helmet. I yelled and I yelled until my throat hurt, and then I was crying.

I lost track of how long I sat there before I stopped. Probably not long. A soldier moved into my line of sight and instinct kicked in. I pulled myself together. We were still in combat, and there was no time, so I mashed all the crap back down inside and struggled to my feet.

I needed to know about the other units, if they'd been hit as hard as we had. If they were, someone would talk some sense into Larsson. We didn't have ten soldiers left who could walk in our platoon. We had wounded we needed to evacuate. If Larsson tried to press forward, the soldiers wouldn't follow her orders. Not now. Not after what we'd gone through.

A shadow crossed my faceplate again and I looked up to see a soldier—my suit identified her as Kapoor—gesturing with her rifle for me to get up. Then a second soldier joined her, and relieved me of my weapon. What the fuck were they thinking? We needed every shooter we could get if we were going to make it off this planet alive. If they understood, if they cared, they didn't show it. Or at least I couldn't hear them. I didn't know what Larsson ordered, or if they'd pushed back at all. What she'd promised them. I was a prisoner, plain and simple, but worse than that was the isolation. Not knowing.

I had no doubt that Larsson meant to kill me. But if that was the case, one of the soldiers could have just shot me. Maybe they balked. Maybe she didn't give them the order because she didn't want to test their loyalty. She could have them bring me to her, and she could do it herself. I considered attacking one of the soldiers, going for a weapon, but that would provoke them. Regardless of their orders, they *hadn't* shot me, and I didn't want to change that. This had ceased to be a combat mission for me and turned into a hostage situation once more.

Of course nobody had told the Cappans that. I started to form the basics of a plan. When they attacked again, that would be my chance. I didn't know where I'd go, stranded on a mostly deserted planet, but I'd use the confusion and get away. Maybe I could hide out and wait for the humans to leave. I could take my chances with the Cappans.

# CHAPTER TWENTY-NINE

WE SORTED THROUGH the carnage of what used to be our platoon. I did my part, helping tend to the wounded. I might have been a glorified prisoner, but I was still a soldier, and so were they, regardless of if they served on the wrong side. I had no right to judge. For all that they'd done since they signed on for this mission, I'd done much worse in the past. I'm a hypocrite, but not *that* much of one.

We separated the dead from the wounded, marked a landing zone, and left the injured but ambulatory to supervise evacuation. They'd be safe enough once the ships could finally make it to our location. I couldn't hear the communication, but I assumed the other units had taken heavy casualties as well. Five of us remained mostly uninjured from our platoon.

Somebody must have decided that it was inconvenient not to be able to speak to me, as a channel opened up and Sergeant Kapoor spoke. The sound of another human voice lifted me, though my situation still sucked. "You still don't have comm access to the command nets, but you can respond on the private channel if somebody else opens it."

"Thanks." I had a dozen other replies ready, from berating to begging, but that's all that came out. Probably smart.

"We're going to move out, soon. I hope you're not going to give us trouble, sir."

"What's the plan?" I asked.

"Don't know," she said. "XO has an idea, but she's not telling us much. We're heading to the original objective."

"To do what? There are five of us and we've got three klicks to go. Who knows what lies in between?"

"Scans show nothing, for whatever that's worth." Her tone said that she understood that the Cappans had been fooling our scans all day, so I didn't push it. But I couldn't just let this lunacy go.

"Why keep going? Why not make the call yourself to abort?" I kept my voice neutral, no judgment. I was curious more than anything, trying to figure out what could keep a soldier moving forward in such a ridiculous situation.

"Because if we don't, there's no exfiltration coming. Not for us, not for the wounded."

"What?" I didn't believe it.

"Exactly what I said, sir. If we keep moving, they evacuate the wounded. If not, then we all sit here together until . . . well, until who knows what."

"Holy shit," I said. "Tough call."

"Not really. Look around." She gestured at the group of dead soldiers at the other side of the clearing. "You think we're not expendable here?"

"This is fucked up."

She nodded. "Yep. I guess we deserved it, though. Picked up a lot of paychecks on easy missions in the past. The bill always comes due though, right?"

"Can I at least have my rifle back?" I asked. "If we get into it again, I can help. I promise I won't shoot any of you."

"I can't."

"If you die, I die. You're my only ticket off of this planet. Let me help save my own life."

She thought about it for a moment. I tried to make out if her lips were moving, if she was asking for another opinion via her comm, but the light glinted off her faceplate, obscuring my view. "Promise that you won't run."

I thought about it for a split second. "I promise I won't try to get away from *you* or do anything to harm your mission. This group here. But if you run, I'm running with you. And if you're all dead, all bets are off."

"Deal." She walked over and got my rifle. "Get yourself as much ammo as you can carry, too."

"Thanks." I went to the pile where we'd collected the platoon's ammunition. I had most of my load, still, but I grabbed some more. Explosive, mostly. With just a few of us, I wanted all the firepower I could muster, little as it was. I meant what I promised Kapoor. She was in this as deep as I was, though for different reasons, and it appeared that our way out lay in the same direction for the moment. If that path diverged sometime in the future, I'd reevaluate.

We set a quick pace, jogging, though the suits made it almost effortless. Somewhere along the way we'd lost one of our drones, but we flew the other one low, zipping in and out of the trees in front of us, for all the good it had done so far. Overhead the engines of our support aircraft echoed, too far away to be distinct or even to allow me to pinpoint them. But close enough to respond.

The woods ended at the crest of a steep drop that fell away about thirty or forty meters into a depression probably ten or twelve kilometers across. Hundreds of off-white, prefabricated buildings sat in not-so-neat groupings that almost resembled small villages, with narrow swaths of grass separating one group from another. We'd arrived unmolested. The Cappans had to know we were close, if not our exact location, but nothing moved other than the calf-high grass rippling in the breeze.

I upped the magnification in my helmet and scanned the area and made an awkward hand-signal to Kapoor to move the drone forward into the bowl to give us video. Here and there tools or other implements leaned against buildings, the remnants of life. Somebody lived here and had been present recently, but nothing specifically suggested the Cappans had been around in the last few hours. Perhaps they'd evacuated when we landed. It would make sense, since we could have easily used rockets and aircraft to attack their vulnerable living area.

"Contact," said Kapoor. A second later, enemy

icons appeared on my display. I used that to guide my search and located half a dozen Cappans in an almost hidden position on the right-most edge of the encampment relative to our location.

"Got them," I said. "Can't tell if they have weapons."

"Assume they do," she said, unnecessarily.

"We have orders?" I asked. The Cappans were out of rifle range, so we had limited options.

"Sit tight and wait," she said. "Observe."

I sighed and went back to scanning. I identified a second outpost of Cappans, this one better hidden— nearly underground, they had dug in so well. I had my system populate the master feed with red icons so the others could see them. I didn't have time to further assess as a group of blue icons appeared, and then almost immediately another, smaller group. The remnants of the two other platoons had come into range. Judging by their numbers, they'd been hit almost as hard as we had. Seven in one group, ten in the other. With our five the total number stood at twenty-two out of an original hundred and sixty. That put us right around an eighty-five percent casualty rate, which well exceeded what any unit could expect to take and still function. But here we were, continuing. If we had been the good guys, people would call it heroic.

We weren't the good guys.

As if to punctuate that thought, the roar of aircraft grew as both our support birds came in fast. I hoped it was just for a show of force. My stomach twisted when they each dropped two objects. The bombs almost appeared to float, like they were leaves on the breeze and not two hundred kilograms of metal and explosive and death. But they only seemed to float because of the speed of the ships that released them and the horror of watching something terrible but inevitable. They slammed into the ground all within two seconds of each other, flashing as they hit and throwing up dirt and chunks of polymer from one little group of structures at the outside of the encampment. The wall of one building, seemingly intact, flew some fifty meters into the air, tumbling several times before falling back to the ground. The sound reached us a couple seconds later, four distinct crunches followed by smaller thuds of falling debris.

The aircraft gained altitude, banked, and headed back toward us on another pass. I flipped my helmet to maximum magnification and scanned the wreckage, but I didn't see any bodies.

"What the hell is she doing?" I asked, forgetting that my microphone was dead. Destroying the settlement wouldn't get us what we needed unless the mission had changed to simple retaliation. I didn't think it had. In theory, someone in those buildings held the key to a multibillion-mark industry. Rational people didn't throw something like that away. Corporations definitely didn't, and I had no doubt that Omicron still held the strings on the mission, one way or another.

The aircraft bore down again before pulling off at the last moment, banking hard and moving into a racetrack pattern, circling the area without ever leaving view. A moment later I understood why, as a loud-speaker sounded from the top of the bowl, maybe ninety degrees around to our left, nearest where the bombs hit.

"Attention! We want to meet with your leadership. You have five minutes to agree or our ships will drop more bombs." It took me a few seconds to realize the words were in Cappan, and I was hearing a translation. Apparently Larsson hadn't shut down that function of my helmet.

For at least two minutes, nothing moved in the set-tlement below us. I wondered if anybody occupied any of the buildings. If the leaders that Larsson demanded to meet had evacuated, it would be a rough day for the Cappan settlement. It did beg the question, though. If they weren't here, where were they? And would de-stroying their homes matter? Someone in my group pointed, and I followed it to a door that had opened in a building. I hadn't noticed it before because of the identical color and prefabricated material, but the building was perhaps four times larger than the other structures. I found myself holding my breath, though I don't know what I expected to happen.

Three Cappans emerged, moved away from the building and waved. I couldn't tell if they meant it as a signal to identify themselves or as a method to forestall the next attack. With only a loudspeaker for communication, we couldn't know.

"We see you," said the loudspeaker. "Wait there and do not move. We will come to you. If anybody fires on us, we will destroy you and your entire settlement."

She lost me. Larsson had to be making some sort of play to get the information, but it appeared to be a sort of mutually assured destruction, assuming she meant to go down herself, which I expected she would. It was a pretty big risk to assume that the Cappans valued their settlement enough to hold their fire. Not something I'd want to bet my life on, which Larsson was doing.

"Let's go," Sergeant Kapoor said, startling me out of my thoughts.

"Me?" I asked.

"You and me," she said. "The others will stay here and provide cover."

"Okay. What's my role?" Larsson might have still wanted me to broker the deal, but she'd resorted to threats, so I didn't have a lot of latitude left with which to work.

"Come with me and don't do anything stupid," said Kapoor.

I wanted to ask, *Like walk into the open without a plan?* but just said, "Roger." Either she didn't know, or she wasn't telling. Regardless, it wouldn't help me to argue.

The steep grade would have been difficult without the assistance of our armor, but our heels dug into the soft parts, making easy, if awkward work of loose dirt and the sixty-degree slope. We reached the bottom of the basin and the first buildings, which measured about three meters by four meters for the most part, though from up close a couple of them were slightly bigger than the others. I peered in a few of the clear polymer windows. From about a dozen buildings, one set of eyes looked back. They'd evacuated, but not completely, which made me wonder if the stay-behinds were part of a plan or had refused to leave. I pushed that out of my head. The Cappans had their reasons, and I couldn't influence them.

We reached what I now considered the command center of the Cappan encampment at the same time as Larsson, who came with two soldiers trailing her. The three Cappans hadn't moved. I'm horrible at reading Cappan body language, but they gave me the impression of calm, which I took as a good sign. Rash decisions at this point on either side would end only one way, and not a good one.

"Are you in charge?" Larsson asked. We all stood a few meters apart, roughly in a triangle. Me and Kapoor, the Cappans, and Larsson and her muscle. I'd have felt a lot better if Tanaka had made it.

"This way," said the Cappan standing slightly ahead of the other two, and he headed toward the building. Larsson followed without hesitation. I looked at Kapoor, who shrugged, then started after them. Larsson's two guards stopped outside, which I assumed was at her order. Kapoor gestured for me to go in, and then she peeled off and waited with the other two, but not before she took my rifle. Larsson must have had a lot of confidence in her plan, going in with just the two of us, and me unarmed. I wondered what she knew that I didn't.

It took a second for my faceplate to lighten in the dimmer interior. A lone Cappan waited for us at the end of a long, rectangular room. Computer terminals lined the walls, eight or nine on each side, but nobody sat in the chairs in front of them. When we reached the Cappan he had a yellow circle around one eye, and though he was dressed differently, I recognized him from our previous meeting back on Talca. I kept my face neutral, but I smiled on the inside. Whatever Larsson knew that I didn't, I had at least one thing on her to make up for it.

"Greetings," she said.

"To you as well," said the Cappan. "Would that it could have been under better circumstances."

"Indeed. But there's still time to salvage the situation."

The Cappan cocked his head slightly. "That would be good. We have both lost enough soldiers."

"We've brought you a gift," said Larsson. "This is Colonel Butler. The destroyer of your world."

My heart pounded in my chest, not because I was offended at being a bargaining chip. I'd been that from the start. Instead, I worried that the Cappan leader would give away that we'd met before, ruining my one advantage.

"You have caused my people much suffering," he said.

"I'm very sorry for that," I said.

"If you give us the information we want, we will leave him with you, to do with as you see fit," said Larsson.

"That is a generous offer," said the Cappan. "But he is here now. You bargain with what we already have."

"My people are still out there," said Larsson. "More importantly, they're still orbiting overhead. If I don't come out with the data I require, they have orders to level this entire island."

So that was the game. They never wanted me to negotiate. They wanted me as barter. For his part, the Cappan's expression didn't change, almost as if he expected her response. He had to have known she wouldn't be without contingencies. He'd as much as told me that he expected this threat. Since my meeting with the Cappan back on Talca, I understood now what I had failed to understand in past years. The Cappans always knew more than we gave them credit for. "Colonel Butler, what is your opinion on this?"

"His opinion doesn't matter," said Larsson.

"It does," said the Cappan. "He knows your people, and how much I can trust them."

"You can't trust them at all," I said.

Larsson turned on me and glared through her clear faceplate, but she was stuck. She'd promised me to the Cappans as a prize, so she couldn't do anything without jeopardizing her proposed offer. I appreciated the opportunity her mistake gave me. "You don't know what you're talking about," she said.

"Sure I do," I said. "As soon as you get what you came for and get off the planet, you're going to lay waste to it anyway."

"Why would we do that? We'd have the technology we want. That's the job."

I turned and looked to the Cappan and spoke to him. "To cover their tracks. If they were serious about their offer, they'd be offering to work together on the project. The Cappans solved more of this in two years than humans solved in twenty. But they can't do that, politically."

"He's lying," said Larsson.

I continued to ignore Larsson, keeping eye contact with the Cappan instead. He was the key to everything. She didn't matter. I'd felt a small connection with him back on Talca, and hoped that he'd felt it too—hoped that he'd act on it.

"He's lying to save his own skin," Larsson repeated, a slight tremor seeping into her voice.

I shook my head. "I gave up on that the moment I walked out of Haverty's office. This ends only one way for me. I just want to do some good before I go."

"He's—" Larsson bit back her response. I could almost see her mind working. "If I don't get what I came for, that's the end of this settlement and all your people on this planet."

"And if she does get what she came for, it's still the end. Why give up your one bargaining chip?"

Larsson raised her rifle toward me. I took a step back, for all the good that would do. I should have seen her response coming, provoking her like that. Then again, she should have shot me an hour ago instead of trying to use me in a false deal. Larsson's face had a look of mixed determination and hatred . . . and then it exploded with two soft pops, gunshots muted by something in the design of the room. I stumbled backward, blood and bits of bone and brain matter spattering my faceplate. One of the Cappans stood behind Larsson, rifle following her body as it sagged to the floor like a sack of dirt.

"The soldiers outside—"

The Cappan with the eye patch waved his hand, cutting me off. "Have been dealt with." I didn't know if that meant they were dead or alive. I hadn't heard shots, but with the soundproofing in the walls, that didn't mean anything. "Those on the ridge, too."

"There's still the ship in orbit," I said. "It carries XM-25s."

"It is as you said. That was always our fate. We have evacuated most of our people underground. We will hope that the damage is limited."

I thought about it. Being underground would help, but it didn't matter. If they survived, Omicron would keep coming back. There was too much money involved for them not to. They were doomed no matter what.

Or maybe not.

"What if there was another way?" I asked.

"I am listening."

# CHAPTER THIRTY

THE NEXT FEW minutes passed in a blur. I didn't know how long we had before the ship would open fire if they didn't hear from Larsson. For everything that had gone on down on the planet, the things that mattered now were spaceside. I hoped that having their own people down here would make them hesitate to pull the trigger, but given what I'd seen of the mercenary group so far, I wouldn't have bet too much on it. It took a Cappan technician almost eight minutes to hack my helmet and get my communication functionality back, and I used that time to propose my plan to the Cappan leader.

"So you want us to simply give away the information," he said, when I finished.

"I think it's our only option. I thought so back when we talked on Talca, and I'm more convinced of it now. Once the information is out there and everybody has it, there's no reason to come after you anymore."

"And you're sure you can get it out in that manner?"

"I'll need your help," I said. "You have people who can get a message to someone off planet, right?"

"Yes, we can manage that. It's difficult to do without it being intercepted, but while they can likely detect it, they can't stop it."

"Then help me get a message to Karen Plazz. I'll write something for you, and you include whatever you want her to know. She'll get it to the rest of the galaxy."

He thought about it for a moment. "Draft your message. I will decide after. And hurry. I do not think we have much time."

I'd thought what I'd say through in my head several times before that moment, so it didn't take me long.

*Karen,*

*Sorry I've been out of contact, but I was kidnapped by Omicron, with the willing participation of VPC—you probably read about their "joint venture"—to go on a mission to extort technology from a Cappan colony. I'm not identifying that location in order to protect the Cappans, though they may choose to share it, and the corporations already know. Omicron has been stealing technology from the Cappans and experimenting on their people in order to facilitate medical research in something called the Phoenix Project. The Cappans perfected the technique that Colonel Elliot was working on back when we were on Cappa—the procedure that helps humans assimilate ortho-robotics. Everything that follows this message is from the Cappans themselves.*

*You can trust what they say is the truth. Please distribute it as widely as possible. Know that if something happens to this group of Cappans, it was Omicron that did it. They have XM-25s on their ship, and they intend to use them. Please hold this for ninety-six hours after you receive it before making anything public.*

*One final request—and this is the most important thing I'm going to say: there's a former employee of VPC named Ganos. She helped me get to this point in the operation, and I have reason to believe that Omicron and/or VPC have targeted her. They might already have her. Find her and keep her safe, whatever the cost. Consider it my price for this information. If a human with Cappan DNA named Sasha contacts you, trust her.*

*Carl*

I showed it to Eye Patch. He nodded. "We will use our assets to keep Ganos safe as well. But I do not understand the ninety-six hours."

"If everything goes to plan, the crew of the ship in orbit will have completed their mission and be headed home by then. They'll be in stasis, so they'll be unable to receive messages once the information becomes public."

"But it will not matter, if they have already fired their missiles."

"Leave that part to me," I said. "I have a plan. But I need to know where your underground locations are."

Eye Patch looked at me with what, if he had been a human, I'd have assumed to be incredulity. "You are asking for a lot of trust."

"I am. But you chose me, back on Talca. Something made you do that."

The Cappan stared at me, and I had to assume he was thinking. Finally, he asked, "You are sure you can protect us?"

"I'm not," I said. "But if I can get back to that ship, I'm the best chance you have."

He stepped away from me then and called to one of his compatriots. They talked in hushed tones, raising their voices once, the newcomer gesturing with his hands, angry. After several minutes of discussion he came back. "We will show you what you want to know. But only you can leave. The others stay here."

"I need to take them with me. As many as possible."

He shook his head. "You ask too much. We trust you, but giving up the soldiers is imprudent."

"What will happen to them?"

"They will be with us. If we live, they live."

I nodded. "What about after?"

"We will need to keep them with us. They will be unharmed, and allowed to live freely. Hopefully there will be a time in the future where we can release them."

I sighed. I was condemning the soldiers to a life in captivity if I allowed the Cappans to keep them. More significant to my plan, with troops alive on the planet, Omicron, and more immediately the ship in orbit, would have more reason to revisit. These soldiers had friends up there, and when you brought emotion into the equation, it changed the calculus. "If they think their own people are still alive down here, they're going to come back for them. It's important to our plan that they don't."

"We could kill them," said Eye Patch.

I tried not to cringe. Despite our recent understanding, there were still some serious differences in how I and the Cappans saw morality. I had to remind myself that these were people who hung their own dead on poles as a warning. "Or you could make it *seem* like they're dead. The sensors in their suits. You'll need to disable the location function anyway. It wouldn't be that much more to alter the other sensors too."

Again he thought on it. "That we could do."

I nodded and turned away, trying to hide my relief. I couldn't let myself get so caught up in working together that I forgot we weren't completely on the same team. I did want to help them, and I think they saw that, but it went only so far. "Then all that's left is to show me your evacuation sites."

"What will you do after that?"

"I'm going to escape with the data, and try to make the people spaceside believe me."

**I SCURRIED UP** the embankment, my feet slipping in the dirt, small chunks of rock skittering down behind me until I reached the top and headed into the forest. I jogged for a kilometer and a half before I initiated contact with the ship. I wanted it to look like I tried to get far enough away from the Cappans to give myself a buffer before I risked a call, as if I feared them tracking me by my signal. The Cappans would start chasing me as soon as I made contact, helping to complete the illusion.

"*Basilisk*, this is Butler." I did my best to put some desperation into my voice. Nobody answered. I checked the channel and tried again. "*Basilisk*, this is Colonel Butler. Come in."

"Go ahead, sir."

"I've got the data."

There was a hesitation on the net, longer than the second or so that it took the message to travel to orbit and back. "Say again."

"The data. The mission. The thing we came here for. I've got it!"

"How?"

"Larsson had it before they killed her. She suspected their treachery and passed it to me. When our troops came in, I ran away in the distraction. I don't know if they're chasing me or not. I could really use a pickup."

Another pause. "Is there anybody else alive?"

"I don't know. Nothing's showing on my sensors, but I'm away from the last known location and moving farther by the minute." It was a blatant lie, but it would force them to check their own systems and reach their own conclusions. They'd believe it more that way. They wouldn't trust me, but they'd trust their machines more than they should. I needed a lot of things to go right for my deception to work, and any one of them failing would blow my plan, so everything I could add in my favor helped.

"We're not picking up any vital signs either. But there are Cappans moving in your direction."

"Shit. Where?" I asked.

"About a klick and a half behind you. They're probably picking up the energy from your transmission. Switch your comm into receive only. They won't be able to track it as easily."

"Roger," I said.

"We're sending coordinates to your heads-up. Move to that location now. Pickup is in fourteen minutes. No response required. Just get there."

My computer calculated the location in a split second and put it on my display. At my current pace I'd reach it with two minutes to spare. I changed direction to the left by nineteen degrees and kept running. The low gravity and my suit feeding me oxygen and powering my legs made travel almost thoughtless—it also helped that I wasn't actually being chased. Those mindless minutes allowed me to run through every scenario that I could envision, knowing I couldn't possibly think of them all. Something would come up that I didn't plan for. Basically, I'd be playing a role from the minute I saw another human until we got a final decision. Or until they vented me out an air-lock. That was a real possibility, regardless if my plan worked, but I found that it didn't bother me. There's something freeing about expecting to die. If I could save the Cappans, I'd call it a success, whatever else happened.

It sounds like bullshit. I know that. A lot of people say they're ready to face death but balk when they actually reach that point. But my life didn't matter anymore. I didn't want to die. I wasn't actively seeking it. But I didn't really want to live, either. If somehow I did survive, I'd have to work out that feeling with Dr. Baqri. One more thing on a long list.

I reached the coordinates and went to one knee at the edge of the clearing, scanning back the direction I'd come for my Cappan "pursuit." They wouldn't catch me since they weren't actually trying to, but I needed to get in the habit of making everything look exactly right. There was almost no chance that any human could see me at that moment, at least not with enough fidelity to see which way I had my rifle pointed. But almost no chance isn't the same as zero chance. I had to take every tiny opportunity I could to eliminate potential exposure. They added up.

The drop ship came in fast, the pilot probably still remembering the anti-aircraft fire that we'd taken on our initial assault on the planet. I wish I'd thought to have the Cappans fire at the ship to make it look better. Probably a good thing I didn't, since with my luck they would have hit it accidentally, ruining everything.

I started sprinting for the craft before it touched down. Reaching the door as it opened, I hurried through, stumbling and ending up on the floor as the ship rose before I got firmly set. Two soldiers helped me to a seat and got me strapped in while another manned a manual pulse cannon, scanning the area we'd just departed. I watched her out of the corner of my eye to see if she fired, to see if she'd picked up the pursuing Cappans. She didn't.

I popped my helmet off now that I was inside the ship, which had its own oxygen supply, and ran my hand over my bald head, wiping the sweat away. Somebody tossed me a towel and I used it thoroughly on my head and neck, taking the time to prepare my opening lines.

"What happened down there, sir?" one of the soldiers who'd helped me asked. He was short, with hair so light that it bordered on white. He looked young, no wrinkles around his eyes, but then everybody on the mission looked young compared to me.

"I've got no fucking idea." The simpler the answer, the easier it is to lie.

"How did—"

"People died," I said, cutting him off before he could finish his question. I said it slowly, in a tone combat veterans would recognize. The tone that accompanied the thousand-kilometer stare of a man who had seen too much. "Just . . . everybody. Fucking rockets, snipers, and potato mines. We should have pulled out."

He watched me for a minute, but not in the way a suspicious interrogator would. More like a soldier—and probably one who agreed with me. That's what I needed them to do. See me as a soldier. Good thing I'd had some practice in the role. For whatever reason, he didn't speak again, and nobody else on the ship approached me. I took that to mean that I'd passed the first test, which was the easiest part, to be sure, but a necessary one. Next would come my meeting with the Ops officer. Since my meeting with Lieutenant Danner had been cut off by Larsson, I hadn't had a chance to get to know him, and now I needed him for the next part of my plan. He'd been in charge of the team left back on the ship. Now he was the commander of the whole mission. More important, he'd be the one communicating back to Omicron for orders.

And he'd probably be the one to operate the airlock if they decided to float me into space.

We landed on the *Basilisk* and waited for the bay to refill with air. I stayed in my seat for a little longer than necessary, letting everyone else unbuckle. I didn't know my status and I didn't want to ask. Their actions would tell me if they saw me as a prisoner or not. I assumed yes but hoped for no. When nobody came to help me out after a few seconds, I unbuckled my belts and stood. I fell in with the others and moved down the ramp, scanning ahead for Danner. Nobody waited for us other than the flight support team, who rushed around checking the exterior of the ship, refueling, and doing the hundred other things they did every time a ship docked. The crew went about their business, ignoring me, which threw me a little. Even if I wasn't a prisoner, I had the data that defined our entire mission. That alone should have been worthy of attention.

Still confused but needing to move, I followed the group as they proceeded to the gear removal room, and I got myself out of my armor with a little help from the guy who'd spoken to me. From there I went to decon in a mini-unit that held three soldiers at a time, which would have been a pain for an entire platoon, but worked fine for me and my lone helper. I'd been on the ground and he'd touched me. I'd forgotten about decon. Even carrying critical information, there were safety protocols for interacting with alien planets. That explained why nobody had approached me. I used the seven-minute procedure as a reprieve.

Danner waited for me when I came out. He wasn't smiling, but he did look happy to see me, in that way that soldiers have. "You need something to eat, sir, or can we get right to your debriefing?" Professional. No bullshit. No way to tell yet if that was good or bad.

"I could use a cup of coffee," I said. "But there's no reason we can't talk at the same time."

He nodded and a soldier behind him hurried off, probably to fetch my beverage. What I really wanted was a drink, but I had to keep my mind sharp. I'd drink when I knew my fate, not before. Once they'd made their decision, I'd get good and drunk.

If I was going out an airlock, I'd be doing it with a buzz.

**I SAT WITH** Danner at a round table, not across from him, but sort of by his side. He picked the seats and then said, "This isn't an interrogation. We're just talking." Exactly what I would have done if I were interrogating someone.

"First things first, sir. You said you had the data?"

"It's in my suit," I said, knowing that they probably already had gone through it and found the chip. I'd taken it from Larsson's body and had the Cappans load it, which fit my story. "I didn't want to take it through decon. I don't know how those things work, but no reason to take a chance, right?"

"Of course, sir. We're going to get it uploaded and send it back to Talca to make sure it's what they need."

"Great," I said. I assumed I had what they wanted, but at that moment, for whatever reason, it flashed through my mind that I had no idea. The Cappans could have loaded anything. Shit, it could be blank, and I wouldn't know it.

"You okay, sir?"

"Yeah. I hope we got the data. All those deaths . . . I don't know if it's worth it, but at least they wouldn't be meaningless."

He nodded. "Yeah. What the hell happened?"

"We got chewed up the whole way. I'm sure you saw the reports." I paused. "Shit was bad. Potato mines . . . I hate those fucking things."

He sat, his face not changing, waiting for me to continue.

"When we got to their encampment, our birds dropped bombs on some of their structures. For a minute that seemed to take the life out of them. They stopped shooting back, and that's when Larsson made the call to go forward to retrieve the information." I did my best to ensure I included everything they could verify. I wanted to keep the lie as small as possible.

"We saw that," he said.

"Kapoor took me down and we linked up with Larsson. They took us inside, and they agreed to give us the data. Then . . . I don't know. People started fucking shooting in an enclosed space. Larsson . . . she was hit, but she took a couple of them down, too. We ended up behind an overturned table and she passed me the data. Her leg was wrecked. I guess she figured I had a better chance of getting away. Last I saw she was providing cover fire, and . . . I don't know. I figured they'd chase me, but they didn't. She's a fucking hero." I added the last touch off the top of my head.

Danner's face relaxed slightly, which led me to believe he'd bought it. The sketchy part was the data handoff, but the Larsson-as-hero thing covered some of that up. They'd want to believe that about her. People always wanted to believe in heroes, though the truth of the stories rarely lived up to the myth. Somewhere somebody would know that she and I didn't get along, so my positive report about her would hold even more credibility.

Of course it wasn't really Danner that I had to fool. He was the second gate. The real test came back at Omicron, and I had almost no way to influence that except through Danner. "We'll know in a few minutes whether the data is good. Let me go update home station with your debrief." He didn't add that he'd be requesting guidance on what to do with me, also, but then again he didn't need to. I sipped my coffee and casually scanned the room. I wanted to know who else was interested, because they'd be the people I needed to watch later. Danner was the most important link, but the way that soldiers had acted down on the planet told me Omicron would have people watching him, too. Nobody stood out.

I got up and walked around, using the excuse of getting more coffee. Nobody paid me any attention, so I took advantage of that and made my way to the Ops center. Danner sat on one side, staring at a terminal, but I avoided him and looked for Lopez. I found her via her buzz cut, and she was sitting at the targeting station. Exactly what I hoped to see.

"You have targeting solutions worked up yet?" I asked.

She closed down a window where she'd been playing a puzzle game and glanced up. "Oh, hi, sir! Targeting solutions for what?"

"The XM-25s. Taking out the Cappan settlement."

Her eyes went wide and her breath hitched. Nobody had told her. To be fair, I was guessing at the order, so it didn't surprise me that she didn't know. "Is that what we're doing?"

"Oh . . . uh . . . never mind. I thought they'd have given you the order." It was a shit thing for me to do to a young soldier, using her like that. It would never cross her mind that I'd lie to her, and she'd assume I knew more than she did. Given my other sins, this one seemed small in comparison.

"Should I be working on that?"

"Not yet. Let's wait for the Ops officer. Maybe there will be another way. That's a tough thing, all those lives down there, if we have to do it. Some of our own, too, maybe. No sensor reports, but I have to believe there's a chance that a few of them made it." I walked away before she had a chance to respond. I'd done what I needed to do. I'd got her thinking about it.

Lieutenant Danner called to me before I got out of the room. "Sir, you have a minute?"

"Sure. Here, or in the other room?"

"Other room," he said.

I nodded and led the way, waiting for him to close the door behind us, then spoke before he could. "Look, before you say anything, I don't want to know. If they told you to kill me . . . or if they do tell you, in the future . . . don't tell me. Just put me in stasis, like we're going home, and take care of it there."

He started to speak, but caught himself, considered his words for a few seconds. "Thank you, sir. I can tell you right now that I don't have that order, but I do understand why it might be under consideration. I hear what you're saying."

It didn't really matter to me. Dead was dead. But I'd made it easier on him. I'd like to think, with all the shitty things I'd done and was continuing to do, that act might help balance the scales a little bit. "So what did they say?"

"The information you retrieved, sir. It checks out. It's exactly what they wanted."

I smiled. "Good. But that look on your face . . . you don't look like a man who got good news."

"They want us to destroy the Cappan settlement."

I nodded. This was the moment I'd planned for. Everything hinged on the next minute of conversation. "How do you feel about that?"

He sighed. "I don't love it. But it's the mission. And if I don't do it, they're going to put somebody else in charge that will."

"You're the only officer left on the ship."

"It's not the military, sir. They can promote anyone they want."

"Good point. You'll want to talk to Lopez, the targeting tech. I think she's going to take this hard. Especially if she had friends down on the planet."

"Shit," he said. "I didn't think about that."

I sipped my coffee, giving it a few seconds to sink in before speaking. "I could do it."

"Tell Lopez? I couldn't ask you to do that, sir. She's my troop."

"No. I mean I could work the targeting. I've got some experience with the machine."

"No doubt about that, sir."

"More important, I've got some experience living with something like this. Trust me, that's much harder than the actual mechanics of it. It's not something I'd wish on anybody. Not Lopez. Not you."

"It's still my authority, sir."

"Sure," I said. "But nobody has to know that. Especially not back in the world. When this gets out—and it *will* get out; everything always does—the media is going to look for somebody to blame. I'll be a convenient target, since they already know me. Shit—once they check the manifest and see me on it, they're going to *assume* it was me."

He thought about it. "Like you said, sir. Things always get out. They'll get the truth."

"Maybe not. Show them the story they want . . ." I shrugged. "Well, show them that, and they tend to stop digging. Besides, the soldiers on board know who I am, but they don't know why I'm here. If I take over, they're likely to think that's part of the plan. Why else bring along a mass murderer?"

He thought about it for several seconds. "It could work."

"If it doesn't, we haven't lost much. It's not like an attempted cover-up is going to make it worse." I watched him closely. So far he hadn't registered even a hint of suspicion, but he'd get there soon. I couldn't get ahead of him. He needed to come up with the problem

himself before I could present him with the solution.
But I could prompt him. I waited until we started to
walk back to Operations. "I'll need the authorization
codes to fire."

His step caught for a fraction of a second. There it
was. He stopped, and hesitated before he spoke. "I'm
not sure this is a good idea."

I pretended to think about it. "Oh! Right. I should
have thought about that. You don't trust me."

"It's not that, sir—"

"It's totally okay. I can see why you'd be worried.
I tell you what. I'll build the firing solution and set
everything except the execution codes. You can verify
what I've got in the system before you authorize." He
bit his bottom lip, but didn't respond. He was close.
"And of course you'll be able to view the target area
via the sensors. You'll see the results clearly enough."

He stood there for several more seconds. I couldn't
read him. Then he nodded. "Let's do it."

"Okay. Let Lopez know."

"Right." He walked over to the soldier and spoke
to her in low tones. She nodded and got up from her
seat. I'm not sure how much he told her, but she didn't
look upset, which was all that mattered. I sat down at
the terminal and pulled up the necessary pages, taking a minute to familiarize myself with the interface.
It nearly mirrored the military system, which didn't
surprise me, given that Omicron made them both. I
punched in the parameters of the mission and selected
the weapon type, and in another frame I pulled up a

three-dimensional map of the island. I chose all four missiles we had on board, which was overkill for that area. I could have done the job with two or three, targeted correctly. Because I chose four, the computer spit out over twenty possible solutions, all of which would satisfy the mission requirements. I'd done it on purpose to get those multiple solutions, because I wanted to pick the one closest to what I wanted. I had information that the computer didn't. I also wanted to expend all the ordnance so they didn't have another shot, just in case.

I studied the numbers for several minutes. I could sense Danner getting nervous, pacing behind me, so I reassured him. "The computer spit out twenty-three effective firing solutions. I'm checking them manually to find the best one."

I selected the solution that was closest to my parameters, and I began manipulating the four aim points. People think targeting with high-yield weapons is a simple thing, and that fusion weapons create such a big explosion that all you have to do is get close. It's subtler than that. As big as the weapons are, the planet is bigger, and moving an impact by a few hundred meters can make a significant difference. A hill or a ridge can divert a shockwave, lessen the impact on a certain area, increase it in another. The energy all has to go somewhere. That's scientific law. Where it goes? That's art. I'm a master artist. The effects of a minor change in aim point grow more significant

if the target is underground. The computer's solution
didn't account for subsurface targets. Mine did.

Not everybody who did targeting could do what I
was attempting. People tended to rely on machines
without knowing the underlying science. They accepted what the computer spit out, and it worked. I
was old-school. I'd learned how to do it manually
before I ever learned it on a computer. I didn't think
Lopez had. I knew Danner hadn't. I moved the impact location of two of the missiles and ran a check
through the computer's simulation. The green circles
lit up, indicating my solution met the mission requirements. According to the computer, it would destroy
everything on the surface. There was no way around
that. But if I'd done it right, people underground in
certain locations would survive. Maybe. Like I said,
it's an art. It's not perfect. It was the best chance I
could give them, and I believed it would work.

"Ready." I stood up to let Danner get at the terminal. I left the green lights up in one corner of the
screen, so he could see that the solution met parameters. "I've highlighted the authorization field. All you
have to do is put your biometrics in."

He stopped behind the chair instead of sitting. "Let
me see the detailed parameters screen."

I hesitated, but only because I hadn't expected it.
"Right, of course." He was smart to check that. If
I'd altered the parameters, the computer would show
green for a different mission. It was a simple thing,

and I'd not thought to try that. Theoretically, if I'd reprogrammed the parameters to leave the settlement undamaged but cause massive damage out over the ocean, I could still get the green bubbles to light up by firing the XM-25s harmlessly into the water. I leaned in and pulled up the parameter screen and let him check it without comment. I hadn't altered it from when Lopez built it. It still showed the settlement and all surface life as the primary target.

"This will kill everyone?" he asked.

"Probably not," I said. "Even with the biggest weapons, there are always survivors. Somebody who is out of the area, or happens to be behind the right giant rock or standing in the right depression at the right time. But there won't be many."

"Shit," he said.

"What's up?"

"Just thinking about our own people, if any of them are still alive. It's hard to believe we lost an entire company."

"Yeah. It sucks," I said, keeping my face as impassive as I could. "On the other hand, you wouldn't want to leave any of our people to the Cappans. You know what they're like."

"Yeah." He sighed deeply. He didn't know firsthand about how some of the Cappans treated prisoners the way I did, but he had certainly heard stories. "Okay. No sense waiting. The attack aircraft are clear of the atmosphere."

I pulled the authorization back up and stood back

as Danner authenticated with first his thumbprint, then his retina. "That will do it."

I hit the fire button before he could rethink anything.

The ship barely vibrated as the four missiles left their bays. Their engines wouldn't fire until they had cleared the ship. From there, the computers inside each one would guide them to the targets I'd programmed. Theoretically they could be recalled, though it would be dicey to try once they entered the atmosphere. At that point the best option would be to neutralize them. We wouldn't be doing that.

"How long until impact?" Danner asked.

I checked the computer. "Just over nine minutes." Missiles didn't need to stick to g-forces that humans could live through, so they accelerated faster than ships.

"Flight control, I want a manned overflight of the target area in fifteen minutes," Danner announced. He looked at me as if to ask if that would be safe. I nodded.

"Roger, sir. Flight control has the mission," responded an older-looking sergeant.

"Intel, I want unmanned drone passes, too. Scan on every type of spectrum we've got."

"Roger, sir." A female voice this time. I didn't turn to look at her. I was sure that everybody would read the nervousness on my face if they saw me, so I stayed focused on the screen in front of me. The outcome had passed from my hands. The Cappans had defeated our drones and our sensors when we'd been down on the planet. I had to trust that they could do it again now. If not . . . well, I bought them a month or so until Omicron could get more assets in place.

The room stayed silent, or as close to it as an Operations room can get. Nobody spoke. It was as if the air itself had hushed, paying respects to those on the planet below. The weight of it would stay with everyone in the room. They hadn't done it, but they'd been there. They'd seen it. It would affect some more than others . . . there was no way to tell. Some would second-guess themselves, their role in things. Some wouldn't ever think about it again. And others . . . others would feel nothing but then wonder why they didn't.

I could release them all from that. I could tell them that, if I did it right, those very expensive missiles would make a huge mess but the people were safe. *Safe*. I almost laughed. It was a stupid thought. If I told them, then Omicron would send another ship. More missiles—

"Impact," someone said.

A couple screens whited out for a half second before going black, their internal systems shutting down the sensors to avoid damage. They'd take several seconds to reawaken. The room stayed totally silent as we waited for them to come back up. The visual-spectrum sensor came back first, treating us to a picture of what used to be the Cappan settlement. The prefab buildings were now so much trash, scattered and melted into unrecognizable slag. One person clapped for a second when the image came up, but quickly broke off when he realized nobody else had joined in.

Young faces stared at the display and then shifted to another when it came up, unspeaking but unable to turn away. I didn't look. I watched the people instead. I hadn't done that the last time, at Cappa. There hadn't been time. Now I had nothing *but* time. I wondered if I looked like they did, if I'd looked that way for the last couple years, carrying the weight of thousands of deaths. More than thousands, in my case. At some point flight ops did their thing and sent ships in close to check things out. Drones, too. They'd either find the Cappans or they wouldn't. I'd done what I could. I walked out of the room without speaking to anybody. Soldiers stepped out of my path, almost stumbling in their haste, as if touching me would somehow infect them.

I reached the medical bay without really knowing that was where I was headed. Almost every bed in the long, narrow room had a soldier in it. I found Matua about halfway down a row of almost twenty along one wall. He looked up as I stood over him.

"You made it, sir." His voice seeped out in a croak.

I smiled at him. "I did. Partly thanks to you."

"No way, sir. You know that's not true."

"You did your job, Matua. That's all any of us can do. Trust me on that."

"I'm so sorry, sir."

I smiled again, thinner this time, and shook my head. I didn't trust myself to speak without losing it.

I headed for the bar.

**I WAS THREE** drinks in when Danner found me. "You might want to slow down, sir. We got word that we're breaking station."

I raised my glass, toasting him. They say that it's not healthy to go into stasis with alcohol in your system. But then they say lots of things aren't healthy, and it's never stopped me before. "So the scans came up clean?"

"They did. No signs of life. We'll leave the satellites in orbit to keep an eye on things, but the folks back home seem pretty happy."

I nodded, and poured myself another drink. He wanted me to ask about my own situation, so he could tell me and unburden himself. I didn't. "How long until stasis?"

"Within the hour."

I looked at him, nodded again, and turned back to my drink. After a few minutes of awkward silence, Danner left me alone.

The Cappans weren't out of danger. They'd have to avoid detection by the satellites and find a way to get off the planet before anybody else came looking. They had assets like Sasha and Riku on Talca, and probably others in other systems. From what I'd seen of their abilities, I liked their odds. I poured a final drink. My biggest fear was for Ganos. She held no value to Omicron, now that the mission was done, but once everything hit the news, I wouldn't put it past them to be petty and go after her in vengeance. But she was smart, and Plazz and the Cappans would look out for her. I had to believe that.

For me, I'd go into stasis and I'd either wake up or I wouldn't. I figured I had a decent chance, depending on how they decided to deal with what just happened. They could try to cover it up, but they'd have to know that wouldn't work. Someone in the crew would talk, and if they didn't, Plazz would figure it out anyway, with the help I'd given her. They might want to keep me around as a scapegoat. Then again, they might not.

I just wanted to sleep, deep and peaceful, without the dreams. I didn't know if that would happen or not, but I hoped.

"Sir?" Someone stood at a respectful distance. "It's time."

I stood up and smiled. "I'm ready."

# ACKNOWLEDGMENTS

As I continue my writing journey, so many people have helped me that I couldn't possibly name them all, but I want to acknowledge some who were especially critical to this project.

I want to thank my agent, Lisa Rodgers, who gives me excellent advice about my writing career in general, and who has a sharp editorial mind that made this specific book better in so many ways. I could not have a better partner in my writing endeavors.

I would like to thank David Pomerico and the entire team at Harper Voyager for their continued belief in my work and their efforts at making it into the product you see here on the page. Without the outstanding editing, this book would be much less than it is. Additional thanks to the art department for the cover, and for all the people who work behind the scenes to bring the book to market. I'd like to thank Andrew Gibeley specifically for his work promoting *Planetside* and getting it in front of more readers than I ever could have on my own. Promoting books is hard, and I couldn't have asked for better support.

I had fewer readers on this book than on my previous work, so each person was, by definition, more important. Red Levine provided essential feedback, especially focused on characters and their behaviors, that added depth that would otherwise be lacking. Rebecca Enzor provided early notes and talked me down off of several ledges. Jason Nelson provided critical insights into the computer-network aspects of the book, as well as specific character thoughts for Butler and Ganos. I could not have done this without them.

Special thanks to Dan Koboldt who came up with the title and gave outstanding notes on this project. More than that, he continues to give me career advice and insight on a regular basis. Years after he mentored me in Pitch Wars, I continue to learn from him.

Thanks to Pancho, who inspired me to create Cisco, Ganos's dog.

I want to thank everyone who read *Planetside,* and especially everyone who read it and told somebody else about it. That continues to overwhelm me—it means so much. Your time is valuable, and the fact that you chose to spend it with my book is amazing to me. Thank you. Really.

Finally, and most significantly, I'd like to thank my wife, Melody. Her support, advice, and understanding are more significant to my success than everything else combined. Without her, I could do none of this.